Zor

Isadora Katz

ZOMBIE BAY

A DIRK DOBBS,
ZOMBIE HUNTER,
MYSTERY

Isadora Katz

Zombie Bay

BY

Isadora Katz

Isadora Katz

Zombie Bay

DEDICATION

To my husband, Rick,
who gave me the idea
to write about zombies
and, he believed in me.
He gave me the weaponry
and tactical information
that made Dirk
what he is today.

~

Also, many thanks to
Sandy
for her superb
editing help on the final draft
and Tamara for helping
on the first draft.
I couldn't have done
It without you.

Isadora Katz

ACKNOWLEDGMENTS

*This Book Would Not
Have Been Possible Without
The World of Information
In*

*"The Zombie Survival Manual"
By Max Brooks*

*Some Information Taken From
The Zombie Survival Guide
By Max Brooks,
Published By Three Rivers Press,
A Division of Random House, Inc., 2003*

Isadora Katz

1

It all began with this news story.

 DELUNA ISLANDER NEWS   *Your Eye on the Island*

----TWO FOUND DEAD AT BAYSIDE PARK

Stan Engle, Staff Reporter

In the wee hours of Thursday morning a husband and wife found more than their quota of fish at Bayside Beach. Instead, they found a gruesome end to their lives. Beach Patrol Officer, David Hatfield, found the mutilated bodies of Sam and Michelle Cherie of New Orleans, LA. The Cheries were vacationing on the Gulf celebrating their 30th anniversary.

Sources say the couple left the Bayside Motel around 6pm for a late picnic and some night fishing in the warm bay waters.

Jane Mitchell, a maid at the motel, reported seeing the two hiking through the undergrowth toward the beach around sundown. The beach patrol called in the county medical examiner and police to take over the scene.

The victims were identified by their driver's licenses found on the bodies. No determination has been made on the cause of death. Due to the horrific damage to the bodies it looks to have been caused or disturbed by animals. "We don't know exactly what we are dealing with here," said Detective John Law, the officer in charge of the scene, "but we strongly advise that safety measures be taken when outdoors, especially in the wooded areas."

Family members of the victims have been notified and the investigation will be pursued.

Continued on Page 6

"Oh, my stars! Did you see today's paper?" Jimmi Dobbs asked as she tossed the paper on the table in front of her brother Dirk. "Interesting." He said, noncommittally as he continued making a sandwich. Few things managed to get a rise out of Dirk Dobbs. Murder, Mayhem and Mangled Corpses were his stock in trade. Jimmi's brother was a mystery writer. Bloody death on the beach was all in a day's work for him.

When he wasn't writing about such things he was either reading about it or watching it. He was an aficionado of the classic B-movies. He loved them all whether horror, gangster, gothic tales, or the classics of Edgar Allen Poe, Dashiell Hammett, Earl Stanley Gardner and the likes. When it came to film he enjoyed everything from Hitchcock to the low budget unforgettable from Roger Corman down to the little known Coleman Francis films. Only a true lover of low budget, ill prepared, badly acted motion pictures could love Coleman Francis, but that was Dirk Dobbs.

That was not all of Dirk Dobbs. Dobbs had a long and varied military career. He entered the Navy in 1972; he served on the U.S.S. Little Rock in the Mediterranean for four years. After being accepted into the SEAL Teams Dirk began developing his tactical and marksmanship skills. After SEAL training he was assigned to SEAL Team II for an additional four years. While there he participated in all types of classified operations. Dirk's SEAL career was cut short in 1984 after being injured in a HALO jump. HALO stands for High Altitude Low Opening procedure where the SEAL operator jumps from altitudes in excess of 20,000 feet but doesn't open the parachute until 3,000 feet or lower. The reason for this is to get the team into an area covertly without the drop aircraft being detected. He was retired from the service due to his injury, though not disabling, did prevent him from jumping. After hospitalization in Wiesbaden, Germany he made a full recovery.

Dirk, now a civilian, was also an avid motorcyclist and musician, though his music had taken a backseat to his other pursuits in recent years. As for his income producing endeavors, he made his living by the royalties from his writing. Fiction and otherwise. Though many knew about his popular books few knew about the research books, articles and seminars he gave under the pen name A.R. Bushmaster. These were not books, articles and seminars for enjoyment or leisure. These were serious studies on serious subjects. Subjects that dealt with life and death and the little known world of the living dead. Dirk was a world renowned expert in his field, but not in the spotlight. His fame was in the shadows of a dark and dangerous world. Few people knew this side of the mild mannered writer. Most people saw

famous mystery writer, the quiet loner. Little did
they know? They were better off not knowing.

Through the sale of his fiction works, research and
instruction books, materials, seminars, as well as
his consulting work on the clandestine cases, Dirk
amassed a sizable fortune that was, also, unknown
to most of the people around him. Even to his
sister, Jimmi. As far as she knew his income came
from his mystery fiction only. What most people,
and that included his sister, Jimmi, did not know
about him was that he was, not only, a very rich
man but he performed a very serious task. This
fortune allowed Dirk to move freely and covertly
about the world to find and eliminate danger.
Danger, lurking in the dark and horrifying places
in the earth; carrying out his true mission in life.
Dirk was an expert Zombie Killer.

2

Jimmi Dobbs was confused. "Well, my lands! What did I do with that paper? I know I put it here on the table before I went out." She scanned the kitchen surfaces with an eagle eye but there was no paper to be seen. "I guess Dirk must've picked it up for the crossword or something." The tiny woman shook her short curls and headed to the den to watch The Price Is Right.

Dirk Dobbs sat in his silver Porsche 996 GT3 in the palm lined drive without turning the key, frowning at the pictures of the man and woman killed at the beach. The news of this attack had set his antenna buzzing. Could it be? Right here in his own back yard?

He had been all over the world to scenes such as described here and had found the same thing at them all. He had to get a look at those bodies and he had to do it fast.

Dr. Randall Durham was the Chief Medical
Examiner of the county. He also was Dirk Dobbs'
oldest friend. They had been friends since they
were kids at school. Durham was one of the very
few people who knew the complete story on
Dobbs. They had shared a few scrapes and
Randall had been called in on a few cases where
secrecy had been essential. Dirk belonged to an
organization called *ZARC* that ferreted out the
undead and their nests all over the world. *ZARC
stood for Zombie Assault Response Corps.* Dirk was
one of the originators of the group and leader of
the North American Command. They were a
clandestine group shrouded in secrecy, for obvious
reasons. Dirk had called on Randall to help with
the forensics in a couple of cases where he needed
someone he could trust completely. It was still a
little unnerving to the doctor, still hard for him to
believe, but he had seen the proof. He had been
face to face with one of them and a few more of
their victims.

Standing in the cold, dank shadows of the county
morgue Durham pulled back the sheet on Sam
Cherie, the first victim from Bayside Beach. It only
took one look to make him go cold inside. With a
more in depth examination he was convinced.
With shaking fingers and a rock in his stomach, he
picked up the phone and dialed Dirk's private
number.

Dirk rarely answered the phone on the first ring. It was a habit he had acquired over the years. He let the phone ring through the second time before he answered it.

"Hello," he snarled into the small cellular contraption. He hated phones, he hated call waiting, and he hated emails. They were all just assaults on his privacy, intrusions into his life that he found increasingly annoying, even though they were all necessary evils. Even at that, as he had said many times, if he had his way we would all be raising carrier pigeons and rolling up notes for pretty blue glass bottles to toss into the bay. "Dobbs here." He growled as he took the curve a little too fast.

"Dirk? It's Randy. I have something here you should see..." the M.E. said.

"If you are talking about the couple from the Bayside, I'm way ahead of you, Durham. I will be in the parking lot in about 30 seconds. Hold the door open for me." He said as he clicked the phone shut without a goodbye. Further words were unnecessary. If it turned out to be what he suspected, they both know what they were dealing with, and it scared the hell out of both of them.

The sun was just going down in a rosy glow as his taillights disappeared into the County Complex parking area off the Bayway Highway on Government Street. When he entered the Emerald County Medical Examiner's office the street lights were just popping on all over the island. It was a warm night. The wind had picked up just enough to ruffle his longish hair. The breeze was warm and soft like a woman's sigh. He could hear the gulls fighting over a fish on the beach, just across the street, and the palm fronds clattering together. Just another night on the island, people would say, but they would be wrong. Nobody could guess that the world was about to go bottom up on the small island in the Gulf, but Dirk didn't have to guess. He knew. All too well.

Randall Durham greeted his friend with a shake of his head. "What'd you do? Fly?" he asked. "You know I would never exceed the speed limit...unless absolutely necessary." Dirk smiled back at his old friend. "Yeah, right." The doctor said as the headed toward the office. They passed it and turned into the hall that led to the cold room. "What've we got?" Dobbs asked as he put on the worn bomber jacket he had grabbed from the car for this purpose. He had been in enough of these places to know how frigid they could get.

"Well, it looks bad." He hesitated, trying to downplay his concern, "It could have been an accident, or maybe murder ...at this point I don't know. Animals could've gotten to the bodies before the patrol found them this morning..." he trailed off. "But, that is not what you think any more than I do, is it?" Dirk asked, knowing the answer. "No, it's a possibility, but a slim one. Take a look." The M.E. answered as he pulled out the drawer and then the one adjacent to it.

The victims were torn beyond recognition with parts of their faces, necks and arms missing. The male victim was minus a hand and a section of his torso from the rib cage to the hipbone. The female fared much worse. If they were alive at the time of the attack, death did not come easily. Hopefully they died from the wounds and not later, from the infection.

Dirk pushed the drawers closed and leaned on the table behind him. "What are you telling the cops?" he asked. "Nothing more than I have to at this point. Falling back on the excuse of testing taking time and all that." Durham shrugged, "I still DO have lots to do to be sure and, besides, they won't believe me when I tell them anyway." Dirk nodded.

The medical tests would need to be done to be positive but Dirk had few doubts as to the outcome. Not after seeing the bodies. He and his friend, the doctor, discussed the details and ran over how to proceed before they went their separate ways, making a plan as to how to proceed. They agreed to meet the next morning and said an uneasy goodbye. "You watch yourself, Durham." Dirk said as he headed out, "Make sure you keep them on ice until we are sure and know what we have on our hands." Durham assured him that he would and they parted with a few unkind words and slaps on the back.

Dirk turned left out of the parking lot of the complex. The site of the bodies had given him reason to worry. Maybe, as Randall said, it could be just an animal mauling, but his gut said no. Maybe I am just becoming paranoid, he thought. With all the unnatural things Dirk had seen in his career as a researcher, writer and zombie expert, it is reasonable that he should be concerned. He had a lot to lose here but he *could* be wrong. That's what he kept telling himself as he wound his way down the Bayway Highway. He wanted to believe his home was still secure, far from the horrors he worked with daily. He had kept Deluna Island as his safe place. It was a place where he could relax and get away from the horrors of his work. A place where the people he cared about could be happy and safe, as well. If his uneasiness turned out to be warranted, as he thought it would be, Deluna Island, his cocoon could be destroyed.

The chill he was feeling was more than the refrigerated air. He had a knot in his gut telling him what to expect. He hoped his gut was wrong.

3

Dirk had moved to the island when he was a grown man, at a time when he had needed a safe place to land. Deluna Island had become that safe place. He loved everything about it, from the sun-bleached sandy dunes to the emerald green waters. He loved the beautiful view from his house on the bluffs, down to the brackish water under the rickety fishing pier at Captain Jack's diner. When he was on the island he felt whole and alive, just like many before him had felt.

The island had a golden history. Deluna Island was a jewel in the Gulf, just off Pensacola Beach, at the mouth of the Gulf of Mexico and the Deluna Bay. It had once been an, all but, uninhabited sand bar in the early 1900's. It wasn't until people from the cities began to make the trek to the beaches and islands for their health that it attracted some attention.

The story goes that a rich merchant from St. Petersburg was sailing his yacht in the warm waters one spring day when he was caught in a freak storm. The boat was run aground on a sand bar and sunk off Deluna Island. The few residents of the island, mostly Indians and a few traders, took the man into their beach shacks and fed him. He fell in love with the island and built a summer home there on the southwestern tip. Later, he expanded and turned it into the first hotel on the island. He started a boat tour that brought passengers from Pensacola and Mobile to the hotel, and back. Soon, people were coming from all over the southeastern states to his beautiful Deluna Island. As the island became more populated, the ferries were established and families began to live there year round, open businesses, form churches and open schools. The rest, as they say, is history.

The, now thriving, island had come a long way from those quaint shacks and flat boat tours. At the time of the *apparent* animal attack on the anniversary couple, Bayside Beach, where the couple had been killed, was a popular spot. It was just past the National Seashore and was just what it implied. It was a long crescent of pure, white sand nestled in the curve of West Deluna Island on Deluna Bay. It was a well-known corner of bayside paradise, facing Pensacola on the west,

Pensacola Beach directly due north and, farther to the east, it faced toward Navarre, Fort Walton and Destin. It was in a perfect place for tourists and travelers who wanted to get away, but, not too far away.

Deluna Bay was a small body of water in between Pensacola Beach and the island. Deluna was a small island, less than ten miles long from one end to the other. There were no connecting bridges to Santa Rosa Island or to the mainland. There was regular ferry service at either end. The East End Ferry took passengers to Navarre and the West End Ferry went across to Pensacola Beach or Downtown Pensacola. This allowed the Deluna Island residents easy access to jobs and shopping without having to live in town and the visitors' access for traveling to the island and other areas nearby. The passage was inexpensive and, usually, uncrowded. Since the island had its own police force, hospital and schools there was less traffic on the ferries than there had been in years past.

Deluna Island was not a part of the other counties like Santa Rosa and Escambia. There were no shared services. Deluna Island was in its own Emerald County. They had a county complex that housed the court house, clerk's offices and other municipal services, that included the medical

examiner and the morgue. Deluna Island residents
needed very little from across the bay.

The island was laid out in several zones. On the
south side of the island, facing the Gulf of Mexico,
they had the residential houses, condominiums
and communities on the East End. The residential
area had a public beach and bath houses for their
use.

The West End on the gulf side was zoned for
commercial purposes, motels, hotels, vacation
homes, restaurants and businesses dealing with the
hospitality industry. There was another public
access beach on that end, as well, that gave
residents and tourists privacy and access to the
Gulf side beaches.

The early planners had seen how the other
vacation spots were selling their souls to the
highest bidders and losing their heart in the
bargain. They were smart enough to know that if
they followed suit, not only would they out price
the family tourists, but they would eventually out
price the local residents who wouldn't be able to
afford to live on the island that was their home.
So they put zoning ordinances on the books that
kept the business on one end and residences at the
other. Along with that they limited not only how
many hotels and condos could be on the beach but
also limited the size. The laws would allow no

buildings to be built over three stories tall or within 50 feet of each other. That allowed for a less restricted view of the beach for those on the sound side. Even though the fees were reasonable all over the island the lodging taxes discouraged most of the rich and obnoxious from staying too long. The taxes were based on income so that the rich paid more to stay on Deluna Island than the middle or low income. It was a line in the Island's by laws that would never pass today but was set in stone for as long as the zoning stayed on the books. If the commission ever voted to annex themselves to Pensacola or the county, that one would be wiped off in a hurry. But most of Deluna Island liked it just the way it was. . Developers and real estate tycoons hated it. It kept the talk lively on Saturday night at the clubs.

It was just one more way to keep this a quaint little island instead of an ice cream colored maze of expensive vacation homes and shops like Pensacola Beach and Navarre were becoming.

The main road on the island was the Bayway Highway. Bayway Highway was not a massive pipeline of transportation; it was in fact a tight two lane road filled with potholes. The soft sandy shoulders that sometimes spilled onto the road were great places to get buried up to your axles. But the name sounded impressive.

By the time that Dirk moved to the island things were settled down into a slow, sleepy pace that soothed him. With all the turmoil in his professional life, it was just what he needed. The moment I set foot in the sand, he thought as he drove through the night, I feel at peace. He hoped that his serenity would not soon be shattered.

4

It was too late to go out to the scene, Dirk thought ruefully. *He* wanted to get a look at the area. His years of experience had taught him that even the most unimportant thing could turn the tide of battle, and battle is what the little strip of sand in the Gulf would be facing if his fears were founded.

God, I hope not, he half prayed in the luxurious interior of his sports car. Look on the bright side, Dobbs; it could just be an animal gone mad or a serial killer! When stress got to him, he always made not-so-funny jokes to himself. This one was really not funny.

He drove on through the dark, his mind on the deaths. What would be so special about them? Or, the place they died, he wondered. His mind conjured up a picture of the Bayside Motel.

The Bayside Motel one of the older and more nostalgic on the bay side, sat at the edge of Bayside

Beach. It was where the couple spent their last night alive. About 1/4 mile inland from the actual beaches it fronted onto Red Point Drive just off of Red Point Road. You could reach the beach by trekking down the winding paths through the woods or by following the road to the National Seashore and turning left onto Beach Street. There are several motels and campgrounds closer to the water but The Bayside is one of the much nicer places. It has a restaurant, a pool and a playground for the kids. The yards and gardens around the rooms are well kept and clean. The centipede grass, which is an island trademark, trails its way across the sand in a wavy zigzag pattern, never quite being thick enough to be called ground cover, much less be called a lawn. Yet, it has its own tropical beauty, as do most of the indigenous plants and trees seen in the area.

He thought about the trails that wound through the undergrowth out to the water. It was not what you might call a dense wood, but you could lose sight of the motel and the water in some of the areas. He could imagine the couple running into an animal, or a pack of animals, in some of those spots and not being seen. They might call for help and not be heard, either, with the wind, the surf and the clatter of the dry fronds. After all, he thought, it was at sundown, or after, when they were out there.

Still, he couldn't imagine anything on the island being that deadly. His mind rambled on, trying to call up stories heard from residents and tourists. For some reason, another one of those random thoughts that come up when under stress, he thought of one of the local plants of which people consistently remained in terror.

In the summer the trails and grassy areas were filled with tall green sprigs of grass bending prettily in the breeze. In the fall all the tall green sprigs are filled with vicious little burrs that have barbed prongs. Lying innocently on the sand, you wouldn't think much about them. Until you step on them. Then you know that they are there to torture any innocent barefoot visitor.

The hills and valleys of white sugar sand hide unseen suffering with each step of the uninitiated. However inviting it might be to tiptoe through the sandy surrounds with your exposed toes, beware, don't do it. You will come hobbling back for tweezers and disinfectant.

Tourists and residents, who know, will tell you not to walk yourself or your pets through the grasses. They will warn you that you will be spending hours trying to free your wriggling pet from the tenacious hold of the barbed burrs.

Dirk had always thought that there should be warning flags put out for sticker season along with the ones announcing rough waves and sharks. Maybe he would bring that up at the next Island Authority meeting. He contemplated the idea for a couple more minutes before he shook himself back to the real problem at hand. Death. No wonder he would much rather let his mind run free for a few minutes. It was not something that he wanted to think about. Not here.

Nevertheless, he thought of the Cheries. A contented couple came to this place to celebrate their happiest day and, now, there will be no more happy days for them, he thought. The questions about their deaths were swirling around in the darkest recesses of Dirk's mind. They should have been safe here. The thoughts made him angry, and frightened. Dirk had many friends on the island. He had his only sibling here; his best friend. How safe are they? He thought. How safe is anyone?

As if to put a punctuation mark on that thought, Dirk pulled into his garage. Turning off the motor, he was aware of the calming silence. No cars, buses or trains up here. Just the sound of the breezes in the palm fronds, seagulls calling out over the bay. The smell of salt air and island sage.

He noticed that his sister's car was gone. It was a night for one of her meetings, he supposed. He

liked having Jimmi here. At first...well, it wasn't
what he had planned but things don't always go
the way you think. He pushed the thoughts of that
time away. He still couldn't think of that time
without pain. He didn't want to muddy the
waters, right now, he thought, and thinking back
to that loss would not leave him with a clear mind.
He let himself in; found a note on the counter. He
was right. Jimmi had a meeting and wouldn't be
back until late. He would have to fend for himself
and find his own supper. He knew exactly where
to go.

 After a long shower, he dressed and had a drink
on the balcony overlooking the water, still thinking
about his home and its beauty. He didn't let his
mind go back to the morgue. He refused to let that
disturb his moment of peace.

A little later, as he headed out for dinner, he
ruminated on this and managed to put aside his
worries for a little longer, Dirk was unaware of
what was happening only a few miles out under
the crystal waters of the gulf.

Isadora Katz

5

It was a warm night. Dirk was headed for Capt.
Jack's Diner on the West Side of the island.
Things should have been perfect if... No, he
thought, I won't go there right, now. He turned up
the radio and returned to enjoying his drive.

Zipping up the Bayway Highway, which was a
pretentious name for the main road that ran the
length of tiny Deluna Island, he had to work to
maintain a decent speed. The Porsche could reach
speeds in excess of 200 miles an hour. If you put
numbers on the thing you could put it on the
racetrack.

On an island that was only eight miles long at the
farthest point, speed was out of the question. He
had often thought that with that kind of
acceleration, a good ramp and this eight mile

runway he might make the mainland without the ferry. But tonight his mind was not on taking a flying leap to nearby Pensacola. Tonight, despite his admonition to himself, his thoughts were on scary things and Dirk was deep in thought.

Dirk followed the Bayway down to Turtle Lake. There he turned right onto Line Drive, taking the long way to the diner. When he came to Red Point Road he turned to the right again. He was driving slow, mentally ticking off the things he might need if this turned bad, when a rusty VW sped around him in the no pass lane, nearly sideswiping him. "Damn kids!" he yelled into the setting sun, along with a few other chosen words.

Most of the kids on the island belonged to one or two groups, the poor kids who had nothing to lose and the rich kids who thought they couldn't be stopped. Either way it was bad news. The good kids just kept to themselves and stayed out of trouble. The kid driving the VW wasn't one of the good ones, he grumbled.

He watched the taillights on the bug disappear as it turned into the National Seashore. He considered following them for a moment, but discarded the impulse. He had better things to do than wrangle some stupid teenagers. They wouldn't listen anyway, he thought gruffly, as he drove on into the night.

He soon forgot all about seeing the kids. Little did he know that he would see them, again. Next time, there would be blood, death and worse. The undead.

6

While the horrifying news of the deaths buzzed through the community, life still went on. People went to work, kids went to school, played ball and they all had plans of their own. There was one plan that was right on track and, even, a dead couple from Louisiana couldn't put a crimp in it if Anna Knox had any say in the matter.

Anna Knox was a senior at Bayside High. Since she was one of the homecoming court contenders, she was in no need of a date period. Yet she turned away more boys than not. Often she stayed in on the weekends but this Friday night if all went as planned, she was going to have the mother of all dates! She had schemed, lied, twisted and manipulated facts and people, begged and borrowed to set this night up with Adam Moore and nothing, or no one was going to mess it up, she thought to herself.

Adam Moore was captain of the football team and the man of her dreams. She'd been crazy about him since middle school. He knew she liked him but had never taken her seriously as a love interest. That did not stop Anna from pursuing him. He had been in her sights for a long time and, now, she would finally hit the bulls-eye.

Unknown to Adam, Anna had been busy setting her plan in motion. The last piece on the game board had fallen into place that very morning. Adam didn't understand what had happened. It had all been so quick, so horrible. His steady girlfriend had just dumped him. It had worked like a charm, Anna thought as she watched him from the third hall doorway. It was all so sad, she thought, sarcastically. "Gee, Adam, what could have come over her?" she planned to say, "She was never good enough for you!" It should be just the right time to go to him, she thought as she saw him walk, dazedly, out of the library.

Somehow his girlfriend, along with the rest of the school, had heard a very nasty rumor that was going around about him. There had even been pictures! The girl had been furious, then devastated. Anna could hardly contain herself. She had broken it off immediately! He was free, now, and she was getting her shot.

She spun her web, trapping him. All she had to do now was go to him and offer her shoulder to him to cry on. Once he accepted, and she knew he would since nobody at school wanted any part of him, now, she would have him all to herself. She had everything ready. She would take him out to Red Point Park that evening. She would bring the food and beer and he would bring his gorgeous body, she thought gleefully. She could hardly wait.

The only dark cloud on the horizon would be if he ever found out who started the rumor and posted the photo shopped pictures on the Internet. If he did, Anna's dreams would turn into nightmares; but she refused to think about that. All she needed was a chance to make him see how much she loved him and how good she was for him and Adam would be hers. It never entered her mind that she had destroyed the boy's life, or that what she did was wrong. She had no idea that she was a very sick person. She could see only the fantasy that she was playing in her head, and it had a happy ending. Meanwhile, the boy's whole world was dissolving with every click of the mouse.

Deluna Island was, basically, a small town that just happened to be surrounded on all four sides by water. Everybody knew everybody, and their whole families. Many of the residents were related, either by blood or marriage. It was a tight knit community. Gossip could run through it like water through a fish net. Right now, the water was running like a fire hydrant.

Adam Moore was confused and heartbroken. Jenna McLain and Adam had been going together for almost a year. They got along great, had a lot in common and thought they would make their relationship permanent someday. Adam had been a little less than faithful in the beginning but Jenna had given him the boot for a week. When they reunited it was for good and Adam never looked away again. When he first began to pick up a little of the rumors he had actually thought it was funny. He knew he hadn't done anything and expected Jenna to trust his word on it. That was how it was between them, but he didn't know how bad the stories were. And, he didn't know about the pictures.

He thought this would be another bump in the road that they would leave behind them. He felt that way right up until she walked into the cafeteria at lunch, slammed his senior ring down on the table and stormed out.

He chased her down in the hall. Spinning her around, he said, "What is this all about, Jenna?" he asked, "You know how gossip is around here. People make things up just to have something to do." He was stunned when she told him about the pictures that she had seen, and that they were on the Internet, too. Who could be doing this? And why were they doing it? He begged her to believe him but, in the end, she shook her head and ran away.

Somehow he made his way back to the library and into one of the computer cubicles. With a few strokes he was seeing himself on screen doing unspeakable things. This was impossible! He never did anything like that! How? He thought. They were faked, of course. He knew that, but no one else would believe it. Or accept it. It just looked too real.

He closed the site just as he heard snickering behind him. Two of his teammates were standing across the room looking into another terminal. Hoots and catcalls erupted from the boys. He had no doubt what they were looking at. He slid out of the chair and made his way out the back before they could see him. Out in the parking lot he sank down on the curb behind a cluster of tall palms and put his head in his hands. What was he going to do? His life was ruined. Nobody would ever believe that those images weren't real. Even if he could convince people that they were fakes, the memory of them would always be in their minds.

From her vantage point by the door, Anna could see that it was time to step in and comfort him.

She had been hearing about it all day. No one else would go to him, now. He was all hers.

Suddenly Adam felt a warm hand on his shoulder. He looked up into the face of Anna Knox.

Usually, he would feel annoyed that he couldn't get away from the blonde girl. She had been his shadow for so long he couldn't even remember when she hadn't been around. She was at practice. She was at the convenience store. She turned up at *The Hangout*, the place where all the kids met on the weekends for burgers and music. She was everywhere. He couldn't shake her. Once, he'd seen her car outside his house after midnight.

Anna Knox was an odd fish. She never fit in with the others in his group, although she was, actually, a pretty cute girl. She had made the homecoming court this year. Yet, there was something...off about her. She wrote him letters, sent him emails, even after he changed his email address, she still found him. She made stalking look easy. But, right now he was glad of a friendly face.

"Oh, Adam! I heard what happened with Jenna. That was so wrong. I just want you to know I don't believe a word of what's going around. Especially the part about the guys...ugh. I know you better than that, even though all the rest of the school doesn't." Anna said as she leaned in close to him. His head dropped a little lower as he realized there was more that he hadn't heard. "You can count on me to stand beside you. Not like those others," she said, cocking her head toward the steps in front of third hall to make sure he would see the crowd that had gathered there, watching them. Adam groaned and leaned back out of their view.

The team and all of them...they wouldn't know the truth if..." she paused, acting uncertain as if she had said too much. "Well, they're saying they couldn't believe it and I told them they better not believe it...But, you know how these things go. They'll forget all about it in a few weeks. And, all those guys in my history class this morning, they said they would find you at the game tonight and...Well, they're all just talking big." She paused again for effect. She wanted to give him time to think about his position. She leaned in next to his ear and put an arm around his shoulders, "And those bitchy cheerleaders! Don't let them get to you either. They laugh at everybody." Adam moaned and squeezed his eyes shut.

"Come on, Adam. I know what you need to do. Let's get out of here." She pulled on him until he rose from the curb. "Don't look back. They are not laughing at you anyway. They are just juveniles. Pointing like that! How stupid they are." She led the dazed boy to her car. "Come on, get in. I'll take you home. You probably shouldn't ride the bus."

Adam was a lamb to the slaughter and she was the wolf.

Adam turned slightly and looked at the group on the steps. God, they were still pointing and laughing. Suddenly he decided he should try to do some damage control and look like all was well. The thought buoyed his spirit, somewhat. He lifted his head, squared his shoulders, and thought, do they think their childish hoots are going to get to me? He would show them he was just fine.

He laid his arm around Anna and leaned in as if telling her a joke. "Follow my lead" he whispered to her and threw back his head and laughed as if he had just heard the joke of the year. Anna never missed a beat. She giggled and cooed, playfully slapping his arm. "Oh, you!" she cried loudly enough for the boys and girls to hear her. The she threw her arms around his neck and kissed him, long and hard. He played along. He didn't know that Anna wasn't playing. This was the kiss she had waited for, for years, and she was making the best of it.

Eventually she broke away feeling exhilarated. Adam seemed a little dazed. This was not what he wanted. Everything was piling up on him. Things were happening way to fast and furious. Anna giggled again and, in a loud stage whisper, said, "Come on. I know just the place where we can...talk." More giggles as she pulled him toward her car.

Neither of them realized there was someone else watching them performs their act. Someone besides the kids on the steps. Jenna McLain sat in her car, hidden from sight by a large green dumpster. She had gone home but was too upset to be still. She came back to talk to Adam. The whole thing seemed so out of character for him. She was beginning to think that is was some sort of bad joke or prank, that is, until she saw the way he was acting. And, with that...witch Anna! If he could act like that with her, then, it was a sure thing that she didn't really know him at all.

While Jenna watched, the pair got into her beat up VW Bug and engaged in one more lengthy kiss. Jenna clenched the steering wheel with all her might, wishing it was Anna Knox's neck. Or, Adam's, she wasn't sure. Of course, she could not know that Anna was orchestrating all of it, telling the boy that they had to 'make it look good' to the crowd if he wanted them to see that the rumors weren't true. She was playing him, but he was in so much pain that he couldn't see it.

"You know, Adam, all this may have been for a reason. The only way to get you to see who was really your friend and who wasn't." she went on talking as she drove, "Now, you can see. Who is standing by you? Me, that's who!" She knew better than to bad mouth Jenna to him, at this point. It was all too sudden. He would still take up for her and Anna didn't want to take a chance on alienating him. After a few minutes of more talk, she drove to Adam's house without a word. She knew to let it sink in for a little while. Adam, in his black cloud of despair, didn't think to ask how she knew the way. The Moore's had just moved into the new house in the upscale neighborhood by the lake. None of his friend's, except Jenna, had been to his house, yet.

When they pulled into the driveway Anna knew this was her big chance and she was going all the way. "Adam, now, you hop out and run around back. You don't want your mom to see you from her sewing room over there." She pointed to the upstairs right window. "She will worry too much if she sees you in this kind of mood. Then, you would have to explain, and she would want to see the pictures...well, of course, that is, if she hasn't already... Well, maybe not...You know how the Island grapevine works." She let that hang for a second.

"Just get your shower like everything is normal and hope for the best. I will pick you up for the ga---...Oh! Sorry! I guess you better not go to the game..." She paused for effect. Adam rubbed his face with his hand, "Well, I know! I'll get us some food and stuff. We can just go hang out at the beach and chill. OK?" Looking for an affirmative answer. She was nothing if not an accomplished sales person.

"Yeah. Yeah, you're right. Can't go..." his voice broke a little. He cleared his throat and turned to her, gratitude in his eyes "Thank you, Anna. I don't know what I would have done..." He cleared his throat, again, trying to regain a shred of his near manhood, "The beach. Cool." He got out of the car. Anna said, "OK, I'll be back at 5:30. Wait out here by the road... by those shrubs...ahem." Digging the hook in a little deeper, insinuating that he should hide.

"You're going to be back, right? Ah, you sure?" he said, doubt creeping over him again. "Sure, baby. I am here for you." She said, without a trace of guilt. "Don't worry. This will all be over soon." She didn't know how true that would turn out to be.

7

Dirk quickly forgot about reckless drivers and the gnawing fear in his gut once he turned onto the shell driveway at the diner. Captain Jack's was one of the best places to eat on the island. The diner is located beside Sundowner RV Park at the west end of the island on the bay side near the ferry dock. The park is owned by Captain "Jack" Jackson. He also runs Capt. Jack's Diner.

The RV Park has 14 large cement pads for small trailers and motor homes. They have their own private beach and a large pool and clubhouse. The park stays full almost year round. Most of the tenants are connected with the military in one way or the other. Quite a few are retired from various branches of the service, as is the owner, Captain Jack.

When Jackson retired from the Navy he came back down to the Pensacola area where he had been stationed for the first part of his hitch. While sightseeing he visited Deluna Island, landing at the West End Ferry Dock. One of his buddies rented a motor home at the dilapidated little RV Park for the weekend. During their stay, Jackson was mesmerized by the island. Seeing the 'For Sale' sign on the office window had made up his mind. He bought the park and the bait shop next to it. Getting it back in shape took most of his savings but he never regretted the decision. Shortly after refurbishing it he met a pretty young woman at a little restaurant on the beach. They fell in love, got married and turned the bait shop next to the park into a café. Now, the café is one of the best on the island.

The café is located just before the west end point, next to the RV Park, where the Gulf meets the bay, on a small fishing pier that juts out into the water. The eating area sits on the land side end of the pier with windows all the way around. It is one long room with tables on either side facing the water with an aisle down the center. The kitchen is at the end nearest the end of the pier, where the cook can buy the fish from the fishermen's daily catch, clean it and cook it, all from the back door. The walkway goes down the side of the café past the kitchen to the fishing area. The fishing area extends 25 feet past the café with benches all around. The end is in a T pattern with a covering over it for foul weather. From there you can look to your right and see the tip of the ferry dock.

Beyond that you see the mouth of the Pensacola Bay and the Naval Air Station and Pensacola in the distance. On your left you can see the emerald water of the Gulf. It is a soothing and restful place to eat and unwind.

The simple menu offers breakfast, lunch and dinner. The Shrimp basket is a lunch time favorite filled with battered gulf shrimp and seasoned fries. Supper time features the best steak on the island. That happened to be Dirk's favorite. The smell wafted out over the parking lot as he pulled in. He was still a bit early. In an hour there wouldn't have been an empty space. The dining room was full most nights.

The food kept the dining room full and the view kept the RV Park full. The Sundowner had few rental pads that were open and even fewer RV's for hire. Military retirees and snowbirds from up north kept them pretty tied up. Capt. Jack and his wife, Selena, were favorites among the locals, especially since so many were ex-military like Jack. The ex-Seal felt right at home.

Dirk sat at his favorite table on the right side end. Selena waved to him from the kitchen window up front and gave him a questioning glance, meaning, "Your usual?" Dirk interpreted the look correctly and gave her the thumbs up signal. She grinned and nodded and went back into the busy kitchen to get it ready for him.

The crowd was growing in the little dining room. He noticed many familiar faces. Some not so familiar faces, too. There was a new couple that parked beside him. Their tags were from New York. Another man, near the kitchen, sat with a large, boisterous group of, obviously military, men. One of them, a stocky built, dark haired man, sat quietly in the corner. His dark eyes took in every corner of the room. Dirk figured him for some sort of Special Forces retiree. While he was observing him the man's eyes met his for just a moment. They nodded to each other and Dirk turned his gaze to a new group of fishermen who had just arrived. The men had, apparently, just come in from an all-day deep sea excursion. They were beet red with their hair in every conceivable direction, stiff with salt spray. When he looked back, the dark man was gone. Dirk didn't know it but he would see the man again, soon.

As the last rays of the sun went down over the Gulf, he looked out over the gold tipped waves. What would the sunrise bring the next day? He thought, morosely. He was usually an upbeat guy with a positive go-getter attitude but something was unsettling him, something deep and dark. Darker than the twilight waters surrounding Deluna Island. Something blacker and much more evil, he feared. When Selena brought his dinner, he forgot everything but the mouth-watering meal in front of him.

While he ate, bad things were going down on the north side of the island. Death and disorder were on the shores of his beautiful island and things would never be the same. Dirk finished his dinner and sat back in the booth. His hunger was satisfied, it was a beautiful night...but, he couldn't rest. He knew things. Things that people, normal people, couldn't imagine.

8

As he paid for his dinner and took a walk on the dock in the moonlight, Dirk thought about how he had come to this place in his life. His path had been set in motion quite by accident. Small things had changed his course. A turn here there a meeting there. Some were good, some not so good. Some were very, very bad.

Dirk Dobbs did not start out in life planning to become a zombie expert or a zombie killer. Quite the opposite in fact. He was planning to become the next rock star. He was far from being a hunter of any type. He had a job, like most young men, but the music was his main focus. He planned to make that his career but fate stepped in and sent him on a different course.

In the last gasping breath of the war in Vietnam, 18 year old Dirk's number came up. It was the last draft of the war, just his luck, he had thought. Rather than ending up in a rice paddy in the middle of a firestorm in Vietnam, he joined the Navy.

Within a year he was in the Mediterranean visiting exotic ports and beginning to learn some of the lessons that would change his life. One lesson proved to be the one that would sculpt his life, move him away from the dreams of his youth into a nightmarish reality.

His ship went out on a cruise and was docked outside Cairo, Egypt. Since they would only be in port a short time, the sailors were given leave time to go ashore and see the sights. Dirk and a few buddies left the ship with no real plan in mind. They wandered around the ancient city for a while until they became a little bored, and a little hungry. They stopped in a local café, a little off the beaten path.

During the meal they were approached by an Egyptian tour guide. He offered his services in showing the young sailors the interesting sights in the area. Dirk remembered the moment well. It was to be one of the turning points in, not only the tour, but in his life.

You want to see the wonders of Cairo?" the man asked, "I know all the places. I will give you good tour! You stick with me!" the man said. The three sailors, bored from weeks at sea, readily agreed.

They haggled over the fee and finally settled on one that was easily split three ways. The man was more than happy with the price. He would have settled for half as much had they pushed the point. It was a hard living in the city and it was, at the moment, a hard living for the guide.

Happily, the guide began with a foot tour of the local landmarks. He was well informed and his English was getting better and better as the tour progressed. They made a circuitous trip that brought them back to the café.

"Now we can take the car and I will show many more wonders of the ancient world, if you would like." The guide said, urging them on to the second leg of the tour, "for a small additional charge." The guys had nothing better to do, so they piled into his rickety, foul smelling car to go farther afield.

 Before the day ended the three sailors and the Egyptian had become friends. They enjoyed the many sights and hidden places that the man showed them along the way. Places that most guides would have never taken them. They ended the day eating in the courtyard of the man's family home. The guide's name was Gassim Al-Fayed.

Gassim, it turned out, was in the Egyptian Air Force but, was grounded temporarily for a leg injury. He was taking over the tour business while he recuperated as a favor to his uncle who had become ill. The three found they had much in common because of their military lives. The bond that was formed in Cairo that week became a long friendship between Al-Fayed and Dobbs. Al-Fayed eventually went back to his service in the Air Force and went on to be involved in Military Intelligence. The two men kept in touch for quite a while. After a couple of years their lives became more complicated and the letters slowed, the calls came less frequently, until they ground to a halt. Dobbs never forgot the friend he made that day at the café' and hoped to get the chance to visit Cairo, again, one day. As it turned out, that day would come, a little sooner than he had imagined.

Late in 1975, Dirk found himself back in Egypt. He was injured in an accident while on a HALO jump with his SEAL unit. He had been flown to a hospital near Cairo and when he was released he decided to do his recuperation in the old city. By this time, Dirk had been writing for various magazines and newspapers in the military world, as well as a mounting list of ones that were civilian. Mostly technical journals and teaching publications, but he had had some success in the fiction genre, as well. He was just starting out on his first mystery novel and planned to use his down time in researching for it. The mysteries of Egypt inspired his creative processes. He was doing just that when, once again, he ran into his old friend, Gassim.

Looking back, Dirk realized what a momentous meeting that proved to be. As he sat, safe and sound, on Deluna Island, he could think of that time and realize how easy it is for just one choice, one decision of where to visit could change the course of a person's whole life.

9

The red ball of the sun was just starting to peek down through the palms and pines in the National Seashore on Deluna Island when Anna Knox left Adam's street headed for Red Point Beach for their picnic. They still had to stop by Bay Grocery to pick up a few last minute items, get gas and pick up more beer. It would be dark before they would get set up, Anna fumed, at herself. After all her planning, she still hadn't been prepared.

Always in a hurry, she was frustrated that the trip took so long. "If it hadn't been for that senior citizen in the silver sports car we could have been here and set up by now!" she thought.

Adam had been quiet and distracted during most of the drive. Anna was feeling a little nervous about how the date was going.

"Adam, honey, don't look so glum. We will get this all figured out." She told him as sweetly as she could muster. "I have a friend that can locate the person who posted those fibs and photos on the web. Then we will Google them, find out where they live and you can go and whip their sorry butts."

"Yeah! You better believe I will, too!" the boy said as he seethed with rage. "Can you really do that, Annie?" he asked, calming down. She hated the nickname Annie. Her grandfather used to call her that and the less she thought about him the better. Yet, she was thrilled when she heard the man of her dreams say it.

"Yeah, baby. I can, and I will! You bet! But, we will have to wait a bit." She said, backing off just a little. "First thing tomorrow morning I will give him a call and get him started on it!" That scared her. If Adam thought this thing was over he might not need her anymore and would go back to ignoring her. She would never let that happen.

It was really a moot point; she smiled in the darkness of the car, considering that SHE was the one who posted the stories and the pictures. It would be kind of silly to turn herself in, she thought, smothering a giggle, as she cut the engine.

"Let's just forget all about the troubles tonight and enjoy our picnic." She said brightly, "We came out here to take your mind off of it all and that's what we are going to do. Come on!" She hopped out of the car and ran around front to open the trunk. She loaded Adam's arms down with blankets, an ice chest and her CD player. She grabbed the food basket, the pillows, her purse, and a flashlight. She slung her dad's old fishing lantern over her shoulder and led the way down the narrow path to the point. Red Point Park was a small finger of land that jutted out into Deluna Bay, just east of Bayside Beach. It had more foliage surrounding it than the other beaches that made it a little more private. It was called Red Point because the sandy soil around the point was the color of red clay. Except for that one beach, the rest of the island's sand was a brilliant sugar white. It was Anna's favorite beach.

They found the small inlet empty, as usual, and set up their things. Anna sent Adam to collect driftwood while she unpacked the food. For months, she had read and clipped pictures out of magazines on how to have a romantic picnic with your heartthrob. She pasted them into her journal, memorizing each part. She set everything out and arranged it just like the pictures. She set out the CD player and her collection of music. The music, surprisingly, was not of the romantic sort that she would have preferred. She had picked the music that Adam liked. His favorites were hard pounding rock and heavy metal. She had two Korn CDs and the latest by a band called

Disturbed. Even though it was an older one, she also brought SlewCiah. She liked them. This is going to be a killer night. She thought. Ironically, she would turn out to be right.

While she set up camp, she couldn't shake the feeling that someone was watching her. Silly, she thought, it is probably Adam looking at her while she didn't know it, she said to herself, smiling. She wouldn't look around. It would only embarrass him and he might stop. She certainly didn't want that!

Adam wandered around the scrub looking for wood. He was not a camper and didn't really know what he was supposed to get. He just tried to find things that were dried out and not green. When he had a small armload he started making his way back to the clearing. Suddenly he heard shuffling off to his left. He stopped to listen but didn't hear anything more. Even at that, it creeped him out and he decided to hurry back.

"Oh good, you found some." Anna took charge of the small collection and put them on the sand where she had made a circle of shells. It looked so pretty, she thought. After the wood was stacked she told Adam to light it. She handed him a beer, unscrewing the top first. She wanted him to know how she tried to serve him. He didn't notice. Oh, well, she thought, he has a lot on his mind. He will see how much I care for him before the night is over.

Amazingly, the fire roared to life with very little coaxing. They sat on the blanket eating the chicken salad sandwiches that she had made. She got the recipe off the Martha Stewart show. The fire was warm, the breeze was blowing gently, and the music was blaring comfortingly. It was perfect.

As they finished the second beer, Adam began to wind down. He kicked back on the pillows and thought, this ain't so bad. He had a good buzz started. He looked over, realizing that Anna was quite fetching in her short gauzy top and low rise blue jean shorts. She had great legs, he thought, wondering why he never noticed before. Anna saw the look in his eye and took advantage of the moment. She snuggled in under his arm and curled up beside him. He turned and forgot all about the problems of the day for a while.

Later, as they lay under the extra blanket, he dozed off. Anna, on the other hand, was still wide awake and ablaze. Shooting stars in the sky could not be as bright as this, she thought. It was all she had dreamed, and more. Adam was an ardent lover. She was about to tell him when he rolled over toward her and opened his eyes. She waited to hear that he felt the things that she was feeling, willing him to speak. "I've gotta pee." He said and got to his feet. She was disappointed for a moment, until he got up. She was awed by the way his body looked in the moonlight, how he walked away almost in time with the driving beat of the music, that she didn't notice he had dumped her purse out onto the sand by the pillow. The girl didn't feel the eyes on her again, either. She was still in such a glow. Eyes watched the scene from the trees. More than one pair of eyes had seen it all. Behind the eyes was a hunger, not a sexual hunger, but a driving force that was set on her.

She lay there listening to the song, dozing in and out. She thought she heard sounds. He must be coming back. She sat up, expectantly. He wasn't there. Strange, she thought. She was sure she'd heard rustling in the dark trees. The boy had taken the flashlight with him so; she was unable to see much by the fire light.

Suddenly, something burst from the trees, coming right at her. It landed almost on top of her. She would have screamed but the force knocked the wind out of her. She was terrified. Adam sprawled across the blanket, laughing hysterically. "Did I scare you?" he wheezed in between peals of mirth. "Yes," she slapped at him, giggling now. "Yes, you did you bad boy! Now I gotta go!"

She was too embarrassed to walk away naked, as he had done, so she rooted around, tossing pillows and blankets, until she found her top and shorts. She pulled the top over her head and wiggled into the shorts, minus any undies. She would be taking them off again as soon as she got back, she thought, sure of herself, now. Taking the flashlight, she picked her way through the wooded trail.

While she was gone Adam sat up. He needed a cigarette. He usually didn't smoke but tonight was a new night. Tonight he wanted to smoke. He rummaged around in the basket for the pack Anna had brought but came up empty. It must be in her purse, he surmised. He picked up the big leather bag, not realizing it was already upside down and partially dumped it out. All the contents spilled out onto the sand.

"Oh, Crap." He said to himself as he tried to get the sand off of the stuff. "God, girls have too much stuff!" He spied the cigarette pack under a large manila envelope. When he reached for the pack the contents of the envelope were showing out the top. He picked it up to put it into the bag and saw pictures. Pictures of him.

He poured them out into his lap. It was several prints of his head, his body, his arms and legs. That is weird, he thought. He fanned them out and saw an equal number of shots of another boy about his age, also, in different positions. And, he was naked. Looking back through the stack he saw that most of the pictures of him were in various stages of undress. He knew Anna was obsessed with him, but pictures of his...parts? He pulled out another pack and sucked in his breath. These shots were like the ones on the Internet! Some were of him, alone, in strange positions! The last one was him with...the other boy! Oh, my God, what did this mean? These were the parts of photos that had been photoshopped together to make the disgusting pictures on the Internet! How did Anna get these pictures? His mind was reeling.

He looked at the pages more closely. The printer had printed the name of the file and the author on the file on the top of each page. He read it slowly. The file name was 'Adam'. Slowly, his eyes read the name of the author of the file of photos that had set this nightmare in motion. It read, "AnnaK"! He let the meaning of this information sink in for a minute.

Anna made the sick photos? He shook his head. She couldn't...could she? If she made the pictures, she, also, had to be the one who posted them on MyFace! It was all becoming real, now. He looked through the other pages, quickly. One was a large block of printed text. Every word of the rumors was there. While his anger burned he looked over the information on the pages. Along

with the file name and author there was a fax
number across the top with the name of the
receiver beside it. It was familiar, he thought.
Then the name of the recipient floored him. M.
McLain. Jenna's dad! These had been faxed to
Jenna's FATHER? From Anna! He was so
furious he didn't know what to do. Anna had
done it all! She had spread the rumors. She had
faked the pictures. She had put them on the
Internet and faxed them to his girlfriend's dad!
Just then he heard the rustle in the bushes. It must
be the witch coming back! Before he could get the
papers back into the folder, he heard a terrified
scream. He crammed the folder into her purse and
put it back under the pillow just as Anna came
running out of the trees.

After that, everything went black.

Adam had heard of people becoming so incensed
with rage that they blacked out but he had never
believed it until now. He had no memory of the
events that followed. From that point, until he
found himself walking in the darkened parking lot,
Adam Moore had no idea what had happened on
the point or since. It was a total black screen. He
didn't know what to do or where to go. His hands
were cut and covered with blood. What had he
done? He was afraid. More afraid than he'd ever
been in his life. He knew something terrible had

happened out there. But what? He put his head in his hands and cried in the darkness.

The breeze picked up and soothed the residents of Deluna Island who sat in their armchairs and slept in their beds. They lived in paradise, where the real world could not touch them. Each day came, and went, in the pure and regular patterns of island life. The recent hurricane had touched on their shores, but, had left them, virtually, unscathed. In their naiveté, they rested in the quiet lull. They slept in peace. For now.

Unknown to the Gulf Coast residents, Deluna Islanders, in particular, the summer storm had brought destruction and disorder to their shores. It was not from the ruinous high winds, surging seas or smashed homes, but, something much more devastating than all those things combined.

Over the sound of the wind rattling the palm fronds at Red Point Park, the driving beat of the rock group, SlewCiah, was playing. The words said more about the future of the community than the writers could have foreseen.

"While the city sleeps,
Death is walking by.
While the dead man creeps,
Murder makes us cry.
Discord, Death and Murder,

Discord, Death and Murder,
Discord, Death and Murder,
Discord, Death and Murder,
It's on our border,
Nothing but disorder.
It's multiplying all the time,
Pretending it's just another crime.
Discord, Death and Murder..."

(SlewCiah, Back for More CD)

Discord, Death and Murder, just like the song said, was coming to their city. It lay beneath the waves just off their sunny shores. It would wreak havoc on their lives as it came. Discord, Death and Murder...

10

When Jenna McLain left the lunchroom she was trying to get herself together. She went home but she couldn't stay there. She had to go back. She wanted to see what Adam had to say for himself. She pulled back into the parking lot. She saw Adam Moore come out looking for her and saw him go back inside. The girl parked her car beside a dumpster where she wouldn't be seen by anyone. She didn't want to talk about what had happened with anyone. It was all just too painful.

A few minutes later she saw him come out of the hall next to the library and sit on the curb behind the palm trees. She could see how distraught he was. She almost went to him until she saw Anna come up to him. She saw her comforting him and touching him, proprietarily. "I guess this is just more of what I don't know about Adam!" She said, out loud, to the air.

Anna Knox! The realization sent physical shock waves throughout her body. Adam wasn't aware that Anna had been harassing Jenna from the time they'd gotten together. The malicious teen told Jenna that she and Adam had a steamy past relationship that would 'never die'.   She told her it was still very much alive. To make matters worse, she had somehow managed to be wherever the two of them went. Whether it was on dates, to church, at school functions, or most any place, Anna was there. Jenna had not mentioned this to Adam. She didn't believe what the girl said. She wrote it off to Anna's warped mind, but it made her very upset.

She warned the girl that if she didn't back off she would MAKE HER back off. Anna took it like she took most things. It rolled right off her back. She kept up her campaign to break them up.

Most everybody thought Anna was a little off the bead. She told so many different stories that you never knew what to believe. Jenna told herself she didn't believe a word of it. She told herself that it didn't matter. Yet...deep down, it did matter to Jenna. If she believed that Anna and Adam had something going, she thought, she didn't know what she'd do. The aggravation had suddenly stopped about a week before and she thought maybe Anna Knox had given up. She couldn't have been more wrong.

When the fax came in to her Dad's machine she was overwhelmed with embarrassment. And, fury! How humiliating to have to sit there while her dad looked at those pictures; pictures of Adam, with other girls, and even a guy, doing those horrible things. When he handed her the pages she saw the identifying address on the top...AnnaK.

Her dad had asked her if she knew who the sender was, if she recognized the name. She told him no, but she lied. She knew exactly who it was and she was sick of her and her lies. She wanted to be done with Adam and done with this dirtiness. Well, that isn't entirely true, she'd thought. She didn't want to be rid of Adam but she could not face what he was doing. Anna and those images, what did it mean? She thought. It must all be related. He obviously had certain 'tastes' that she didn't want to think about. Anna had hinted at their unrestrained 'lovemaking'...maybe this is what she meant...Ugh. It made her sick. She had rushed out of the school determined to end it all and never look back.

When she saw Adam by the steps, she almost softened. He looked so hurt and confused. She waited in the car until he came out. She was working up her nerve to go over to him when Anna showed up.

Seeing them together, her arms around him, it made her angry all over again. When he kissed her, well that was it. She had never been so furious. He wasn't upset at all about losing her! His sad face had been an act! He was laughing! They were laughing! "Look at them together!" she said out loud in the confines of her car, "the way she is joking with him and him...walking to her car like nothing has happened!"

Had their whole relationship been a lie? She wondered. Had Anna been telling the truth? They'd made a fool of her. She put her head down on the steering wheel and started to cry. The more she cried the angrier she became. Just then she saw the Volkswagen pull out of the parking lot. She slammed her Toyota into gear and followed them.

Adam's house was on a winding residential street with thick pines lining the road. Jenna didn't have a problem hiding her car from sight. She saw Adam go into the house. When he didn't come back out Jenna drove to Anna's house. She sat in the shadows of a large stand of palms contemplating her next move. Should she confront the girl or just wait to see what happened next? Were they meeting later at the game? While these thoughts whirled around in Jenna's head she saw Anna come back out of the house with a basket and blankets. She got out of her car and slid noiselessly around the neighbor's house to the cover of the old garage beside Anna's car. Anna was talking on her cell phone while she packed the car.

"It is so wonderful, Girl! Adam is the sweetest guy in the whole world. He can't wait till we get to Red Point tonight. I almost couldn't drive the car. He was ALL over me!" she giggled into the receiver. "I mean, once he was rid of that DEAD WEIGHT, Jenna! Ha! He practically flew into my arms."
The hidden girl listened quietly, her nails biting into her palms. It was true, she thought, it's all true. Jenna knew, as most of the local teens knew, what Anna meant by Red Point. It was a small cove at Red Point Park. They all went there in the summertime to picnic, drink and party. It was secluded and the water was shallow enough for even the non-swimmers. "So, that is where they are going later." She whispered to herself as she made her way back to the car, stealthily. Well, she thought as she pulled away from the curb, dialing her cell phone, I will have a big surprise for Miss Anna and her new boyfriend!

11

The morning sun shone through the front windows of the Jackson kitchen. It was a beautiful gulf day that forgot the storms of the past week, that didn't acknowledge the dangers of the darkness. Capt. Jack greeted his old friend with a big smile and a hot cup of coffee. His friend, Angus Murphy, was a regular visitor to the Jackson household. The two men had similar backgrounds, likes and dislikes. They'd known each other for many years and were glad to rekindle that friendship when the burly Scotsman had rented one of the Captain's RV's for the summer several years ago. The summer turned to fall, and, eventually, Murphy decided to retire on the island. During that time they began the ritual of meeting for coffee nearly every morning and jogged the paths through the park together. This morning Angus had gone out early, alone.

Angus Murphy was retired from the S.A.S., the Special Air Service. The Special Air Service Regiment (S.A.S.) is the principal unit of the

British Army. It is a small and secretive institution. The S.A.S. forms a significant part of the United Kingdom Special Forces, much like our Navy Seals or Delta Force units. The S.A.S. can trace its existence back to 1941, when British Army volunteers conducted raids behind enemy lines in the North African Campaign in World War II. The Regiment's motto is "Who Dares Wins". Currently the S.A.S. is believed to be involved in many areas that are classified including counter terrorism within the United Kingdom and its concerns, training special-forces from other nations, protection of senior British dignitaries and VIPs, and intelligence collection in deep battle space. Training of other Special Forces units was where Angus Murphy met Jack Jackson. Captain Jack was a Master Navy Salvage Diver. He came in contact with Murphy in the Falklands when Jackson was on special assignment with the Royal Navy. He was on the Damage Control Team on one of the British Carriers.

Angus Murphy stood side by side with Captain Jack at the dining room table in the kitchen. They were both looking at a large, flat, blue plastic case that Murphy had found half submerged in the sand on Little White Key.

"I was out doing a walk along the beach, pickin' up the rubbish, and all, when I spied this sticking up outa' the sand." He told the Captain, "It is someone's computer notebook, possibly from some vessel that had trouble in the storms. It has the look of it."

Little White Key was a short strip of sand just off the westernmost tip of the island between the West End Ferry dock and Capt. Jack's Café. It wasn't unusual to find articles on the key. It was sort of a catch-all for debris.

There, where the Gulf waters meet the bay waters, the currents meet, beating up against each other, swirling around, washing all manner of rubbish up onto the tail end of the island. Several years ago, after Hurricane Ivan, two bags filled with cash had been recovered there. It was thought to be drug money from a smuggling vessel that cut his chances too close in the squall. After a storm residents follow the coastline looking for useable items and cleaning up anything that could be dangerous.

That is what Angus Murphy had been doing in the early morning hours when he came across the box. He knew the laptop was probably ruined but he thought it might be worth a try to see what was on it. He took it over to his friend, Jack.

"The plastic is in good shape, so I wouldna' think it had been in the water a long period of time." The Scotsman said in his melodic Scottish accent. "I can bet that it will still be working, if it hasn'a gotten the sea water into it." Jack agreed and they set about to open the case and check it out.

The Captain agreed, "The seal is still in good shape. I can see that you haven't opened it. Good evidence work, Murphy." He quipped. Angus smiled.

They both knew how to handle items that could be used as evidence, but, neither expected this little computer to be anything important to anyone but its owner. Who knew who that could be, he thought. The only way to find that out was to get it running.

Jack opened the box. Inside he found a perfectly dry but battered laptop. Opening it up, he typed in the startup commands. The machine opened its files without hesitation, but the two were dismayed to find it was in Russian.

Angus had some knowledge of the language he had gleaned during his international days. Sitting down before the tiny screen, he picked out the first file he recognized.

It was a personal journal. It was more than they had hoped for, or imagined. Translated, this is what they read. The writer was a head cook named Boris.

JOURNAL: Head Cook, Boris Zalenski
CARGO SHIP: USSR Katarina
LAST PORT: Port of Tampico, Northern Mexico
NEXT SCHEDULED PORT: Pensacola Harbor, FL
DATE: JULY 7

*We are today leaving the Mexico port of Tampico.
Leaving this place was a great thrill. It was a bad time
there.*
*Our crew had been restless after so long a voyage and was
very persistent about asking for leave. There was some
trouble in the city but the Commander allowed leave,
provided the men avoided the city. This was not a
problem for them as the destination they wanted was a
house of ill repute on the outskirts and secluded from the
city.*
*Most of the company went ashore after we unloaded our
cargo. I am sorry to be one of the ones left behind as I
haven't been ashore in many months. Maybe I will go
tomorrow, if the weather holds. The others will be back
in the morning and the rest of us will go then. We will
have only a short time, since we will be putting out if the
storm turns eastward.*

July 8 0800 hours

*Only a few of the men have arrived back on board. The
commander is in a rage. The local police cannot be
found and there are not enough men left on board to have
a search party for them. Some of the men came back
early in the evening. There is some sort of sickness in the*

port and they did not wait to see what it was about. They did not want to get sick so they returned. Fifteen men went ahead to socialize with the women and have not returned.

One man, who was to stay on duty, sneaked away in the night and was caught boarding this morning. He is in the confinement area. I was not to go there but I went down to see him. He is a friend to me. He seems to be sick. He has scratched his arm and wanted me to get disinfectant for him. I cleaned his wound and bandaged it. The orderlies are very loose and will not tell the officers. I would get in trouble. So would he, so I will not tell them. He was sleeping now, so I will go back up.

July 9 0730 hours

Only three of the men have returned and they are not in good shape. Two are in serious condition, one died shortly after boarding. We put his body in the refrigerated room for now.

We are not sure what has happened to them. They have not been coherent. They are running high fevers and have severe wounds to their bodies that we cannot identify.

They look like animal biting or scratching. The men tell of being attacked by monsters that are men. It does not make sense.

We are leaving port today. The men need hospital care and the hospitals here are abandoned. We don't know why the doctors would leave unless the sickness has become worse in other parts and they have gone.

The officials have warned that the sickness is great and, if our men have not returned, they are most likely dead. We can only assume the others were killed in some kind of attack or have come down with the sickness. There is no medicine here for this and we must not take it on board. The men on board are injured and need care. The captain said we will put out and take them today to the U.S. hospital in Corpus Christi, Texas. He said it is the best we can do.

July 9 1300 hours

The crew now consists of only twelve healthy men. Three became ill and died. My friend in the infirmary has died. We found him and the others with high fevers. They had convulsions and died. The injured crew members have died the same.

We are not going into port in Texas. There is no need now. The sick are now gone.

We have set our course now on to Pensacola, which is our next stop. I don't know if we will be able to land there with this sickness but there is a Navy hospital there that works with the merchant ships. I am hoping they can help us before it spreads to us all.

July 10 0500 hours - *31 hours since Mexico*

We have radioed for help but nobody comes.

I have found out why. The radio man is sick with the fever. He would not let me in the room to answer the calls. He is out of his head. They will not know who or where we are. We are lost.

The things I have seen today I hope never to see again. I am locked in the supply pantry in the mess hall, now. It is a small lock but I hope it holds.

This illness makes monsters of men. The ones we thought were dead were not. They all walk again and kill. I do not understand this. They attack all in their path and kill them. The captain is dead. They eat the men they kill. They do so much damage to the Captain. I do not think he will walk, again. I may be the only one left.

July10 1030 hours

I tried to get out to the radio. I cannot.

I killed one of the horrible men. I shot him in the chest twice. I saw his chest open up but he kept coming. I shot him once more in the forehead and he fell. He does not walk now.

It is a bad thing to kill a man so closely. Even one such as this. The blood splattered over me. It went into my eyes.
I must stop now. I am feeling ill. At least the creature didn't get me. ..

That was the last entry into the log. The men looked at each other. There was seriousness on both sides. The men had been in faraway places and seen extraordinary things. They knew there were things that didn't seem possible in this world that would seem like nightmares, delusions or delirium to most citizens, but these two knew they were true.

"It looks like Boris was in big trouble." Jack Jackson said. "Yes, my friend. The question is this. Did he bring it to our shores? If their last port of call was to be Pensacola and this is washed up onto our wee little key, chances of the ship getting this close are great." Angus answered.

"I think we better get a call into Moselle at the Coast Guard office and see what he has heard about a floundering ship with sick men or injured men on board." Jack pulled out his cell phone and dialed one of his tenants, Roger Moselle.

Moselle was a dispatch officer at the Pensacola Coast Guard at the office on Slemmer Avenue, at NAS Pensacola. He is one of the many that ferry across to the base every day from Deluna Island. He was one of the tenants at the Sundowner.

Moselle had heard of a ship. He knew that Jack and Angus wouldn't be asking for information if it wasn't important. He found the record of the calls and faxed them over within a few minutes.

They received the faxes and sat quietly as they perused the reports.

Coast Guard Report: July 13 0800 hours

Russian Cargo Ship missing in Gulf. Last port of call in Tampico, Mexico
Unloaded cargo there. Unable to verify. No response to our calls to harbormaster. Possibly damaged by Hurricane Rhonda.
Next port of call reported to be Pensacola, FL but has not docked.
Received garbled, incoherent messages referring to injuries and or sickness on board, crewmen missing. Unable to ascertain complete information on the 8th and 9th of July, then nothing more. Search and rescue crews were unable to find ship, survivors or identifiable debris in radius due to excess debris in water from storms. Nothing more can be done at present since we are tied up with survivors from other vessels in trouble from storm.

Coast Guard Report: July 14 1300 hours

Report received of a vessel adrift off of Mobile Bay, AL but not authenticated.

Coast Guard Report: July 15 0900 hours

Large vessel reported to be listing in the Gulf at the mouth of Pensacola and Deluna Bays.

Search and rescue crews were dispatched but no ship was detected, no debris or survivors in water. Slight oil slick near west point of Deluna Island. But is considered to be from the storm currents drifting in from oil rigs off of Louisiana and South Texas....End of Report

----

"Well, looks like we have a sick ship somewhere on the bottom between Mobile and Deluna Bay." Jackson said a little louder than he meant.

"What kind of 'sick' is the question? There is no doubting that it is infectious and transmits within a prescribed set of hours. Delirium must cause the men to do the awful things Boris describes, but I am likely to believe that some of what the cook is saying is fever induced as well. Monster men eating the crew. Sounds like the poison is contact generated. He must have gotten it when the blood was sprayed into his eyes. Poor bastard." Angus looked out the window in thought.

The Captain and Angus didn't realize that Selena, the Captain's wife, had heard part of the conversation from the hallway. "Jack, what is it? What about a ship and monster men?" Selena Jackson came into the room, quickly, obviously agitated. Selena was not a strong woman. She was high strung and couldn't handle a lot of stress at once. Her husband went out of his way to keep her happy and content. Jack wondered how much she had heard.

"Selena, now, angel, there is no need for you to worry. There was a ship out off Mobile Bay that had a flu epidemic on it, that's all. Some of the men were hallucinating from the fevers, saying crazy stuff. The ship was lost in the storm. Way over there on the west side. The Coast Guard knows all about it and has gone out to quarantine the site." He said, patting her on the shoulder, and kissing her head. Selena wasn't fooled. She knew something was up and she wanted to know what. The key was one of the favorite places for the kids on the island. They went there to swim, fish, and snorkel. If there was danger there, she needed to know, to warn the parents. Jack tried to keep everything from her but not this, she decided. She nodded to him, trying to smile, to make him think she was buying it.

Seeing that she wasn't assured, Angus chimed in, "Ah, lass, it is nothing but a tempest in a teakettle. We found this man's little journal out at the key and we are on our way, now, to take it to Moselle. He will take care of it. You don't have to worry."

"But, the box. It washed up at the key..." she started. Angus cut her off.

"You know how that channel runs from over there done the Panhandle from those bad girls, Erin and Opal. It washes the stuff in all the way from Louisiana onto our fair shores. It wasn't close enough for you to worry about, my girl."

Hurricanes Erin and Opal had hit the coast, years back, one right after the other. It had done considerable damage and had dredged out a trench down the coast. The trench caused severe rip tides and changed the currents all around the area, with the tip of Deluna Island being right in the middle of it.

Captain Jack and his cohort were stretching the effects a bit to soothe Selena's mind. Neither had any idea how close the ship was to the island. They didn't want to alarm her, or the other residents. Yet.

Angus went on, as he walked her to the door, "Doncha' worry. The ship wouldna' got this far in that wee storm." Selena ducked her head, smiling as best she could. He went away, sure that she was pacified.

Angus Murphy was a slight man. He stood less than five and a half feet tall and weighed around 150 pounds but his chest rumbled with a deep baritone voice that captured all listeners' attention. His accent sounded like a cross between Sean Connery and Shrek. It delighted the ladies and when turned on an enemy or an underling, it could stop them in their tracks. Usually, when he talked to Selena in that Gaelic purr, she listened, mesmerized. Not this time. But, Angus didn't realize that his charm had failed. He was used to getting his way, whether for personal reasons or in his work.

Angus' life was filled with people following his orders. He was a professional. He gave orders, people moved. He had been an officer in the SAS for 25 years and had been involved in many covert activities around the globe. It was hard to imagine that he could know so many ways to kill a man. In his line of work it was necessary.

His job had been to train men to quell the threat and dispatch the aggressor. He was 'retired', now, at least on record, but he was still very active behind the scenes. His contact list included generals, admirals, politicians, Navy Seals, Delta

Force operatives and lots of people with the three initials after their names; CIA.

Selena let him think she was no longer concerned. If she wanted to know something, she thought, she would have to find out for herself. She hugged her husband and her friend, grabbed the keys off the hook by the door and told them she would see them later at the café.

Preoccupied with the danger, Angus sat back down at the table and looked at the electronic journal. He had a bad feeling about the cook's story. He was going to have to make a few calls. Jack hesitated, watching his wife walk to the van. He didn't know that it would be the last time he would see her on this earth.

12

One thing about the Panhandle area in NW Florida, with the bases surrounding them on each end, there was no lack of trained military personnel. With half its population military or ex-military they had a host of possibilities, Captain Jack thought, as he made up a list. On Deluna Island, alone, there was a couple of retired Navy Seals, one of them an expert in underwater demolition; one former member of the Army's Delta Force, and several others from the regular Navy and other service ranks. Angus, former SAS, had run covert missions all over the world and was still an active consultant on current movements. Angus had offered to take control of the situation.

If anyone could get it done... the Captain thought, he was beginning to feel a little better. Things were beginning to take shape. He had given the list to Murphy and he had added a few names from his book. In just a few hours they had called in several favors and talked a few retirees back into service. They had divers, supervised by Captain

Jack, and underwater demolition guys. Angus was handling the supplies, ammunition and intelligence. Everyone that was contacted was sworn to secrecy. They weren't told the nature of the problem, other than it was a disabled ship with contaminants.

The plan was simple. They would blow up the ship and the infected person or persons inside. From what they had learned, the sickness was highly contagious and spreads rapidly. They were taking no chances. If they could, contain and destroy them before they got to the island, the island would be safe.

While they planned, unknown to them, the infection had mutated to the brains of the dead seaman. It brought the men back from the dead. It woke them into a mutated state where they were not affected by the depths of water over their heads. They merely got up and had already walked the bottoms of the bay surfacing on the island. They were practically on their doorsteps. Neither Jack Jackson nor Angus Murphy realized it was too late.

While the mutants were making their way to the quiet cove on Deluna Island, important things had been happening between interested parties in Sudanese capital of Khartoum. Angus Murphy had called on an old friend to get the weapons and supplies they needed to do the job on the contaminated ship, but, as the heavens would have it, the strands of the web of destiny were intertwined, silently, behind the scenes. These strands came from a time long past, a time when one man performed a heroic act that formed them and would soon find them winding, curling, and intersecting to form the safety net that was needed to save Deluna Island and its inhabitants. It all started long ago.

Ibrahim Pasha, the adopted son of Muhammad Ali of Egypt founded Khartoum in 1821 as an outpost for the Egyptian Army. It was made the capital of Anglo-Egyptian Sudan in 1899.

In 1973 it was the site of the attack in which a group called *Black September* held ten hostages at the Saudi Embassy, five of whom were diplomats. The US ambassador, the US deputy ambassador, and the Belgian Chargé d'affaires were murdered. The remaining hostages were still being held.

The Sudanese government continued to negotiate with the terrorists, but refused to compromise or to meet any of the group's demands. Within sixty hours, the eight gunmen released the remaining hostages, all of whom were Arab, and surrendered to Sudanese authorities.

One of the consultants to the hostage negotiators was a young SAS trooper named Angus Murphy. In one of the unknown stories that you find behind many crisis situations, one of the servants, employed in the embassy made her way to the office where the negotiators are working. She was beside herself with fear and worry. Her young daughter was in the embassy. The guards pushed her away, thinking she was just a hysterical woman, speaking gibberish. When she was refused entry, she waited in the hallway by the men's lavatory. She tried to talk to several of the men as they came into the passageway but was ignored or refused. Exhausted and frantic, she sat on the floor by the doorway and collapsed into wrenching sobs. Angus Murphy saw her there on his way to the lounge and, moved by her state, he knelt to ask her what was the matter. He learned that the woman's 10 year old daughter was inside the embassy with the hostages and the terrorists. When the takeover happened, she explained, many of the servants hid in the servant's hall and were able to escape through a little known larder door into the back courtyard. From there they were in cover from the trees and shrubs all the way to a small opening in the garden wall. The servants often used the opening as a shortcut to the kitchens when coming to and from work. In a frantic moment, as the terrorists unexpectedly opened the door to the hall, she pushed her daughter into a small closet by the back door. It was too small for the both of them so she fled into the garden to hide until she could come back to get her and flee. Later, she had gone back but one of the terrorists came into the hall before she could get her out. One of her co-workers, who had only just then made their way down from the upper floors, pulled her out with him despite her efforts to stay with her child. Now, she was afraid that the men would find her daughter harm or even kill her.

Angus assured the woman that the group had mentioned nothing about children except the Saudi Arabian Ambassador's four children who were still inside. That did not appease the mother. She knew the nature of people who would do these things, she told him. "They will not hesitate to do what they want to an unimportant child who can gain them nothing." She said, "They will not even mention that she is there." Something in the woman's words rang true in Murphy's heart. He told the woman to draw a map to the hole in the fence and the way to the hallway where the child was secreted away. She quickly drew the diagram and pressed it into his hand. "Please save my little girl." She said simply. She believed that he could do it. It made him believe it, as well.

Angus had training in search and rescue missions. He had been in a few of the search parties that had spirited away a man and his wife under the noses of a maniacal madman in Belfast only a few weeks before. This wouldn't be his first rodeo.

Assuring the mother he would do his best, he slipped away from the hotel and made his way down to the dusty alleyway. He followed her directions to the fence that surrounded the embassy grounds. He found the gap and went through it, carefully. He skirted the courtyard, crouching behind bushes and barrels. He found the door into the kitchens. The hallway was visible through the window. It was empty. Quietly, Angus twisted the knob and slid the door open. The closet door was the second door on the left, across from a coat rack full of hanging cloaks and scarves.

Just as he reached the closet door he heard footsteps coming down the stairs. He flattened himself against the wall behind the cloaks and held his breath. A head appeared around the corner. It was a tall man. The man was one of the militants. He was carrying a tray of empty bowls and dishes. He clattered the glassware together as he juggled it to open the door into the kitchen, jangling Murphy's nerves as well. The man stayed in the room only a minute before he returned going back up the stairs, empty handed, the way he came.

Angus expelled his breath and stood listening for a moment. He heard nothing. He crept across the

hall to the closet and whispered the girl's name.
"Be very quiet." He told her, "Your mother has
sent me to get you out of here, little one. Do not be
afraid." He burred the R's in his soft Scottish
brogue. He slipped open the door and looked into
the child's frightened eyes. He put his finger to his
lips and picked her up. In a few steps he had
opened the back door again and slipped, with the
child, into the garden. After checking out the area
completely, he flew across the grass like a gazelle.
Holding the frightened girl tightly, he squeezed
through the hole and into the alleyway, down to
the corner and out onto the main thoroughfare.

The mother and her young son met them, running
down the street in tears. She took her daughter
and they made their way back to a safer distance.
The mother vowed to do anything she could to pay
him for his help. The man looked at her relieved
face and told her that she owed him nothing. The
son, who had grabbed his hand and forearm in a
bear-like grip, looked him in the eyes and vowed,
"I will be your friend for the longest part of your
life", he said, "call on me when you need
assistance and it will be yours."

This son grew up to be an international arms
dealer. He had been instrumental in helping
Angus in many clandestine activities over the
years. He was the one Angus called when he
found himself in danger on the island.

While Angus was calling in favors, Dirk was
having his supper at the Captain's café and a
confused teenage boy was finding out the sad truth
about the world at a picnic on the bay.

 Angus has called in some men and was now,
contacting an old friend who was an arms dealer.
The man who dealt with the weapons had once
promised the Scotsman help, if he was ever in
need. Angus didn't know how to contact the
dealer. It had been many years. The word around
the service was the he worked both sides of the
street, as many did to make money and to increase
the security of his family. Angus contacted an old
buddy from the CIA who was working a case in
Alexandria, Egypt.

The agent met with the trafficker in a café on the
outskirts of Khartoum. "Your old friend is in
trouble. He is calling in his note." The undercover
agent told the young man. "My mother still speaks
of Angus Murphy. He saved my sister's life," he
said, "Anything he wants I will get."

Murphy's CIA friend explained the problem. He
told him about an illness that made men able to
walk under the water, and laughed, doubtfully. "I
am having a little trouble believing the story,
myself" he said with a self- conscious laugh, "I've
known Murphy for a long time, and I have never

known him to...exaggerate...but this one..." The other man scowled at him. "There are many things in this world that we may not believe, but even so, Angus Murphy says that this is so, this is so."

While the two men drank their strong coffee, the distributor made note of the lethal grocery list. As he struggled with the foreign names he asked "How would you write this name of the island?" The agent told him once more, "It is Deluna Island, Florida, spelled D E L U N A." he explained.

Two tables over a dark haired man sat drinking a small cup of coffee. He was just close enough that snatches of the conversation reached his ears. He was paying no attention to the men. In his country, and this area of the world, covert sales of guns and other black market items were not uncommon. At the mention of an illness and walking under water, his ears pricked up. When he heard the name, Deluna Island, Florida, he signaled for the waiter, paid his check and left. In two hours he was on an international flight to New York with a connecting flight to Mobile, Alabama. The ticket agent called ahead and reserved a rental car at the airport with a map of the Florida Panhandle.

As he sat in the uncomfortable airliner seat he thought over the situation. Dirk Dobbs lived on Deluna Island. If someone on that island needed that kind of firepower for men who could live underwater, his friend would need help. His friend would need all the help he could get. Gassim Al-Fayed closed his eyes to sleep while the 747 cut through the dark sky.

13

On his return trip to Cairo, Dirk had taken up writing as a way to keep his mind busy during his convalescence. The book he was building needed spicing up. What better place to find mysterious happenings to write about than ancient Egypt, he thought. While Dirk was busily weaving his story-world, his friend, Gassim, was reliving his own horror story. It had begun a month before on, what was supposed to be a routine recon mission. It turned out to be much more.

Reports had come in about trouble in Khamudi, a small village 70 miles south of Cairo named after an ancient Hyksos king. Gassim Al-Fayed was sent, with a troop of soldiers, to check out the accounts of violence in the area. A passing caravan reported that the village was in disarray. The authorities were not to be found. A woman, one of the residents, was found in the desert, wandering, sick, with horrific wounds to her body. She died soon after being discovered and was buried, the people told them.

The men went out into the village and found it as
the nomads had described. While searching the
huts, Al-Fayed and his men found carnage. They
found the sands soaked in blood. And, they found
something else. They found the walking dead.

Gassim entered Khamudi with a small force of six
men.
At first they thought the village was deserted. The
streets were emptied and the houses dark.
Everyday articles were strewn about as if the users
had simply dropped them where they were
working and run off.   As they passed empty hut
after hut, they were taken by how totally quiet it
was. The center of the village was formed in a
semicircle of the larger residences. Entering the
homes they were horrified. Mutilated bodies of
men, women and children littered the homes and
dusty inner courtyards. The unit, resuming their
search, met back on the main track. Gassim
instructed his men to continue through the town.

After several minutes they came to a fork in the
dusty road. Two ramshackle buildings and an old
rusted out truck blocked the view beyond. Al-
Fayed held up his hand to stop the men.
Suddenly, they heard noises. Noises they couldn't
identify. It sounded like a dog lapping up water.
The commander silently directed two men to go
around the back of the building while he took two

more around the side. The remaining two were to stay in the street and keep a lookout.

As he and the two soldiers made their way around the building they heard the reports of several shots being fired. They turned and ran toward the corner of the building as the air was pierced with screams. The team moved in a low crouch between cover of the buildings and rusted cars. Before they could reach their comrades Al-Fayed caught movement off to his right. He turned. What he saw defied reality.

There on the ground he saw one of his men. Crouched over him was what looked like a man, but with sunken eyes, rotted skin and grotesque features. He looked half dead. He was ripping into the soldier's neck with his rotted teeth. He could tell it was too late to save the soldier but he could do something about the thing that was attacking him. Al-Fayed pointed his military issue AK 47 into the creature's face and blew its head away. That was Gassim Al-Fayed's first zombie kill.

He would destroy many more before the nightmare was over. He and his men had walked into a nest of the living dead. The zombies were feasting on the villagers who, in turn, were then falling prey to the sickness and become zombies, as well. The numbers had increased daily with no one to take action to quell the plague. The men used their elite military training to destroy as many as possible.

After being cornered in an old market, the fight went on. Somehow Gassim managed to survive. The rest of his force did not. He had been forced to shoot two of his men when they had become reanimated into the flesh eating walking dead. He fled the market and would not have escaped had he not been taken in by two of the villagers who had managed to stay alive and uninfected. The survivors had barricaded themselves into a mosque with six other survivors. They stayed alive until help came fourteen days later. After being hospitalized, debriefed and released, on leave, with orders to take it easy, Gassim ran into his old friend, Dirk at the café in Cairo.

"My old friend!" the Egyptian said as he hurried forward, hand outstretched. Dirk looked up from his Stella, surprised. "Gassim! I never expected to see you! I thought you were on a mission?" he said as they clasped hand and took their seats around the little table. "I was, my friend." The Egyptian answered, solemnly. The sallow look of his friend told Dirk that he had been through some sort of ordeal. He seemed shaken to his core, not the strong, confident man he had known. After many drinks and many hours, Gassim opened up.

He told Dobbs everything that had happened in Khamudi.

Dirk, upon hearing the story, rejected it out of hand. There was no such thing as zombies. His old chum had just spent a little too much time in the desert sun and drank a little too much Stella. Dirk patronized his friend, not wanting to hurt him. "Ah, Gassim, you have obviously had a very bad experience on this last mission. It has...caused you to become more... imaginative. You will be feeling more yourself soon..." he trailed off at the look in the man's eyes.

"I know this is hard for you to believe. It is hard for me and I have seen it. It haunts me at night, the faces..." he trailed off. Dirk knew that Al-Fayed was not easily frightened. There must be something to this, he thought, just not ... that. He knew he must go there himself. His good sense told him to stay away but his inquiring mind wanted him to go. Al-Fayed resisted, at first. He explained it was too much of a danger but, deep down, he, too, wanted to return. He had to put the fears to rest, and, he had to be sure they had destroyed them all. At length, he agreed to take Dirk there.

Al-Fayed set up the trip to Khamudi in secret. The officers over him would not want him to go back there; much less take a civilian with him. The man didn't look forward to going back there, either, but he felt he had to. He had to face the fears that came at him in the night. If not he would be lost and, if he had to go back there, there was no one he would rather have at his side than his SEAL trained friend, Dirk Dobbs.

Early the next morning they set out in Al-Fayed's, once again, rusted and foul smelling car. The trip was hot and miserable. By the time they made the rise to the village the sun was beating down on them like a jackhammer. The village had been devastated and the security forces, in their haste to quell the situation, had burned it to the ground. No one had dared go back there since. The official explanation was a 'plague of unknown origin'. Actually, considering what Dirk would learn later in life that would be a correct description.

Inside the village the smell was sickening. Dirk was regretting his decision to visit the site. Be careful what you ask for, he thought, cryptically. Al-Fayed glanced at his friend. He knew what they were getting into. He knew the scene that would soon unfold. Would it be sending the American running? He didn't know. Even with all his qualifications, there was no training for this. There was little he could do to truly prepare him. The truth of the matter defied description.

He parked the vehicle just outside of the first line of buildings, about the same spot he and his troops had stood more than a month before. The smell of death and burned flesh still hung in the air.

"Well, my friend, this is where you will lose your innocence in this world." He said quietly. "Only this will not be to a woman, as it should be. This will be to evil." Dobbs felt a rush of adrenaline. Maybe he was only now taking this seriously. The word 'plague' had thrown him. Were they prepared for this? What should they have done to protect themselves from the virus? He thought, too late.

"Gassim, maybe we should not go into the village. If there has been a plague..." he broke off, fighting an enemy was one thing, Dirk had done that, but fighting a sickness was another thing. You couldn't shoot a virus. Gassim broke in to his thoughts.

"This was no plague, Dirk. Not in the conventional way that is said. I have told you. You must believe me. This was the work of the walking dead, zombies. I know it is hard for you to believe. That is why we are here. We must find out more about this thing. Make sure that they are wiped out. Learn how they come into being so they can be destroyed." He stopped to take a breath. He was sweating profusely. It was not from the heat. "My good friend, I would not bring you to this place just to prove my words. You are a smart man. You have a mind that works. You are the person who will help me stop these creatures. It is our work in this world. The gods have put us in this place."

He opened his door and got out. Dirk felt the passion in his words. They propelled him forward. Gassim lifted the trunk and Dirk looked down at an array of weapons. From inside the compartment they selected two AK 47 rifles, several 30 round mags each. The assortment of weaponry had seen better days. Gassim handed Dobbs a Makarov 9x18 semi-automatic hand gun, two eight round mags and took the same for himself.

Dirk attached the holster to his belt, put the extra ammunition in his jacket pocket and slung the rifle over his shoulder. Gassim did the same. Once armed Dirk's training kicked in. Gassim explained, as they prepared, about the way the infection is passed. "Do not let the fluids get on you, in your eyes, or let yourself become wounded." He looked into his friend's eyes. "It is death." He told him not to aim for the body or extremities. "The creature will continue to come. You must shoot the head." He motioned for Dirk to follow and they started out.

They made their way quietly around the buildings, stopping to listen every few feet. There was total silence. Al-Fayed fought the urge to panic that was aroused by the feeling of déjà vu. The sandy street wound around into an alley between the remains of two buildings. Guns at the ready, they stepped out.

The village had been burned to the ground in an effort to kill the remaining creatures. Blackened corpses incinerated by the blaze, still lay where they fell. Dirk was beginning to realize that the story his friend told was true. "My God, Gassim..." he said loudly. "Shhh!" Al-Fayed rebuked him. "Any noise will bring the things, if there are any left."

Dirk felt the sting in the censure. His friend had never spoken to him in such a way. He realized he was not with his friend now. He was with the battle commander. He was a soldier in a battle zone. This thought sobered him. His military training returned, and he centered his attention.

Al-Fayed motioned for him to watch the darkened doorways and openings. Just as he nodded, he caught movement on his left. A dark shape was moving out of one of the doors. The being he saw shuffling toward him wasn't a man, although it looked as if it once had been. It was in the full stages of decomposition. He wore the woven woolen robe of the desert and there was one sandal on his right foot. His left foot was missing most of the digits and was turned in, toward the other. His arms hung straight down from the shoulder, one dangling at an awkward angle. His head, mostly skull with rotted flesh, was jutted forward and down, giving him the look of a starved dog. He was making a low sound that couldn't accurately be called a moan or a growl. It was something in between.

He was moving very slowly, which was a very good thing since Dirk was rooted to the spot in horror. Suddenly the ghoul's head exploded as Al-Fayed put two rounds into its forehead. Dirk spun toward his friend. "Always shoot for the head. It is the only way to stop them." He said as he pulled the shocked man away.

"My God, Gassim..." this time Dirk whispered.

He heard a scraping noise behind him and whirled around, this time he was ready. Another of the zombies was shambling toward them, stepping over the former one on the ground. There was no acknowledgment of its fallen comrade. It just continued forward toward the prey. Namely Dirk and Gassim.

Dirk raised the AK 47 to his shoulder and put the front site on the center of the zombie's head as it moved across the road 25 yards away. He pressed the trigger and the beast fell. Dirk had eliminated his first Zombie.

At the end of the day the two men had ferreted out and dispatched over a dozen of the undead that had somehow managed to secret themselves away during the onslaught and fire. Later that night the two sat in a tiny bar on the outskirts of Cairo eating Hawawshi, liver and vegetable sandwiches Hushari, turnovers with pasta, rice and lentils, and tea. The stall that served the sandwiches was on the street corner in front of the bar, adjacent to the butcher shop. Gassim finished his tea and ordered a licorice drink favored by the locals. Dirk wondered at his friend's appetite after the day's experiences. He had barely touched the turnover and the liver sandwich was out of the question for him.

"One thing I don't understand, Gassim. Why didn't the creatures die in the fire?" he asked as they walked along the ancient streets. "Zombies will be destroyed with fire IF they are caught in the actual flames. The problem with that is that many of them are in out of the way places, sewers, caves, underground cellars, and are protected from the flames." He explained. "How do they know to hide?" Dobbs asked. "Do they understand such concepts?" The Egyptian shook his head, "No, no. They do not plan. They do not fear. They do not hide, as such. They merely are where they are when the fire comes, you see. They do not have the capacity to...strategize. They were, I guess you could say, lucky. They were in a better place and did not come out."

Dirk was beginning to understand the problems with destroying and clearing a town or area from the things. They were not necessarily hard to destroy, if you could prepare and wait for them. They were not fast. They were quite slow, in fact. Since they could not comprehend danger they would continue to walk into the path of the attack. They also did not feel pain. When they were wounded in a way that would be fatal to a normal human being they would not fall. They would be slowed down by each injury because they would not move as well. Even horrendous wounds to the body would not put them down. They could lose limbs, have gaping chest wounds but they would keep coming.

Only by killing the brain could you kill the zombie. You could shoot them in the head, chop off their head, or crush their skull to kill them. Any of those acts would stop them because the brain would be destroyed. Or, if you actually were able to totally engulf their bodies in fire, fire would destroy them as well.

The two men talked on and on through the night. When the sun rose on the land of the Kings, Dirk Dobbs had a new calling on his life. Zombie Killer.

14

From the first kill in Egypt, Dirk learned all he
could about the living dead. He learned about the
virus that mutated the brain and re-animated the
dead humans into the creatures, about all the ways
to prevent the infestation, and about the tactical
procedures needed to destroy them in their nests.
The intervening years found him in many faraway
places hunting and destroying zombies.

During this time his only solace came from his
writing. He escaped the horror and blood filled
world of zombie killing by inventing intricate plots
of mystery and intrigue. His books found an
audience and were soon topping the best seller
lists. The income from his books added to his
mercenary work and soon amassed a large fortune
for him. The money was nice to have but it wasn't
the central focus of his life. His work was the core
of his existence but it was wearing on him. He
longed for a place of peace and solitude to which

he could escape. After a series of harrowing encounters he took an extended vacation. It was on this leave of absence that he found it. Now, he resided there full time.

Dirk Dobbs lived on one of the only bluffs on the island. He found the spot many years ago while on vacation after a particularly brutal encounter in Alaska. After the death and the cold he had wanted to soak in the sun, see the emerald sea, watch the gulls and just lay back for a while. He rented one of the nostalgic little cinder block houses with wide crank out windows all around to let in the breeze, tongue and groove hard pine paneled walls, and small, attached carports. He spent his days on the beach or exploring the dunes. One day he came out of his reverie to find himself on the top of the bluff overlooking the little inlet and the bay. The view was spectacular. He made up his mind that morning that he wanted to make his home right there on that pile of gleaming sand.

He called the number on the sign that read, "Deluna Developers", and within 30 days the bluff was his. He began construction the day after closing. It took the best part of a year before the home was finished. The slow pace of island time leaked over onto the contractors and laborers. Irritated, he complained to his sister, Jimmi. "I swear, had I built this any place else'," he exclaimed, "The house would have been done in six months!" It was a frustrating time for the "get it done" kind of guy that Dirk was, but, eventually, it was done and everything fell into place.

At the time that Dirk was building the house, he had hidden plans about his future. He did not plan to live in the house alone. Known only to his closest friends, Dirk had already asked someone that all important question. But, fate, once again, stepped in and changed his plans.

Dirk's work took him to Afghanistan, which led to Tunisia, then into South Africa. The work was nearly done on the house and he knew he would be away for a while. He phoned his sister, Jimmi, and asked her to come take care of things while he was away. She flew in from Atlanta to supervise. She was thrilled about coming to the island and to be staying at his beautiful island home.

The woman he was planning to marry, Alexandra Kent,   was out of the country on a mission trip. She was scheduled to return in two weeks. They were to be married the following month. When she departed Dirk's plan was to be on the island but plans change. He got the call and readied himself to take off. His new plan had been to finish up the job in Afghanistan quickly and return to supervise the finishing touches to the house. It had been thought to be a small outbreak. The mission where Alex had gone was too far out for cell phone reception and the contact in the closest town couldn't get to her before he left. He left a message for her to call Jimmi at the bluff house. He left his itinerary with his sister with instructions to have her contact him when she returned to the states. Jimmi was a good woman but she was a little flaky when it came to getting information correct. When his fiancé called things became jumbled. Flustered, Jimmi gave her the itinerary, but instead of telling her to CALL, she told her that Dirk said to COME to where he was when she returned. It was a critical error.

The fiancé, in hopes of surprising her soon to be husband on what she thought was a research trip for his newest book, ended up flying straight into the middle of the infestation. It was only with his superior skills and expertise that he was able to save her life and keep her from becoming infected.

He saved her life but was unable to save her sanity. The terror and fear that she had experienced and the gruesome sights that she had seen caused her to retreat inside. She left in a catatonic state that lasted for months. Despite her cataplexy he hoped for her return to her former self.

At first, horrified by the danger she had been in because of his work, he stayed by her side, night and day. He was stricken with guilt for the lasting damage done to her psyche. When she began to show signs of life she would become hysterical when she saw him by her bed. He saw that his presence only reminded her of her ordeal. He went back to the island, alone and broken. He made arrangements for her care. He made sure she had every comfort he could give her, but he never went back to her side. He left his private numbers with the doctors in case of emergency, or, if, on the off chance, she asked for him. No calls ever came.

He was sent progress reports monthly. Other than that, there was no contact. After a couple of years he received a letter stating that she was being released. It said that she had requested that he be notified and thanked him for his kindness. The only personal note was a handwritten addition asking him to refrain from contacting her. He abided by her wishes. For the first few years, the house on the bluff was a double edged sword, joy and sadness, comfort and pain. Jimmi, insisting, stayed on to help him out and eventually, she just stayed.

The house was a modern two story structure made of steel beams, concrete and glass. He had the plans drawn up by one of the area's foremost design and engineering firms. It was designed to withstand the worst of the hurricane season. The entire side facing the bay was floor to ceiling tempered glass with steel beams crisscrossing the expanse. The front of the house, which would be most exposed to the hurricane force winds coming off of the Gulf, was poured concrete reinforced with rebar mesh. It was a startling white block and stucco façade in the Aegean style with blue shutters. All of the windows were fitted with motorized roll shutters, made of high impact resistant material. Automated to rise and descend at preset times or by the touch of the remote control, Dirk had allowed for the house to be filled with the sun all day long. In case of storms they were also set to close when the wind reached a certain speed. Dirk could enjoy the beautiful view while still being assured of the safety of his home and his sister.

The master bedroom was on the second floor facing the water. It had a sitting area that was nearest the windows and the bedroom and dressing area farther away. A set of slide away doors separated the sitting area from the sleeping area. The ceiling rose to a peak of sixteen feet in the center. The shutters could be closed at six, ten, twelve and fourteen foot increments, depending on the amount of light or what type of view was preferred. The tinted slide away glass walls could be closed in varying heights as well. For privacy and, as with all the windows in the house, the tinting increased from clear to smoky golden to espresso brown by digital control.

The bedroom had a king size black and brown wrought iron bed. The headboard and foot board was wound with intricate details of vines and leaves interlocking with braided rope. The bed was covered in a black and gold fleur de lis patterned jacquard comforter and pillows. The massive armoire was in dark teak with the same wrought iron scroll work around the doors. The master bath had a solid onyx lighted tub with Jacuzzi jets. The walk in shower was tiled in the same golden cream onyx, offering deep seats on either side and water jets directed from both sides at six inch intervals. The entire wall around the tub was glass giving the bather a full view of the bay with mirrored tinting for privacy. Dirk had not designed the bathroom for himself but he had found the jetted tub and the surrounding spray in the shower quite relaxing after a stressful trip. Beyond the bedroom was a connecting walkway across the length of the house that led to his office and library.

Downstairs the living room dining room and kitchen were mostly one big open space that looked out onto the bluffs and the bay beyond. In the center of the area a circular couch covered in sand colored leather looked into an indoor pond filled with Koi. It was encased in glass and lighted from the bottom. The corners were filled with potted palms in massive stone urns. The dining area, in the corner, was surrounded by the full view of the outside and held a large glass table with brass upholstered chairs. The glass and openness gave the impression of becoming one with the outside world.

Jimmi had chosen to make her rooms in the maid's quarters off the back of the kitchen. Although it did not look down on the bay, it opened up onto the side of the house where Dirk had installed a large garden area. Winding paths flowed through the various flower beds and indigenous plant life. A six foot white picket fence with an ornate Victorian gate surrounded the garden and opened onto the pool deck. Jimmi, when she wasn't cooking for Dirk or supervising the staff, spent most of her days puttering around in the garden or swimming laps in the pool. She had many outside interests and belonged to several of the clubs on the beach but she was basically a homebody. She enjoyed the quiet life and domestic duties.

Jimmi never knew that her mistake had been the reason for Dirk's canceled wedding plans. She knew that the woman he loved had met him in South Africa and become very ill afterwards but never knew any of the details. Dirk never let her know that it was her fault. If she had known she would have never forgiven herself. Plus, Dirk could not explain the cause of the terror, or why he was in such a place. He knew that, ultimately, the fault was not Jimmi's but his alone.

Because of his involvement with such horrors he vowed to stay a solitary man. His life was too dangerous to take someone else into it. Jimmi could be kept safe and in the dark here on the island. It would not be that easy with a wife. He could never take that chance again. His work was critical to the well-being of the world. He could not back away. Dirk would remain a zombie hunter, a zombie killer. Dirk would remain alone.

These thoughts are just making me depressed, Dirk thought. Dobbs was not one to let negative thoughts linger. If he found himself thinking dark thoughts he would find something to keep him busy. That is exactly what he decided to do tonight. He had work to do. He had a seminar video half done that was due in less than a week. He pulled out his laptop and went to work.

Two hours later, the work was not getting any closer to being done. Dirk tried to work but his mind was not on it, at least not in the way he needed it to be. Time was passing but it seemed as if it was sitting still. The computer screen blinked at him as if it was trying to get his attention. He shook his head to clear it and answered its summons. He had to finish this article. It was supposed to be in to the publisher soon.

"Zombiism is caused by a rare and lethal virus called Solanum. The virus is carried through the blood stream to the brain where it mutates over a short period. The symptoms start in just a few hours and within 24 hours the victim dies. The difference in this virus and a host of other deadly diseases is the fact that after the victim succumbs to death his body is reanimated. The body will rise again to live, walk and feed. The reanimated bodies of the victims of Solanum are called Zombies, the walking dead.

The Zombie lives only to move and feed. It feeds on flesh, alive or dead. As long as the flesh has not totally decomposed the Zombie will eat it. It has a voracious appetite that cannot be slaked. Zombies do not eat for nutrition or fuel. Their bodies do not convert the food to nutrition. Their digestive system is dormant. Therefore, it cannot turn it into fuel either. The system that digests food, extracts nutrition and converts it into useable nutrients is completely shut down. The body is dead. It is only the brain that functions in a limited capacity. When it eats the food sits in the digestive tract and builds up upon itself until the weight of it pushes the matter out of the body through the channels made for that process. In some extreme cases it is not unheard of that the stomach of a Zombie will explode. This would be thought to put an end to the creature but it will not.

Because Zombies are animated by the mutation in the brain, it can sustain blows and injury that would kill a human. It will be impaired as a result but it will continue on. If a Zombie should lose a foot it would go on, dragging the appendage along. It would slow his progress but it would not stop him. There are stories of Zombies being shot in the chest, stomach, and back, suffering horrendous wounds and still continue to 'live'.

The only way to 'kill' a zombie is to detach the brain from the body. You must shoot it in the head, crush the head, remove the head or otherwise destroy the head.

As far as saving a victim from a Zombie attack, once blood or saliva has splattered onto the victim or otherwise made its way into the bloodstream of the victim, there is little that can be done. Once the virus has been passed it is 100% lethal. There is no cure, no antidote. The victim will not only die but will become a Zombie, too. A zombie who, just like the one before him, that has no sense of danger, who has no fear, who is tireless and relentless, and who lives to feast on human flesh.

Common misconceptions about Zombies are that they are strong, they move fast, that they have supernatural powers, and other actions that the living dead cannot do. First of all, they are not strong, unless the person who contacted the virus and reanimated was strong. The zombie only has the capabilities that the person had in life and those break down fairly rapidly after infection. When the person dies the body begins to decompose. Reanimation doesn't stop the process although it may prolong it. The average life span of a zombie can be up to five years, depending on the rate of decomposition and the climate in which the creature "lives". It is suggested that they cannot be sustained as long in tropical, hot or humid climates as they could in say a cold, dry climate. They can live in extreme cold but they will freeze if kept inanimate in a below freezing environment for any length of time. That is why the dead bodies of the host should be burned. Being refrigerated or even frozen cannot guarantee there will be no reanimation. Infected humans must be destroyed. They will not regain their health. They will become zombies who will kill and infect others.

  The mutated brain keeps the body function only on the lowest level. For the most part, the body is dead only the brain is alive. The mutant feeds and moves about seeking to feed. That is about the extent of the function of the zombie body. They cannot run, scale walls like a spider, climb steps, jump, fly or any other activity of the sort. They do not have supernatural powers. Their eyes do not glow red. They cannot read minds, move objects, cast spells or expel lightning from their fingertips or any other part of their rancid bodies. They don't think or speak. They can moan and they make a sound like a growl once their vocal chords have deteriorated to a certain point. The virus does not cross species. Animals that are infected will die from the virus but they will not reanimate. Dead bodies cannot be infected and become zombies because the virus must be carried to the brain via the blood system. If the blood is not flowing through the veins the virus will have no transportation device. All of these types of myths usually came from Hollywood movies but do not have any basis in fact, according to the research at this time.

Zombies can see, only not very well, as their visual signals to the brain are altered by decomposition. Although it is indicated that they do have night vision since they are prone to night feeding. The absence of light is no help in trying to hide from a zombie. Do not stake your life on that fallacy.

The zombie has an acute sense of smell. It is indicated that this attribute is heightened as their other functions deteriorate. This is one of the ways they find their prey. You will see a zombie lift his nose and turn in the direction of the target even when he no longer has vision.

Hearing is also advanced in the zombie. Although many brain functions have ceased or are limited, they can hear and detect the direction of the sound. This would also help explain their ability to hunt and feed in total darkness.

Zombies have little if any sense of touch. That is why they are relentless adversaries. They feel no fear. They do not understand danger. They do not feel pain. Until their physical bodies are totally useless from injury or deterioration, the zombie will continue its pursuit of food.

Concerning this, another myth is that they can regenerate limbs, organs or even the brain. That is untrue. It can lose limbs or major organs and continue to drag itself on to its appointed target. That is why the only way to stop them is by shooting them in the head or otherwise totally destroying the entire brain. The brain will not regenerate.

As for respiration, they do breath. Air is taken in and expelled, but the process of extracting oxygen and removing carbon dioxide is not operating. Zombies can move and stay underwater because of this. They do not need oxygen. This may be the reason some have erroneously believed that the ghouls have some type of supernatural power since they can move about underwater. There is no way to drown a zombie. The air taken in and expelled allows them to moan as it moves through their vocal cords but they do not have the power of speech. They have no language skills. They have no emotional needs. They have no reproduction ability. They have no social skills. You cannot be friends with nor have a sexual relationship with a zombie. They cannot recognize the concept. If anyone were to attempt to communicate with a zombie he would not survive the venture. The only relationship a zombie wants to have with a human being is as his dinner.

To survive a zombie outbreak you must be prepared, educated and skilled in ways to destroy the creature, protect yourself and your party, as well as handle and dispose of victims before and after reanimation.

"This concludes the Part 1 segment on the zombie. Please do study your materials carefully, do the exercises in the workbook and rejoin me afterwards for part two of your disc or tape."

Dirk turned off the video camera, folded his notes and leaned back in his leather office chair.

He was currently working on a series of taped seminars for the law enforcement officers in Mexico City. The city had recently had a small outbreak that had been quelled quickly. They were able to control the flare-up easily, mainly because the virus was introduced in a small rural area. The local farmers, who were very superstitious, burned the home and barn with the infected inside. The authorities were called in and arrived in time to see the creatures attack one farmer before the blaze started. They contacted ZARC; the Zombie Attack Response Corps, the agency Dirk had helped to create, and asked for help. Unknown to most of the citizenry, *ZARC* had affiliates in most major cities that offer help and assistance to affected communities. Dirk was the co-founder of the agency in its inception and has initiated the formation of affiliates throughout the states and the world as they had become necessary.

"Funny," he mused, "I never thought I would be considering forming one here on Deluna Island." He hoped that he would be wrong and that it was not going to be needed.
He returned to the chair, gathered his thoughts and flipped on the recorder. "Part Two of your seminar will begin with a few more facts." And he began his lecture.

"Once a victim has been infected it takes only a short time, depending on the person's age, health and environment, to become ill. The site of the wounding will be painful and turn brownish purple with instantaneous clotting. Within a very few hours there will be a fever, chills, nausea, vomiting, slight dementia and acute joint and muscle pain, much like a severe flu. In even less time than it took to set in, the victim will feel numbness in their extremities and the infected area. The fever will increase, the dementia and delirium will multiply and there will be a marked loss of muscular coordination. Few victims are coherent at this point. They may still be moving around at this point but will not be likely to understand the reality of what is happening to them or going on around them. These symptoms are followed over the next several hours by paralysis in the lower body, numbness and lowered heart rate, until they lapse into a coma. Then, their heart will stop, their brain activity will end and they will die. At some point, usually after several hours, their body will reanimate into a full-fledged walking, feeding Zombie. A Zombie that will infect, kill and eat whomever is in its way. It will not matter who it happens to be. That is the reason that no sentimentality can be attached to a former loved one who has become infected. That person that you love, and who loved you, is gone.

The reanimated body will not recognize you, have feelings for you, or have sympathy for you. In these cases, you must have no sympathy for it. It is, now, just a shell with a ravenous creature inside. You must destroy it as quickly and completely as possible to save your life and the lives of countless others. Every time a Zombie makes a meal out of a human being, that human becomes one more Zombie who will make more and more. The exponential growth of the Zombie population can become staggering. And, it happens very quickly. It is like the wheat germ and honey shampoo advertisement from the 1970's. It said "You tell one person, and they tell one person" as the screen showed picture after picture of the cute blonde saying, in unison, "and so on. And so on. And so on. And so on." Eventually the entire screen was filled with a multitude of cute blondes. In this case, one Zombie bites one person who then becomes a Zombie. That Zombie bites another person who then becomes a Zombie and bites, or otherwise infects, another person...and so on, and so on. And so on."

Dirk hit the save button and turned from the screen. He closed the books on his desk, including "The Zombie Survival Guide" by Max Brooks. It was the zombie hunters' bible. Everyone in his organization was issued a copy when inducted. The information it held could save their lives. It had saved his, many times. Dirk slowly closed it and leaned back in the chair.

He was tired and he was worried. His own words brought a deep feeling of dread to him. He knew how this could add up. For the people on Deluna Island this could become a math lesson that would never be forgotten. If there was anyone left to tell the tale.

He rose to stretch his legs and collect his notes for the next section when his private line began to ring. He was about to find out that his worst fears were coming true.

15

Back on the island the residents were unaware of the dangers that had washed up on their shores. They didn't have the knowledge that Dirk Dobbs had. If someone had told them, they wouldn't have believed it, but, that was soon to change for some people there. Some would soon be coming up close and personal, looking into the blank, rheumy eyes of the undead.

Selena Jackson sat in the front seat of the old Suburban van, the precursor to the late model SUV's. She knew that her husband and his friend were just trying to keep her from worrying. Jack thought she was a coward. He thought she would go all to pieces if there was a problem; just because she had crashed a few years ago when their baby died.

That was different. She wasn't scared then. She was guilty. When she found the 3 month old in her crib, dead; she was sure it was her fault. It had

to be something she had done wrong, or
something she had not done right. It had taken
her six years to convince herself that it wasn't true.
Crib death. It has a name. And even the doctors
aren't sure what causes it. They have new theories
every few years but they can't pin it down. She
could recite the pamphlets and articles, word for
word, she did it quite often, but it really never
could get to the sick pain deep down inside of her.

Selena shook her black curls. Stop. Don't think
about that. Keep your mind on the problem at
hand. She was sure that more was going on here
than the men were telling her. She heard Angus
say he found that box off of Little White Key.
What else was there? She thought, I will just have
to go see for myself!

She would go out to the point and see if there were
any more clues about the ship. She wanted to
know what was coming and be prepared. More
than that, she wanted to make sure the others
would be cautious. There were so many children
on the island. Most of them played along the
beaches. If she found anything else from that ship
she was going to make the Sheriff alert the parents
about the danger. She turned the big truck down
the track behind the Ferry dock and bounced over
the sandy road. She turned off the path and
followed the track down to the water. At the little
key, there were tall stands of trees that went right

down to the water, their roots exposed, reaching down into the sandy soil. Looking out toward the key, Selena could see the tip of the ferry dock on her right and the end of the pier by the café on her left. Straight ahead she could see big piles of trash that had washed up onto the sand at low tide. On the right she saw a large rusty refrigeration unit like the one she had at the café. It was turned on its side and mostly submerged in the sand. The large coils were facing toward her and dark hole where the door should have been was turned out, toward the bay.

She went around to the back of the truck and opened the doors. She pulled out an old pair of fishing gloves, a plastic bag to hold anything she should find, and a long shovel.

Heading toward the debris, she flipped off her flip flops at the edge of the sand and padded barefoot down the warm sand. At the farthest end the water lapped slowly on the pile that was still slightly submerged. She started there. Digging through the twisted pile she found nothing of use. She back tracked to the pile on the left, facing the dock and her café. She saw something shiny in the sand. She cleared away the sand and saw that it was the top of a trophy.

The top of the trophy was a swimmer in a diving position. When she looked closer it was the engraving that got her attention as she wiped the sand off,   it listed, apparently, the name of the ship and what looked like a list of names below it. "This is from that ship." She said out loud. "And this is a list of their swim team members." How sad. She thought.

She put the award in the plastic bag and tied it to her belt loop. She hummed to herself as she dug through the rest of the heap. Behind her the ferry let out a loud blast on the whistle, startling her. She thought she heard movement somewhere behind her but when she looked around she could see nothing but the trees, the refrigerator unit and the trash.   A flock of seagulls flew overhead, crying out. The birds caught her attention for a moment and their cries muffled the sounds of the creature climbing out of the refrigerator.

The 'man', if you could still call him that, was one of the impetuous sailors who had gone ashore in Tampico. He had been very sick when he returned to the ship. Later, that night, he died and they put his body into the galley refrigerator. When the storm struck, and sunk, the ship, the unit had been ripped from the craft, severing the electrical cords. With no power to the unit the body slowly began to defrost. After a night in the warm gulf waters and a long morning in the hot sun on the key, the process was complete. The man's body thawed out, the reanimation process was set on its way.

The body went in human. It crawled out...A Zombie.

He was dressed in the uniform of a merchant seaman. His clothes were covered with dried blood and were torn. His face showed several deep gashes and part of his cheek was gone and the rest hung loose. It was beginning to decompose and was white and bloated from being in the water so long. His eyes held a vacant stare, moving slowly from side to side, scanning the beach. Abruptly, he stopped. He put his nose holes into the air, smelling his prey. He turned sluggishly and began to move toward her in ungainly movements. The woman turned just as he reached her, his putrid smell reaching her nostrils. He reached out with his fleshless finger and closed them around her forearm. She struggled, screaming, as the ferry blasted its horn again. In terror she pulled the bag loose from her belt and swung the heavy award into the side of the zombies head with a sickening slushy thud. The beast collapsed onto his knees, raking his bony fingers down her arm drawing blood.

Selena picked up the shovel and smashed it against its head, again and again. Then, exhausted, she threw the grisly implement into the water and ran toward the truck. Her only thought was to get back to Jack. She had to tell him about the...thing! In her terrible fear she had become turned around.

Instead of running up the beach she had run into
the undergrowth. Blind with panic she crashed
into a low limb. The impact knocked her cold.
She lay in the bushes, for hours.

Selena came back to consciousness slowly. The
prickly palm fronds fallen on the ground stabbed at
her back. She opened her eyes. Her head was
sliced with pain from the collision with the limb.
She got to her feet, looking around, unsure of
where she was. Then the memory flooded back.
That thing! She scanned the trees but saw nothing
but the van. It was just a few yards away. She ran
even though each step was torture. She had to get
out of there!

She opened the door and jumped into the driver's
seat. She was becoming woozy but she battled on
to stay conscious. She clicked the electric locks
and cranked the engine. Throwing the truck into
reverse she sped backward into a U-turn. Jerking
the handle down into drive she hit the gas, hard.
Sand exploded around the thick tires, feathering
into the air. Her head spun and she felt as if her
head was as heavy as an anvil. Halfway back up
the wooded road Selena passed out and the truck
crashed into the undergrowth. The engine died.
The trees closed up around her van like a mother
cradling her baby.

While Selena lay unconscious, again, in the Suburban, the tide crept in covering the key. It covered the trash. It covered the refrigerator. It covered the body of the dead zombie and floated it out to sea. The contamination in the woman's blood stream washed through her like the tide. It carried in the horrible sickness and flooded her body, taking the life with it as it flowed away.

While his wife was gone Captain Jack and his friend had been very busy. They had made phone calls to several of the other ex-military personnel who lived on the island, as well as to some of Angus' friends in high places. They had reports coming in by fax, email and phone. The room had become a war room.

The reports they were receiving had led them to the unbelievable conclusion that they were not dealing with a simple sickness. They were dealing with much worse. They studied the records of similar outbreaks around the world, including one in Egypt in 1975.

Dirk's name was not mentioned so the men had no reason to associate that, or any other outbreak, to him or the island. What they read did make them sit up and take notice.

The descriptions of the illness and the symptoms sounded very much like what the young Russian was describing in his journal. The last port of call before the ship was lost had been in Tampico, Mexico. One of the outbreaks listed most recently had been in a small rural village 25 miles south of Tampico called Cabo Blanca. Since both were near the water, it was thought that the infection had come in by ship or boat. Angus looked at the web page, and the papers, then up at his friend. "Jack, I know this seems unbelievable but the signs are all there. There are horrible beasties in that ship. And the vessel is sitting out there off the point somewhere." He said quietly. "I told your sweet wife that story about the currents, and most of it is the God's honest truth, but it was mostly to settle her mind." He swiveled around in the chair. "I am not anxious to give credence to these tales but these are faithful sources they are coming from, and I am convinced they wouldn't be making them up."

"I know it says the creatures are just infected people who have somehow gotten the virus into their bloodstream, but if the infection was on the ship and it is gone down. Why should we be worried?" Jackson went on, "The ship went down and they were all drowned. The infection is not water born. There is no way for it to get onto the island."

Angus shook his head, "It says here that the zombie creatures canna drown. They can breathe underwater somehow. So that means they are still out there in the ship."

"The ship could be recovered when the Coast Guard has time. How long can they last out there?' he asked

"Says they can make it an indefinite time underwater, and, Jack...It says they canna float or swim, but they can WALK. Right across the sandy bottom up onto the shore." The Scotsman's eyes were wide and he was looking at a point over the top of his friend's head as if he could see the picture of the monsters coming closer.

"We can't take a chance that the Guard will pull that thing up. They will let loose those things onto Pensacola or Mobile if they do. With that kind of dense population and the rapid onset of the mutation...There would be no stopping them." The captain said. He thought of all the innocent people out there that had no idea. They could try to tell the authorities but there was little chance that they would believe them. At least not in time enough to check the population explosion of flesh eaters. My God, he thought, it is a nightmare. He shared his thoughts with Murphy.

"What do you think we should do, then, Angus?" the Captain asked.

"I think my friend, I should call on a few of our acquaintances from the 'services' and get out there and blow that bloody thing to Hades." Murphy said, shaken but firm.

The retired Navy officer was already thinking of whom else he could put on the list.

16

Anna Knox's mother was frantic. Her daughter had not come home last night. She demanded the sheriff's deputy get a search party out and find her little girl. The harried officer took the information and asked her all the questions that were usually asked in these situations. Who are her friends? When did you see her last? Where was she going when she left the home? Had she ever done anything like this before?

"Now, you listen here, Officer. Anna may be harsh and a little wild but she wouldn't just go off and leave me with no cigarettes or food all night!" the woman crowed. "She knew I had to go to the bingo game this morning, too. I want you to find her. I've only got till noon time to get there or all the good cards will be gone."

The officer stopped writing and looked at the grizzled old woman. Gertie Knox had hair like a Brillo pad and she smelled like a brewery. "If I was Anna, I'd take off, too." She thought. "Mrs.

Knox, we will get this out to all the patrol cars and they will be on the lookout for her but that is the best we can do until she has been gone 24 hours." The policewoman told her firmly. "Now, I will have Sgt. Beeker drive you home and we will call you the minute we hear anything."

"Can they stop at the Pic n Save and get me some cigarettes and some groceries?" she asked as the woman escorted her to the door. "Maybe they could just drop me off at the Hoot n Holler Bingo. I can get a ride from there later."

The desk officer sent the flyer on Anna Knox out to the other station and called it in to dispatch, wondering all the time if the girl had made a break for it. Good luck, girl, she thought as she put the phone down.

An hour later Yolanda Moore, Adam Moore's mother, put in a similar call to the same officer. Officer Denton recognized Mrs. Moore's name. Benjamin and Yolanda Moore were well known on Deluna Island. Benjamin Moore was one of the Island Authority managers and Yolanda was on the board and a very visible participant in the local club and social scene. She directed the Annual Mardi Gras Parade and the Krewe Dance at the Elks Club. Their son Adam was the rising star quarterback of the Bayside Marlins.

Mrs. Moore sounded worried but controlled as she spoke into the receiver, "I am very concerned about my son, Adam." She said, "He came by the house yesterday after school and was back out the door without a word. I assumed he was off with Jenna, Jenna McLain, that is...was his girlfriend. You see they broke up yesterday." She stammered a little. One of the parents from the decorating team, a good friend, had called earlier that day to see how Adam was taking the break up. When she found the mother unaware of the situation, she told her about the rumors and pictures. Mrs. Moore was horrified for her son. It was the piece of information that spurred her to call the police. "I thought when he wasn't in for supper that he had gone on to the game for early practice but I found out this morning that he didn't show up for the game, and, he'd...he'd had some bad news on Friday. I am very concerned. This is very unlike him. Now, this morning I realized that he didn't come home at all last night, either.... I...well, could you send an officer out to the house? My husband will be home by then and we would like to see what can be done." She finished, a bit out of breath. "Yes, Ma'am, Mrs. Moore. I will get someone out there as soon as possible." Denton disconnected the call and got on to Dispatch. Within minutes a car was on its way to the Moore home.

Officer Denton did not connect the two missing kids so she did not mention it to dispatch. It would not occur to her until later.

17

Early the next morning, Parks and Recreation Officer Benny Green made his rounds through the sites along the beach at the National Seashore. He did this every morning, looking for anything out of order, campfires left burning, trash left behind by partying teenagers, regular summer issues.

Benny liked his job. He was a solitary person and it worked for him to be out on his own, doing his job without someone on his back all the time. Green saw the VW sitting at the end of the wooded path as he got out of his truck. "Damn teenagers." He thought as he spied the mess around the campsite. There were beer bottles in the sand, the remains of a picnic scattered in the bushes and a pile of blankets. The CD player was on its side and the case holding the CD's was spilled out beside it, the music still playing.

Beside the burned out fire there was someone rolled up in blankets with nothing sticking out but blonde hair at the top and bare feet at the bottom.

Beside the blanket was shredded paper, a manila envelope and a pile of beer bottles, one near the blanket was broken.

"OK, kid, wake up! Time to go home." Officer Green shouted. The figure in the blanket did not move. He stepped a little closer and shouted again. "Hey Kid! Wake up! Time to go!" Still nothing.

Looking around at the feminine underthings, the purse and shoes, he knew this was likely to be a female. A little apprehensive because of all the legal wrangling people had to deal with these days; he hesitated about actually touching her. It was pretty apparent that she would be undressed under there and he didn't want to try explaining why he had his hands on a naked teenage girl.

He remembered what his grandfather used to say. "Son, discretion is the better part of valor. In everything you do, exercise caution. Don't take unnecessary risks. Proper judgment is always better than unwarranted bravado..." Green did not think the words were original but heeding them helped him make many decisions in his life. He was going to heed them today.

He walked back to his truck and called the sheriff's office. "Hey, Ortiz? Yeah, this is Green with P and R out at Red Point. I got a situation down

here that requires a female officer. Looks to be a
teenage girl, passed out in a blanket, with...uh,
without any clothes." Rubbing his head, he could
hear the guys at the Elks Club dinner tonight.
Well, he thought, it's better than possibly listening
to the guys on the cell block. Nope, he was taking
no chances.

Deputies Lennon and Ortiz arrived in a black and
white a few minutes later to find Officer Green
leaning up against his Parks and Recreation
vehicle. They got out with serious looks on their
faces and he felt his stomach flip. They were
taking this seriously. It was not the attitude he
expected. He anticipated them getting out and
making jokes, embarrassing him, then sending him
on his way to finish his rounds. Didn't look like it
would play out that way, he thought, dismally.

"Green." Ortiz said, genially. The female cop,
Lennon, nodded toward him in acknowledgment
and said, "You say you think this is a girl and she
is not responding?" He nodded.

"I couldn't get her to wake up or move when I
called out to her. It was obvious there was
drinking and...sex. I just thought... I'd better let a
woman officer handle it..." He broke off. "You
did the right thing, Green." She said,
empathetically. "Where is the camp?"

The two deputies followed the man around the
stand of trees to the VW. Beyond the car they
could see the rumpled blankets, the empty beer
bottles and the discarded clothing. Deputy Fiona
Lennon walked over to the still form. She leaned
down to shake her. The minute her hand touched
the cover she knew that whoever was underneath
it was no longer alive. She had heard the calls this
morning about the missing teenager. Gingerly she
pulled back the blanket. The face she uncovered
was the one she'd seen on the missing person's
bulletin. The music was still playing as they called
in for a crime scene unit and the medical
examiner.

"Discord, Death and Murder,
Discord, Death and Murder,
It's on our border,
Nothing but disorder.
It's multiplying all the time,
Pretending it's just another crime.
Discord, Death and Murder..."

Anna's body had been so bloodied it was hard to
tell exactly what happened here. M.E. Randall
Durham had arrived shortly after the call and had
done a cursory examination of the girl.

"Well, what's the cause of death?" the cocky
investigator asked the doctor. Durham gave him a
sidelong look. He'd had more dealings with

Detective Law than he wanted to remember. No matter what the circumstances, it was never pleasant. The man was a grade "A" jerk. Durham struggled to maintain a professional attitude.

"It's obvious that she was attacked in some way. I will have to do a more in depth exam at the office." He answered as vaguely as possible. With the suspicions he had about the couple at Bayside he was afraid that this would turn out to be the same.

"Well, Durham, you said the same thing about the last one." He said, nastily, "Is that your pat answer, now, or are you in over your head?" Law had no great love for Randall, either. Of course, he had no great love for anybody, as far as anyone could tell. The M.E. ignored the jab snapped off his gloves and trudged up the beach to his car to wait for the unit. He had more important things to worry about than sparring with the surly detective.

He thought over what he'd seen. There was hardly a spot that was fully intact on the front of her body and there were long deep scratches that scored her arms and back. Her clothes were all next to the blanket. There was very little blood on them, more like they had been sprayed there by an impact blow. Her underwear lay just off the blanket in the sand as though she had just stepped out of them. Apparently she did not have them on during the attack.

There were shreds of paper lying here and there, but nothing large enough to see what had been on them. In the cold campfire there had been ashes of burned paper and the corner of a yellow manila envelope. The kind with the metal closure. The ground was littered with beer bottles and a broken one was found underneath the girl. There were puncture wounds on her back at about the point where the body was lying on the glass. The wounds were not deep enough to have been intentional. Detective Law thought it looked like the bottle had been there when she fell, causing the superficial wounds. The blood on the bottle came from those wounds. The massive amount of blood she lost during the frontal attack was not under her except for around the edges of the body, leading Randall to believe that she was attacked while still lying down, and was unable to get up.

It was obvious there was at least one other person here on the beach with her, Detective Law was saying. It was equally obvious that it was a male, he went on, and that some sort of sexual encounter took place. The ME would be able to tell more about it after the autopsy but Law was pretty sure about his theory on the situation.

John Law liked to look like he was doing
something, when, in fact, he was doing nothing.
"Looks like to me we have some high school kids
with a little too much alcohol. Hormones get
going and we got some sort of sexual activity,
whether consensual or not, don't know. Have to let
the ME figure that one out." Law said, to the
officers while waiting on the crime scene unit, as if
he were lecturing a class of rookies. He picked up
one of the beer bottles and flung it into the water.

"Sir, do you think that might have been another
source of information?" Officer Lennon said, as
nonjudgmentally as possible. The detective was a
pompous jack ass, she thought, standing here
lecturing US like rookies while he tosses evidence
into the bay! Detective Law looked sharply at her,
then, out toward the choppy waves and offered no
comment. He turned and walked across the sand
to the tech van as it pulled in. He waited until they
got out, made a few notes in his notebook, and
turned. He called out to the officers, still by the
body, "Stay put until the CSI unit is done and
make sure the crime scene is not compromised."
With that he got into his car and drove away. The
two officers looked at each other and shook their
heads. "Jack Ass." Lennon said under her breath.

Anna Knox's body was zipped into a body bag by
the crime scene tech and lifted onto the gurney.
Detectives Lennon and Ortiz watched as they

rolled the cart through the sandy soil and up to the ambulance. The unit wrapped up the scene, put the body in and left the park in time for the sun to start casting a golden-pink glow over the terra-cotta colored sand on Red Point Park.

18

Gerald Johnson grimaced as he twisted the top off of a long neck beer. "Rack them up again!" he shouted, drunkenly, to the guy at the pool table. He had been in the bar since noon, drinking beer and shots, shooting pool. At the beginning he was running the table, which meant his opponent hardly had a chance to shoot. He was sinking every ball. But, as the day wore on and the beer bottles collected on the table, he began to miss more than he got. He didn't care by this point; he was in his own blurry world where he was the champion of all things. He grinned like a possum and ordered another round. He wasn't legal yet but he had a very good phony ID card and the bartenders at this little hole in the wall didn't have the best eyesight.

'G', as his friends called him, hadn't always lived in this way. It wasn't long ago that he had been a high school football star for the Milton High School team with great expectations of a future in college ball, possibly even in the professional arena. His grades were good and he had plenty of friends to hang out with on the weekends. In the world of teenagers, he had it all. He had it all, that is, until he met Anna Knox.

In his junior year, Gerry Johnson and his family went to Deluna Island for a short vacation. Nothing fancy, just a long weekend at the Sand and Sea Motel on the Bayway Highway. With their parents on the beach for the day, Gerry and his little brother went exploring the dunes, crossing the highway over onto the sound side at Bayside Beach. They wandered around the trails in the National Seashore, catching lizards and feeding the birds. A wonderful day.

He was chasing his brother across a dune when he crested the top and ran smack into a thin blonde girl carrying a beach chair and a bag that was bigger than she was. The girl's name was Anna Knox. They hit it off right away and spent the rest of the weekend seeing the sights on the island. When it came time for the Johnson's to leave, he was a little sad about it, but, it was just a summer fling. He never expected to hear from her again. He was wrong.

From that time on Anna Knox became his worst nightmare. She called him every day, several times a day. She emailed him, she wrote long,

romantic letters, and sent cards. Since it was only
a thirty minute drive from Navarre, she borrowed
her mom's car, caught the ferry and came up
highway 87 to Milton three or four times a week.
At first, he was flattered that she liked him enough
to go to all that trouble, but soon he regretted ever
meeting her.

 She became jealous of any girl he was around,
even his cousins. If she came and he was at ball
practice, she would beg him to leave early and go
with her. She wouldn't accept that he was serious
about the team and his prospects for the future.
She would rant and rave, throwing things, making
a big scene. It was embarrassing. He wanted it to
stop. He told her that if she continued to act this
way she could not come to practice any longer.
She was immediately contrite. She promised to be
better, and for a few days or a week, she would be.
Then, it would start all over again. Eventually, he
called it quits. In total frustration, he told her it
was over. He ordered her to stay away from him.
She was wild with anger and pain. She begged
him to change his mind. When he refused she
berated and belittled him, attacking his manhood,
his family, anything she could think of that would
hurt him. When that did not get the results she
wanted, she began to threaten him.

She tormented him for weeks. He finally, became
desensitized to her words and browbeating. When

she told him, once again, after a particularly nasty scene at What-A-Burger, that he would be sorry, he thought it was only more intimidation tactics. He was wrong, again.

The next day the school was abuzz. Someone had taped pictures of Gerry Johnson all over the walls and breezeways of the high school. The pictures showed him in compromising activities with another male student who was known to be gay. Worse yet, the boy, Jay Walker, had a gigantic crush on Gerry Johnson and made no secret of it. Jay had told half the class about his feelings for Gerry. Of course, the feelings had never been reciprocated, but, nevertheless, made Gerry's life miserable for a while. . Gerry had, innocently, confided in Anna about the trouble this boy had caused him. It had ruined his sophomore year. The jokes and barbs were just settling down when Anna pulled her tricks. Gerry had hoped the horrible time was behind him. Thanks to Anna Knox it would never be behind him.

The kids at school were viciously amused. Many believed the story the doctored photos told, many didn't care whether they were true or not. That group loved tasty gossip, the more twisted, the better. His life became a living hell. He tried everything to refute the stories but it seemed it only made it worse. He began to skip school. His grades fell. He prayed it would be over.

But, Anna Knox was not through, yet. She updated the pictures every few weeks, putting them in people's cars in the parking lot, or in mailboxes in the neighborhoods of the football team members. He couldn't escape it. He skipped school more than he attended. He was failing in two classes. He was dropped from the football team. In the end of his junior year he quit school, vacationed at his aunt's house in Alabama and tried to recuperate. When he came back to town he moved to another area into a nearby community called Pace. Although it wasn't far away, it was a different school zone. No one knew his story there so he could find friends, get a job and try to forget his dreams. He had managed to do that fairly well. He had forgotten about his college dreams, his football dreams, his future plans. But he had not forgotten Anna Knox.

When he left so abruptly, she lost touch with him. With no further outlet for her perverse affections she turned back to the boy she had been after before Gerry came along. Adam Moore. She turned her affections back to him just as fervently as she had with Gerry. Only this time she would not be pushed aside for football, school, or anything. Or anyone, either. She would have her man no matter what it might take. "I'll have Adam" she said to her girlfriend on the cell phone the day that Jenna followed her home, "I'll have him even if it kills me." She didn't know how prophetic that would be.

19

Jenna McLain had only met Gerald Johnson once. It had been a few months back. Jenna's mother had a sister who lived in Pace at the old Floridatown Mobile Home Park. The sister was in her 70's and could no longer drive. Mrs. McLain often sent Jenna to her tiny trailer in the dilapidated park to take her to buy her groceries, go to the doctor and run errands when she was unable to go. The mobile home park sat on the shores of the bay between North Pensacola and Pace. By the condition of most of the homes in the park it was easy to see that the area had caught its share of hurricane winds and storms. The destroyed homes, with sagging roofs and sheared siding, sat where they were after the storm, no matter what their damage. The owners of the park, an elderly couple, didn't have the money or the inclination to have them torn down or removed. So, there they sat like they were in a big trailer graveyard. They encircled the few homes that were stable. Jenna's aunt lived in one of the few still relatively livable.

After the latest storm, the owners had received some assistance to clean up the debris and had hired one of their tenants to cut limbs and drag them to the road for pickup. He was just finishing up the aunt's yard when Jenna drove up. He introduced himself as "G". His real name was Gerry Johnson. They talked for a bit until Jenna excused herself to take her aunt shopping.

"Are you gonna be back any time soon?" 'G' asked. "Yes, we're only going up to 90 to the Pic-n-Save. Are you going to be working for a while?" she asked. "I can be." He said, grinning. She liked him for some reason. He reminded her a little of Adam, in a grungy, run down, sort of way. Plus, he seemed like he needed a friend, and a friend was all Jenna was looking for at the moment. She was, still, in love with Adam, but she had many other male friends. She seemed to relate to guys more than girls for some reason. Adam had not been the jealous type and he understood.

"OK, I'll be back in about a half hour", she looked at the trailer door and saw her aunt slowly making her way through it, and modified her statement, with a grin, "or let's say, an hour!" "G" laughed, following her gaze. "Right! In 'bout an hour and a HALF... I will be back around here looking for you." The girl smiled in agreement. They said goodbye.

Later, that afternoon, about two hours after they had parted, Gerry Johnson was sitting on the splintery wooden deck when Jenna pulled back into the driveway. After settling the old lady and putting up the groceries, Jenna and G sat out under the live oak trees, looking out at Pensacola Bay, talking. It was such a beautiful view, if you didn't look behind you at the crumbling homes on wheels, she thought, and her thoughts were a jumble.

She found out that he had been a football player, but he failed to mention which school he'd played for. He left that detail out on purpose. She told him about Adam and his football highlights. She was a cheerleader, so that was something else they had in common. His girlfriend had been a cheerleader, also, he said. He respected her relationship with Adam and didn't want to interfere, although he would have gladly dated her had she been free.

In the flow of the conversation they got around to their troubles and she began to tell him about the girl who was harassing her over Adam. When she described her and told him some of the things she had done he went white. "Was this girl's name, Anna?" he asked, on the edge of his seat.

"Yes! How did you know?" she responded, puzzled. He told her about the stalking and how he had tried to get rid of her to no avail last year. He didn't tell her about all of it. It was still too emotional for him. He didn't want any of his new acquaintances and friends to know. He was afraid it would start all over again. He did tell her that he would love to get his hands on the little blonde witch. Jenna said, "So would I." When they parted later that night, they had become good friends. "You just remember that if you ever need any help with that little witch, if she hurts you or causes you any trouble...you call "G". I'll come running." The day had come.

Jenna composed herself enough to drive and listened to the ringing on the end of the phone in her hand. "Crap! He's not home." She said. "C'mon "G" you said to call you if I needed help and I really need help." She was just about to hang up when an out of breath Gerry answered. "Hello", he said. "Oh! "G" you are there! I was about to hang up." She spouted. He heard the strain in her voice and asked, "What's wrong?"

She told him the short version of what was going on and what she'd seen. About the photos, the faxes and how Adam and Anna were together in the parking lot. By the time she finished she had dissolved into tears. "Where are you?" he asked tersely. "On the ferry coming across." She answered, sniffling. "I was going to come look for you if you didn't answer."

He told her to come on. "I'll wait right here. I think it is time to have a long talk with this little girl, and her boyfriend." He had learned a lot about life in the last year. He wasn't the broken high school boy he had been. Anna's reign of terror needed to come to a halt. He felt sorry for Adam. He knew that this was probably none of his doing. Yet, he wondered if the quarterback didn't have something going on the side with her. He may not realize how far she would go to get him. It was certainly unfathomable how anyone could be that cruel. Her brutality was not just confined to her latest fool. Not this time. This time she was harassing Jenna. He hated seeing Jenna hurt. That made him even angrier at the crazy witch. It was time for her to face her problems and he was going to be the biggest problem she'd ever faced, he thought while he sat on the stoop waiting for Jenna. Anna Knox was going to pay.

20

Jenna pulled up in the broken asphalt drive around 7 p.m. Gerry jumped in and they headed out down Highway 90, back across the bridge to Scenic Boulevard. The two lane road ran around the east side of Pensacola past I-10, past the bluffs, until it turned into Cervantes Street. They followed it to 17th Street, passed under Graffiti Bridge and turned left onto Three Mile Bridge. The long bridge connected Pensacola to Gulf Breeze.

The usual congestion in Gulf Breeze Proper held them up for a few minutes longer. Jenna was getting impatient. If they were late they would miss the ferry. Gerry talked her down. The traffic began to flow and the tension eased. While they drove they talked. Or, rather, Gerry talked. He told Jenna the whole story about what Anna had done to him. How he'd had to leave to get any peace.

"When I came back and moved over to the trailer, I started introducing myself as "G". There are so many Johnson's here; nobody ever connected it to my old life in Milton." He said sadly, "I never go back over there. I stay out here or in Pensacola. I don't have that many friends that are my age. They are mostly older so they don't hear the crap that goes around in schools." He finished, lit a cigarette and tossed the match out the window.

"Gerry," Jenna said, purposely using his real name to let him know that she liked both "G" and Gerry, "how horrible for you. She's doing the same thing, again. This time she is doing it to Adam. But, I'm not sure that he isn't involved in it, you know? They are awful chummy." Jenna wasn't sure exactly what she believed. She knew one thing, though. Anna Knox was an evil person and she deserved to pay for what she had done to a nice guy like Gerry, and probably what she was doing to Adam.

The two finally got through the traffic and made the curve that passed the 'big fish', the giant sign that had announced the direction to Pensacola Beach for over thirty years. The car flew over the connecting bridge. She tossed a dollar at the toll agent and sped through the gate when the arm went up. They boarded the ferry just in time. Jenna pulled her car onto the ferry ramp as the attendant closed the bar behind her. It took a half hour to get across the bay and dock on the island, so they had plenty of time to make their plans. It was just getting dark when they got off the shuttle and onto the Bayway.

While they were plotting their next move, Dirk was heading home on the Bayway after his dinner; Anna and Adam were setting up camp at Red Point Beach. None of them realized that they would soon be involved in something bigger than their own problems. Something that would ruin some lives and end others.

The darkness was folding over Deluna Island like a blanket when Gerry and Jenna got off the transport. They headed down the Bayway toward The National Seashore. Gerry remembered most of the key areas from his trip, but Jenna, nervous about the encounter, rambled on pointing out each attraction like a tour guide.

When she turned the car into the entrance of the park she stopped talking. The gravity of all that she had learned weighed on her. Adam. She wanted to cry. She missed him and she would probably never be with him again.

"How could he do this to me? To us?" she asked Gerry. He looked over at the anger and pain he could see in her face by the glow of the dashboard lights. He felt sorry for her. She was an innocent in all this. She was a nice girl. It wasn't fair. He clenched his fists in the darkness. "Try to remember that it is more Anna's fault than his." He told her through the gritted teeth of his own anger. "She's the one who started all this stuff, whether he went along or not. She is the biggest problem, here. She is ruining him, just like she ruined me."

Jenna knew Gerry was right, but, she could still remember the pain she felt when she saw Adam kissing Anna in the parking lot. She saw him laugh and play games with her, just like he laughed and teased her! The thought infuriated her! He knew what he was doing, she thought. Anna came after him, but he made the decision to go with her. Jenna held Adam responsible for his decision and it made her sick. Sick and angry.

Jenna parked the car in the darkest corner, closest to the woods bordering the point. She turned off her headlights and pulled into the space silently. "The camp where they probably set up is right on the other side of this little patch of trees she told the boy. They got out of the car and slipped into the velvety night.

Gerald Johnson had been simmering throughout the long journey to the island. He remembered and relived all the insults, slurs and abuses he had suffered since he met Anna Knox. He charged her with the indignity, the humiliation he had endured on account of his chance meeting on this very island.

His hopes for the future and his dreams had come to an end because of her. Now, he thought as he looked at Jenna, now, she was torturing and ruining someone else. Another who was unfortunate enough to believe her lies. "Don't worry, Jenna," he said, in a strangely strangled voice, "this will be the last time she hurts you, or anyone else." Yes, Jenna thought, it will be. In her agitation she forgot the edge in his voice.

As they neared the camp they could hear the pounding beat of the music and the faint sound of laughter. It made them both furious as they crept closer. Peering through the trees they could see Anna and Adam in the throes of desire on the blankets. Adam rolled away and lay on his back. He said something to the girl then got up, naked, and started toward them.

He had seen them! They were both taken aback by his sudden movement in their direction, and his exposure. They scampered back toward the car and took shelter behind a dilapidated shed. Hearts pounding, they realized he was not looking for them. He had not seen them. He was only relieving himself in the trees. Embarrassed, Jenna looked away. Her thoughts and emotions were swirling. She only resumed her surveillance after he returned to the camp. Shortly after that they saw Anna getting dressed and coming out into the woods as well.

Gerry almost jumped out to grab her but Jenna stopped him. She wasn't ready for the confrontation, yet. She hadn't composed herself enough to say what she wanted to say to Adam and the girl. "Why did you do that?" he hissed under his breath at her. "I could have gotten her away from him so that you could go talk to him alone." He added, "I could have...taken her...for a walk, for a while." Jenna looked at him, sharply. She felt suddenly uncomfortable with his tone. "What? I don't want to talk to him!" she exclaimed, panicking. "Then what are we doing here?" he asked gruffly.

Jenna put her face in her hands and began to cry, "I don't know, really. I just don't know." Her anger was funneling away, leaving only the pain. "Look, if you aren't up for a fight with him, I understand that, but I am up for confronting this b..."he stopped, trying to control himself. "I have things to say to her and I came all this way to do it. Why don't you go back to the car and wait. I'll come back out in a little bit, when I am done...telling her off."

Jenna, totally wrung out, acquiesced. She made her way back through the woods to the car. She just wasn't ready for a big screaming scene with Adam and the girl. She thought that was what she wanted but, when she actually saw them together, saw him there...naked, running back playfully to tussle with her, kiss her...she just couldn't do it. She just felt sick.

Why did it all have to end like this, she thought. I really loved him and thought he loved me. How could he be so deceitful, she asked herself? She slumped into the seat and cried out into the darkened car until, exhausted, she fell asleep. Before she dropped off she remembered the coldness in Gerry's tone in the woods. It frightened her. She hoped he would not go too far when he faced down the girl who ruined his life.

She had abandoned her plan but her partner had not. He had plans of his own and he would not stop until it was finished. Jenna's hope would not be fulfilled this night. Gerald Johnson was out for justice and he would go as far as his wrath would take him.

Gerald Johnson watched Jenna make her way through the trees toward the parking lot. He felt sorry for her. Her heart was broken. Because of Anna Knox! How many people would she hurt to get her way, he fumed. The single street light gave just enough illumination for him to see that she got into the vehicle. In the quiet night he could hear the click of the electric locks engaging. Satisfied that his friend was out of harm's way, and earshot, he crept back into the woods. He didn't want her to hear anything that was going to take place. She had been hurt enough. She didn't need to hear what Anna would say to Adam, or to him. He was going to face down that bitch, once and for all! She would probably try to lie her way out of it and he didn't want Jenna to hear it. He was going to make Anna Knox admit all that she had done! And, she would get what she wanted! She wanted him so bad! She wanted to be with him all the time! She would be begging to get away from him, tonight!

While he had been distracted with Jenna, the rendezvous at the beach had gone wrong for Anna. Adam had found the proof that the girl was the one who had started the rumors and sent the fake pictures. The football player was furious. As Gerry got nearer to them he could hear them arguing. Aha! He almost said it out loud before he could stop himself. She finally was going to get what she deserved! Someone had finally caught on to her game!

By the firelight he saw the boy shaking the pictures in her face. The girl got up from the tousled blankets and stood, naked, begging Adam to forgive her.

Don't go for it, boy, Gerry silently implored him. He saw Adam throw the beer bottle, breaking it against something on the ground. He should have put it upside her head, 'G' thought, angrily. Finally, he saw the boy push her off of him and walk away. The girl fell onto the blankets, crying out.

Yeah, cry, you bitch! Gerry had no sympathy for the deranged girl. She had stolen his life; his dreams, everything, and she had done it to Adam, too! She has to pay! The thoughts swirled around in his head. Rage pumped through him. He rose and set out to the camp.

Back in the car, Jenna had cried until she was exhausted. She curled up into a fetal curve, wrapping her arms around herself, and fell into a fitful sleep. While she slept she was unaware of the violence and death that would go on around her. The night held more than the broken dreams and fantasies of revenge. The night held horrors that no one could imagine on this idyllic sandbar in the gulf.

21

Anna Knox lay curled up on the blankets, crying. She couldn't believe that Adam had attacked her like that. He had to know that she loved him! It was his own fault that she had to go to such lengths to get him! He had ignored her, pushed her away, hurt her every day! All she wanted to do was love him! She knew that she could take care of him better than that skinny witch, Jenna! Why couldn't he see that? She did it all for him, she cried out to herself.

Suddenly she heard a rustle in the trees. He came back! She wrapped the blanket around her and sat up, looking toward the noise. "Adam? You came..." she stopped. It wasn't Adam. She sat up straighter, pulling the blanket tighter. "Who is it? What do you want? This is not a party, it is private. Go away!" She said sternly, peering into the darkness. The man came closer, into the glow of the firelight. She gasped. It was Gerry!

"Not Adam, Anna." He said, advancing toward the blankets. "You ran him down. Just like you ran me down! You wanted me and when you couldn't have me, you destroyed my life. Just like you are destroying his!" Anna, confused at the change of circumstances, cowered back. "Gerry!" she tried to sound cheerful, "What are you doing out here? I haven't seen you in a long time." She tried to smile, but she was afraid. He seemed different. Bigger. Angrier.

"I came to see you, Anna. I came to stop you from causing anyone else any more trouble." He growled, "Do you have any idea how much pain you have caused? Does it ever enter your mind?" He grabbed her arm and shook her. She screamed out in pain.

"Gerry, what are you doing? What do you mean? I never..." he cut her off by jerking her up to her feet. The blanket fell to the ground, exposing her. She reached down but he seized her arm and picked her up off her feet. Shaking her, he yelled into her frightened face. "You BITCH! You LYING SLUT! There is no need for you to cover up because I am not interested in seeing your nasty body! I just want to see you admit that you ruined my life! And, that guy's life, too!" he said, jerking his head toward the path that Adam had used to leave.

"How do you know about Adam?" she asked, forgetting her fear for a moment. "I know about Adam! I heard him. I saw the pictures he was shaking in your face. Just like the pictures you used on me! What is wrong with you that you do these things?" He began to shake her again. The girl couldn't answer. Her head was snapping back and forth and the world was starting to spin. He threw her to the ground, knocking the breath out of her.

She lay, stunned, for a moment. When she tried to get up and run, Gerry threw himself on top and her. She beat at him with her fists. He grabbed her arms, clasping both her wrist in his hand, pulling them over her head. He slapped her with his other hand. He berated and accused her of all the horrible things she had done. She tried to get free but it was no use.

"You wanted me with you, remember? You wouldn't leave me alone. You followed me around and tried to weasel your way into my life every way you could. Well, here I am! You got me!" Anna cried out, begging him to let her go, begging him to stop. It just fueled his rage. Everything went black. He loosed his rage and fury on the girl.

Later, he got up. The girl was making whimpering noises but he was past caring about her pain. He walked into the bay to wash away any memory of Anna Knox. He felt like he was floating up in the trees, looking down at himself and the girl in the blankets. His head was buzzing and he felt light and free. He could no longer feel the anger and pain that had driven him. He didn't feel guilt or shame for what he had done. It was her penalty for the scorn his classmates had shown him and the pain it had caused in him. There were noises in the night, on the beach; he could no longer hear them. He was drifting over it all.

He walked down into the gently lapping waters of the bay and cleansed himself from the past and the pain...and the blood. He didn't hear the undulating water as it washed against the zombie who was emerging from the surf only feet away to join the other in the trees. He didn't see the putrefied and decomposing face that turned his way as he dipped into the salty lagoon.

Only as the clammy wet hand closed around his arm did the insensible man wake up. He came to his senses with a jolt. Danger screamed in his head. He turned and swung wide with his right fist catching the creature off balance, as the rotted teeth got a small nip at his flesh. The ghoul went down and before it could regain its balance in the surf, Gerry turned and tore off up the beach. He was on the path, running for his life before the zombie could get out of the water.

The man sprinted into the night. He veered off the
road to take a shortcut. The kids had made the
woods between the point and the main drive of the
park on the west side a 'make out' spot. It was
private land there, enclosed from prying eyes by a
deep gully that ran alongside of the rest stop. He
knew the area like the back of his hand.

He pushed on never giving a thought to the girl on
the beach or the other girl only yards away in the
car, awaiting his return. He didn't give a thought
to her safety. He was in his own world of terror
and there was only room for one. He was running
for his life. He had not had time to realize that he
was a murderer, or that his life was over. He didn't
know that the small wound on his arm made by
the creature had sealed his fate. As he ran the
virus was invading his bloodstream. All he knew
was to run! He had been wrenched from the
altered state of his rage and frustration and had
been jerked into another type of unreality. A type
that had monsters coming out of the water to
devour him. He had no time to feel guilt or worry
for the dead girl or fear for Jenna's safety. He was
in a nightmare from which he could not wake.
Everything else blurred into the background sound
of terror.

As he came out of the first stand of trees his foot
hit the deep bed of pine needles. He slid down the

embankment, striking his head one of the hard roots protruding from the ground. The blow knocked him unconscious. His body rolled down into the ditch and rested against the sloping wall of sand. The zombie, long since outpaced had wandered out of the water onto the beach.

The body of the girl lay motionless, more dead than alive. She moaned softly. The sound or the slight movements of her ravaged body alerted the mutant to the presence of live prey. The creature shambled across the reddish sand to the helpless girl and fell on her like the night. The last moments of Anna Knox's life was sucked from her by a zombie.

Not far away in the gully Gerry lay quietly, seemingly at peace. But, as the night wore on, inside his body the Solanum virus was not peaceful. It was ravaging his body and settling in to destroy all vestiges of Gerald Johnson, the damaged victim of a stalker, the caring friend of a broken hearted girl, the murderer. Gerald Johnson was in the throes of the virus. In time the fever would turn to coma, the coma to death. His body would die, but it would rise to walk again. Not as Gerald Johnson, he would not be the same. He would become a zombie. A creature just like the one who had attacked him on the beach. One of the walking dead.

22

Early in the morning the phones at the sheriff's office were ringing off the hook. People all along the west end were calling in about seeing strange looking people wandering around. One woman was locked in her upstairs apartment looking down on the courtyard where there were two strange looking men wandering around aimlessly. They looked, from her vantage point, as if they had been in an accident. She was requesting an ambulance.

"Please, send an ambulance! There are two men in the yard who have been badly injured." The frightened woman told the dispatcher. "Oh, wait. There is someone at my door..." the dispatcher held the line. Suddenly, there was a shriek. "Hello, ma'am, are you there?" the operator asked. He could hear sounds of a struggle, then nothing. Silence, except for a strange rattling sound.

When the ambulance arrived they found a man, critically injured, on the grass. They entered the house at the address from which the woman had called. They found her, or what was left of her, sprawled, unceremoniously, across her Persian rug in the front hall. The perpetrators were nowhere to be seen.

The patrol cars logged in five calls, three suspicious people and one attack. The last call was another report of a missing person. It was a report on Jenna McLain.

Jenna McLain, Adam Moore's girlfriend had not been seen since Friday night. She told her parents that she was spending the night with a friend and would be home the following day. When she did not show up the parents became worried. They phoned the friend. The teenage girl, trying to cover for her friend, told them their daughter had gone to the local Wal-Mart.

Hours went by. When Jenna still had not returned their call, they went to the girl's home. She confessed that she had not seen the girl since before the game early on Friday night. The McLain's called all her other friends. No one had seen her.

Mr. McLain, knowing what had passed between Adam and his daughter on Friday, did not think Jenna would go to him. Now, with all other avenues closed, he called the boy's cell phone.

There was no answer. He tried the home number he had in his contact list. Mrs. Moore answered on the first ring. "Hello, Yolanda?" he spoke into the tiny microphone, "This is Jenna's dad. I haven't been able to contact Jenna and I wondered if Adam has seen her?" Yolanda Moore sucked in her breath. "No, no...I don't know. You see, Adam hasn't been home since after school on Friday." When the harried father heard the worries in the woman's voice, he knew it was time to call the police.

The Shift Supervisor took the call. He told the worried man that he was sure that the two would be found in perfect health. "Don't worry too much, Mr. McLain. The two kids probably made up and are hiding out somewhere talking things over." The officer was trying to soothe their fears, but, he was, obviously, not a parent. Part of the worries the teenager's parents were experiencing involved visions of just such a scenario.

Unknown to them, the Supervisor had bigger concerns for the teens. The calls that had been coming in, in the last twelve hours, gave him good reason to keep the truth from the distressed parents. Something worse than teenage romance was happening on Deluna Island, and he just hoped that these two kids weren't going to be the next victims.

Jenna woke up with a start, unsure of where she was. Her head ached and her eyes were swollen from crying. The rush of memories brought fresh tears, stinging them. It was getting light outside. She wondered where Gerry could be. The memories of all that had happened that day flooded her mind. She couldn't believe it had only been one day. She shook off the pain and put the thoughts out of her mind. She needed to get Gerry and get out of there before she ran into Adam. She was in no frame of mind to deal with anything else.

She slid out of the car and made herself follow the path she had treaded earlier in the night. She didn't see Gerry anywhere. She went deeper into the woods, silently moving from tree to tree, pausing at each to listen. She could hear nothing but the lapping of the water and the breeze in the tops of the palms. The campground was straight ahead. The fire had burned low but gave just enough of a glow by which she could see. There was no movement. She crept closer.

She could see the CD player lying on its side; the cooler was turned over, beer bottles and soft drinks spilled out. The blankets were piled and pillows thrown about the area. They must have had a fight, she thought. Maybe Gerry had confronted Anna and Adam stood up for her. She pushed that thought away. She didn't like to think of her

Adam protecting that girl. She walked into the camp, scanning the area to make sure she was alone. She saw nothing.

She saw papers lying on the ground and pieces of cardboard ripped and scattered around the fire. She picked up one of the pages and saw the faxed pages that she had seen come across her father's fax. She did do it! The bitch! It was all true. Adam was really one of her victims. She, nevertheless, remembered the way he laughed and went with her at school. She didn't understand it but it was a small comfort to see proof that all the rumors had been lies cooked up by Anna.

As she turned the firelight's glow fell on the blankets. There, on the bloody blankets lay what was left of Anna Knox. Jenna was too stunned to scream, to run, to move. The girl was covered in blood, with gaping wounds all over her body. The first thought in her head was for Adam. Had Adam become so enraged when he found out that he could have done this? Or Gerry? She remembered how intensely angry he was with her. She turned to run, but, stopped. She couldn't leave the girl lying there, exposed, like that. The girl, however evil she was, didn't deserve to be exhibited like that.

Jenna leaned down, picking up an edge of the blanket that was free of blood, and pulled it over, wrapping the girl. All that was left showing was her hair and feet. Jenna was in shock. She was walking like someone in a dream. She couldn't feel the roughness of the blanket or the grit left on her hands. She followed the trail back through the woods to the parking lot without thought. She was on auto pilot.

Just as she reached the car a hand clamped down on her shoulder. Surprise jolted her from her trance. She screamed and began to fight. She didn't know why she was fighting. She was reacting to all the stress and shock she had endured. The fingers tightened on her arm and another wound around her neck and covered her mouth. She couldn't breathe. Even in the vice-like grip, she found the strength to kick out with her foot, connecting with the attacker's leg.

"Ow! Damn it!" he said, pulling her tighter. "Jenna! Stop! It's me, Adam!" The boy hissed in a loud whisper, "Be quiet! Or you will get us killed." He said, as she shuddered to a stop. She relaxed in his arms and he removed his hand from her mouth. "Now, don't scream or make any noise. It might bring them out." He whispered. Jenna turned his grip loosening. Her eyes wide, "What? Who?" she asked, her heart racing ahead with her thoughts. Maybe Adam or Gerry didn't do that to Anna! Her heart was already hoping, but what he said next wiped those thoughts from her mind.

"I know you won't believe what I am going to say but it is true. There is something, a thing, things...they are killing people. It is horrible. They try to eat, biting..." he stopped. Jenna was staring at him, speechless. "I had to kill...two of the things." Jenna pulled back. "Anna!" she hissed, "Did you kill Anna?"

"Anna? No! What do you mean killed?" he grasped her again. She looked toward the camp. "I found her...body...down there." She jerked her head toward the woods. Horror gripped him. "She was...torn up...bloody." She stopped and began to cry. Adam pulled her toward him. He would have to get the whole story later. "Come on, get in the car." He walked her to the passenger side and put her in. He got in on the driver side and locked the doors. "We'll drive down there and see." He told her, cranking the car. "No!" Jenna cried out, "No, don't go down there! It's horrible."

"OK, OK. We won't go." He tried to calm her. He would have to go back later. Right now they needed to get out of there. He shuddered to remember what he had seen and done, only a few yards away. He cranked the car and left the park by the opposite direction. He didn't want to go back by it. He didn't want to see it, again.

Jenna stared out the windshield, obviously in shock. Adam made several attempts to get her to talk but she sat, silent. Adam drove. He didn't know where to go or what to do. He knew that the things he killed weren't really some unknown monsters. They were men, or were at one time. They had gone crazy, been sick. He thought it must be some sort of terrible sickness that ate away at their bodies and minds, but, they were alive and he had killed them. Would that make him a murderer? How would he explain it? And, what about Anna? The boy was frightened, in shock himself, and worried about what Jenna had said. Anna was dead and he was the last person with her. He had fought with her. Parts of it were still foggy. He didn't exactly know what had happened. He was so angry. It was like a movie screen that had gone black.

He didn't want to tell Jenna about any of it. Or the police. Would anyone believe that he didn't kill her if he told them that the last thing he remembered about the scene at the beach was a broken bottle and wiping blood on his jeans? He looked down. It was still there. Anna's blood on his pants? What had he done? Could he have? He shook the thought out of his head. She was alive when he left. As he walked away through the woods, he had heard her screaming. He'd assumed she was just venting her anger and frustration for being caught. Now, he wasn't sure. The idea chilled him.

His thoughts swirled. He forced himself to put things in order. He left the camp and trudged through the woods, furiously angry. It was a long walk through the park to the main road. The woods pressed in from every side with dark arms snaking out to scratch his face and claw at his arms.

Half way up the road it opened out into another small camp ground with six or seven pads for travel trailers or tents. There were two trailers there that were year round rentals. They were empty now because of the recent storm. Also, the couple who had been found dead nearby probably had something to do with it. Suddenly Adam was afraid. In all the turmoil of the day he had forgotten about that. It was eerily quiet. He could hear each of his footsteps on the gravel. He had seen some headlights, and there was a car at the far end of the lot. It was dark and looked empty. That was almost as creepy as seeing nothing. He went on, seeing more nothing. Blackness surrounded him. No lights, no people. Just trees and darkness. He picked up his pace.

Suddenly, he heard yelling and screaming behind him. It made him jump. Where that had come from, he wondered. He thought it could have come from the direction of his camp with Anna but he wasn't sure. He stood rooted to the spot for a moment. Then, his upbringing took over. He didn't care what the girl had done to him he couldn't stand by and let anything happen to another person without trying to help.

He crept back down the trail. He hadn't realized how far he had gone away from it. His thoughts were so muddled, he had lost track of time and distance. He could just make out the glow from the firelight. He didn't want to go back down there and get back into it with her so he climbed up on a water shed and looked down to the camp. He saw Anna lying on the ground on the blanket. He could see her hair. He was too far away to see any detail. He guessed she had screamed out in anger. He scanned the area again and thought he caught a glimpse of some movement by the water, but it was too dark to see. He looked over the campsite, again. Funny, he thought, the sand looked like it had dark ribbons in it around the blanket from this angle, then, shook his head, amazed that he could have such a frivolous thought at a time like this. He noticed Anna hadn't moved so he guessed the movement he saw was just a fish jumping.

He jumped down from the shed and froze. He saw someone moving through the trees toward the other end of the parking lot. The moon came out from behind the cloud just at that moment and illuminated the white sand. That is when he'd seen Jenna.

He couldn't believe his eyes. What is she doing out here, he'd wondered. He hadn't wanted her to see him, not out here with Anna, naked down there. If he tried to explain, Anna would hear and come up here. Then he'd be back in the middle of that mess, only worse. Jenna would be there to hear Anna screaming and begging. He'd hidden himself and waited for her to get out of sight and then he slid silently down and crept out of the trees.

The sight of Jenna out here had done nothing to make this excursion through the pitch black woods any easier. Now, he had to be afraid of running into her and trying to explain. What in the world was she doing out here? He'd wondered. He figured she must've followed them. Then, for a moment, he brightened. That must mean she still loves me. But, just as quickly, the realization came to him. If she followed, she had seen him making love to the other girl. The thought of her seeing them had broken him. He'd realized there was no way out of this nightmare. His life was done. He trudged on thinking black thoughts in the black night.

Dejected, he set off back toward the main road. He stayed on the asphalt this time, skirting the dark woods. He came around the curve, just below another camping area, cutting across the grass by the maintenance shed. He rounded the little building but, by instinct, he stepped back into its shadow. He thought he heard rustling in the bushes. The sound became louder. He moved to the edge of the asphalt and looked behind the small outbuilding that housed the public restrooms.

Thinking back on the scene frightened him all over again, even in the relative safety of the car. What he'd seen had driven all thoughts of his own problems, of Anna, of Jenna and of reality from his mind. He could not comprehend the horrifying scene in front of him. A man about his size was lying prone on the ground with two other men attacking him, trying to devour him. His blood spilled out in black rivulets in the moonlight around his arms and legs where they were ripping at him. The man was still alive and thrashing about, trying to free himself.

Adam instinctively moved to help him. He grabbed up a 20 inch piece of steel rod that must have been left behind by a weekend boater and swung it at the back of the nearest head. It connected with a loud crack. The attacker fell forward and didn't move. Expecting the other attacker to defend himself and his cohort, Adam ran back a step. The football player repositioned himself in a fighting stance, but the other one didn't move. He continued on in his grisly business, without a glimmer of recognition that there was any danger. This had disconcerted Adam momentarily. He looked around, scanning the area for others who might be there as backup. Nothing.

He looked back at the man on the ground. He was still moving, only obviously getting weaker. Adam drew back and flew at the other assailant. Putting all his body weight behind the blow, he swung and united the pipe with the skull. The rotten head burst under the impact and the body fell to the side. Unsure of what to do, he paused. Then, the victim jerked a couple of times and Adam was back on task. He started to the man's aid. As he passed the shed, another one shambled out and grasped his sleeve. In a flash he saw himself lying on the sand with the ebony ribbons of blood around him while this decaying corpse gorged itself on his flesh. The thought so unnerved him that he had forgot all about the dying man. He forgot about Jenna. He forgot about Anna and the pictures. He forgot everything except how to run. He ran like it was the last minute of the game and he had the ball. He'd run for his life. He had run until he found himself at the entrance to the park. By this time he had calmed down a little. He'd had time to think about Jenna. She was back there somewhere. She didn't know about the danger. Despite his fear, Adam had gone back.

Now, he was sitting in the little car, Jenna's car, and safe. At least for the moment. Safe. That was sort of a joke. He was in a car, in the park, late at night, with one girl who left him and one who would do anything to get with him. Added to that, he had recently crushed the skulls of two very sick men and left a dying one behind. Was that 'safe'? He had to fight the terrible urge to giggle. The hysteria was trying to set in. He curbed the impulse.

He looked at Jenna, again. She still had not spoken. He pulled the car out onto the main road and started toward home. Where did he think he was going? They couldn't go to his house and they couldn't go to Jenna's house. Where could they go? He wondered. As he passed the high school, it hit him. School. They would go to the gym! Being on the football team, and being an honor student, had it perks. One of them was being the owner of a key to the gym. They often allowed the star players access to the workout machines after hours. He had the key in his pocket. He pulled into the dark lot behind the school and parked the car.

"Jenna? Jen?" he spoke quietly to her, "Come on, Jen. We are going to be all right. Come on." He pulled her, gently, from the car and they disappeared into the shadows of the building. For now, the trouble was behind them, but they would have to face it, again. Soon.

23

Back at the RV Park, the Captain and Angus Murphy began calling their contacts from their military and covert Ops days. "We need help and we need it NOW", Murphy growled as he punched in a familiar number. The Captain knew the Scotsman was right. "We need people with underwater demolition experience and some counter terrorism work behind them", was the Captain's answer, although it hadn't needed to be said. After what they had seen, neither man had any doubts that this was to be a difficult job. Each had begun to formulate their plans on the ride back to the cabin.

Angus Murphy planned to take one group of men to Little Key. He thought it would be the best spot on the island to get to the downed ship. After only a few calls, Angus had the people he needed and enough explosives, detonators, timers and firearms to level a small city. All he had to do now, was wait. Wait and plan.

The supplies and equipment should arrive early the next morning. The men should be in place at that point. By noon, they would be on the beach. Angus and the divers would go out in his fishing boat. It was equipped with sonar and depth finding instruments. Murphy loved fishing and had spared no expense when rigging out his boat, but hadn't gotten a chance to use, yet. Now, he thought, I will be fishing for something bigger than a fish for his dinner. They would be trying to locate the sunken vessel that must carry some sort of sickness. They could not know that it was full of deadly, inhuman creatures. The merchant ship should, by the Captain's calculations, be about a mile or so off the west end of the island. The vessel was in the Intercoastal Canal at the mouth of Pensacola Bay. It was where Deluna Bay met the Gulf. The channel was dredged deeply in that area to accommodate the cargo ship that docked at Pensacola Harbor. The ship was on the bottom in about 100 feet of water.

"It might get a little tricky out there," the retired Captain told him, "but, I don't think it is anything you can't handle. Go on and take a nap before it is time. You will need your rest." The Scotsman agreed, thinking that he would lie down, but didn't expect to get a wink of sleep. He was wrong. He was so exhausted that he went to sleep before his head hit the pillow. The Captain stayed up, working out the details and calculating each move they would make the next day. They had gotten some information when they took the boat out that way for a quick perusal of the area.

Capt. Jack remembered the feeling he'd had when he looked at the scene. From the shapes brought up on the ultrasound, it looked like the ship was torn into two pieces. It had a huge gaping hole that opened it up like a tin can in the middle. It was hard to tell by the fuzzy images on the screen exactly what was down there, but he had had a few moments when he wasn't too sure about his own eyesight. He had seen something strange. He did not mention it to Murphy, he could have been mistaken. It had been a long day and it was not state of the art...Still, he could feel that finger of icy fear when he saw what he saw.

He'd zoomed in on the debris. Near the ship there were other smaller shapes, pieces of the ship, bits of cargo, scattered around the bottom. He had scanned the area, starting at one end and going to the outer edges. That is when he saw it.

He had paused as he squinted at the small screen. He backed the viewer up a few feet, examining the bottom again. Jack had retired from the Navy as the head of the underwater dive team. He was used to how the bottom of the sea looked. He could see the vessel, lying broken on the sea floor. Beside it, scattered across the screen were groups of objects of varying sizes. "Hmmm....I could have sworn..." he whispered to himself as he panned back and forth across the area. Suddenly, he stopped and swore under his breath, "What the .... ?", he pulled the viewer back again. He wasn't seeing things. He was right. Things were moving around down there!

He was almost positive...The smaller objects were not in the same places when he panned the area! Icy fingers trailed down his back. In all his years in service, he had never seen anything like this! Before he was through with the thought, he rejected it. No, he thought, that is not possible. It had to be something to do with the currents out there in the mouth of the bay. Or, it could be the viewer. He chided himself for over-reacting. "Apparently, " Jack had told himself, "there is a glitch in the set. Not being an expert with the new apparatus, he was unsure of how to correct the problem.

"Well, we seem to have a small issue with the viewer, but, at least, we have a location." He told Angus when he returned to the bow. "We will just have to figure the rest out when you and the team recon the area." Murphy agreed, "We will take the supplies down, stow them in a safe place away from the ship. The men will place the explosives and we will blow the thing out of the water." He pounded his fist on the table. He went on, "the first thing we will need to do is to find out where the infected creatures are hiding. Then they can decide how to install the devices closest to that area."

The retired officer shook his head, "I wish I could go down and do the final work, but I will be on shore directing the operation." Angus Murphy did not want to admit to himself that his underwater days were over, but, he knew it was true. He'd had to give up diving after his last mission. Things had gone awry and he'd been forced to surface too soon. The damage to his lungs put him out of the program. Although he was still an active and virile 64, his doctors had warned him against diving anymore. He had to be satisfied with teaching and leading other crews. It wasn't easy, especially this time. The crew had little time to plan, much less, train. He knew exactly what needed to be done and how to do it.

Angus turned away when he heard a horn sound outside. "That will be our truck." He said. The two men went out into the shed behind the house and greeted the man in the truck. James Allen was one of the residents of the trailer park and an ex-Navy diver. His specialty was underwater demolition. It had taken a little convincing to get him to come on board for this operation. After he read some of the reports the two men had received from their Coast Guard and other contacts, he agreed. Allen didn't really get the whole, 'flesh eating monster' aspect of it, but, he did understand epidemic. He wasn't alone in that area, neither did the Captain and Angus. They didn't realize the depths of the troubles that the ship had brought to their shores. They could understand that there was a nasty viral infection that mutated in the system, a sickness that allowed the victims to, somehow, stay alive in the ship under the water. They understood that the virus caused them to be in a violent delirium that led them to attack other humans. They did not comprehend that these men were no longer human, that they were real, living-dead people. Unfortunately for their team, they would realize it too late.

Jackson opened the back of the truck and helped load the supplies. He was shocked and amazed at what Angus had been able to put his hands on without legal or military agreement. They had 200 pounds of Semtex plastic explosive. The possession of that alone would get them all a stint in Federal Prison; yet, he knew deep in his gut that it was necessary to keep the people of Deluna Island safe. They didn't have time to go through official channels. By the time the paperwork got out of the fax it could be too late.

Looking at the explosive, Angus would have preferred C-4 to Semtex, but it was impossible to get without more questions than he wanted to answer. Semtex is the Soviet Block equivalent of C-4, and a little easier to come by. Especially, if you have a buddy who is an international arms dealer in Egypt. Luckily, Angus had one. There were few things he couldn't get his hands on, for the right price, Murphy had learned. Included in the shipments were the detonators and timers needed to discharge the explosives. He had received a good deal and the price was right. In this case, the price was tempered by favors his friend had called in.

The divers were going over the procedures they would follow to set the charges. First, they would use the Semtex. Semtex is a moldable substance that can be shaped around the object or adhered to the surface of the target. The substance by itself will not blow up. It must have a detonator attached to set it off. A timer is then connected to give the explosives technician time to vacate to a safer area. Along with the explosives, the men loaded in scuba gear, underwater lighting, ropes, knives and, last of all, the guns.

Thanks to Angus' friends, they were also in possession of two boxes of suppressed H & K MP5's. H & K's are 9mm sub machine guns with a silencer, or suppresser to muffle the sounds of gunfire. If disaster struck and they were forced to fire the weapons on the key or surrounding areas without the suppressers, they would be heard. That would bring down the law and more questions than the team wanted to try to answer. The sound muffler would not completely silence the weapons, but, it would help. None of the crew wanted to discuss the operation with the authorities. All the operatives knew the operations they were conducting were illegal as hell. They were going to blow up a Russian merchant ship in American waters. They were carrying explosive and weapons that only the military were allowed to have, legally, and they were planning on shooting to kill any infected person that they encountered on that ship, or on the ground. It was the only way to stop the infection from getting loose on the island. The last thing they wanted was for Grandma down the road to call in the sheriff about hearing gunshots, possibly lots of gunshots, at the key.

Angus had discussed the possibility of calling in local law enforcement or even military to aid in their plight. The contacts he spoke to offered no assistance in that area, and even less support. With the crossover of agencies, the international difficulties and time factor involved in the situation, it would not work. The islanders would be infected or killed. It was not a chance they were willing to take.

Very few of the agencies actually understood the urgency, or believed the likelihood of the men being alive underwater. As far as they were concerned, the conversations had never taken place. Angus and the men were on their own. Once they blew the ship, the gig would be up. That is why they would leave no clues to whom or why the ship exploded. If they were caught before they could destroy the ship or prove the danger, they would be sunk deeper than the infected ship.

The other divers, Sam Waters and Don Josephs, along with the other teammates, met at the park with Angus for instructions. When he explained to them about the demented behavior and that they might encounter live infected men underwater in the ship, they exchanged unbelieving glances, as he turned. Angus explained the steps to take in searching and placing the explosives to achieve the destruction needed. They became more attentive as he told them that the most likely places where they might find the sick men would be in air pockets around the ruptured cargo holds. They were able to grab onto a scenario where there might be some oxygen. He warned them that there would likely be stragglers who would be trapped in other areas of the ship, ones that hadn't been able to get down to the ship floor because of their illness.

"The main thing to remember here, boys, is that the infection is a nasty bit of work and you don't want to be infected. Keep yourselves from harm, get the stuff attached to the area where most of them are and get out!" He told them earnestly, "We don't want to lose anyone in this thing. Put down your gear at the safe place, recon the area, place the stuff, and get out!" he reiterated strongly. He turned to the last man who had jumped out of the truck. "Phil and I will be on the beach keeping an eye out for any of the ones who might have gotten to shore. So if you are ready?" He motioned to the door. Captain Jack followed him and the men out.

"I would like to be going down with you, but I have to try to find Selena." Jackson said, sadly. His wife had been gone for over twenty four hours. At first, he'd thought that she was at the diner or just staying away to make him worry about her. Since he hadn't heard from her he'd put in a call to the sheriff.

"The sheriff has had no leads on her. Nobody has seen her. I am afraid something terrible has happened." Jack Jackson choked up. His friend put a hand on his shoulder and said, "Jack, my prayers go out to the saints for you and Selena. I know how hard this has been on you. Keep your head up. Go look for your wife, I have this under control. You have my cell number. Call me if you have any updates or any info on the operation I need to know…or anything on Selena." The men shook hands and the truck headed to the little key.

Captain Jack went back into the house and called the diner. Selena wasn't there and no one there had heard from her. Where did she go? He wondered, half angrily. She shouldn't have gone off, like this, he thought, not with all that they feared was going on. He stopped, the phone in his hand, she didn't know about the dangers, he remembered, with a start, he didn't tell her. She didn't know the truth. If she had known she would have stayed home, where she would have been safe. This was his fault. He did coddle her; wrap her up in cotton wool, as his mother would have said. Instead of protecting her, now he had left her open to danger. He put his head into his hands. If anything happened to his wife…

After a few dark moments the captain got his bearings. He was being silly. She was probably at the beach, drinking a Mai-Tai, like she had done last time, or, riding around, listening to her favorite music, letting him worry, he told himself. He wasn't convinced, but he put the thoughts out of his mind and called in an extra hand to work the lunch crowd at the diner. He flipped Selena's old fashioned rolodex to one of the kitchen helper's number and dialed. The action gave him a feeling of normalcy, removed him for a moment, from the worry and fear, but his respite would be short lived. He would soon hear news from the key that would confirm his worst fears.

The men in the truck drew closer to the key. Angus Murphy directed the team to the sandy inlet. Murphy's mind was on the supervision of the task at hand; his head was in the maps and charts as they bumped along the trail. As they passed the clump of trees that marked the turn, he failed to see the roof of Selena's wrecked van peeking out over the foliage. None of the other men were as familiar with the area behind the ferry docks. Even if they had seen it, none of them would have recognized it or that it might be out of place. But, even if they had, it was too late to help the Captain's wife.

The pickup truck skidded and bumped down the track over the sandy trail rattling the occupants' teeth. They pulled the truck to the side at a clump of trees. The tide had come and gone since Selena had killed the zombie there. There was no clue left on the shoreline. The tide had washed it clean of everything except the refrigeration unit. As the men emptied the truck, Angus checked the area around the key and made sure the rusting unit was empty. It was.

Captain Jack had moored his boat to the tree at the edge of the water to take them out. Although it was only a short way out, they would have to have it to take the equipment. Phil Stanley would bring it back to shore after the drop. When the men finished, without the heavy equipment to haul, they would swim back to shore, easily, leaving Angus and Stanley to monitor from the beach. The three divers suited up. Angus and the other man loaded the boat. After checking the location maps once more, to be sure of their directions, the frogmen crawled into the boat.

The light craft skipped along the shining waters to the point on the chart where the shipwreck was indicated. The water, usually crystal clear, was slightly cloudy from the storm and the disturbed silt on the bottom. They could only see down about 10 feet with any reliable visibility. They tossed over the net with the Semtex and the cache of supplies into the water. The yellow buoy that was attached to the rope on the bundle popped to the surface. Each diver had a strong underwater light and a sharp knife in a waterproof sheath. Many divers have been saved from a desperate situation by having an implement to severe seaweed, fishing line or other objects that have wrapped themselves around a leg or arm in the deep. The divers had no expectation that they would encounter anything more violent than sea plants on this excursion. The stories of the attacks had been little more than hysterical ravings of a few frightened fisherman, they thought. The most they expected to find in the downed ship were a few bloated bodies of the unfortunate sailors. The virus would be diluted by the tons of water. They weighed the anchor and each one, grabbing their mask, fell backward into the briny water.

The men pulled themselves through the water with long strokes and flipping feet, bubbles of air rising to the surface. The water was not as bad as it could have been after a tempest like the one that had just passed, but it was hard to see beyond a short distance. The divers could see each other fairly clearly up to about 20 feet, or so. They found the bundle of explosives and untied the top. Sorting out what would be needed first they laid it out on the sand behind the sea grass. Diver one motioned to his compatriots, pointing to himself and away in the direction of the dark shape they assumed to be the ship, off to his left. He slapped his chest, and pointed his index and second finger toward his eyes, then back toward the ship, denoting his intention of going over to take a look at the ship. The oldest of the three men, a retired coast guard diver, pointed at him, shoved his fist into the palm of his other hand, closing the fingers tightly over it. Then, he made a quick gesture, pulling the fist back out of the other hand. The younger diver laughed and nodded his head, swimming away. The hand movement meant "Pull your head out of your ass"; a well-known sign, indicating a need to be on your guard and pay attention to what's going on around you.

The men finished with the gear and started toward the ship. They could see the hull, ripped apart in the middle and twisted at an awkward angle, sitting open, ahead of them. The two openings facing them were nothing more than huge dark, cavernous holes in the sea. The visibility here was much lower than at the safe site. The two men can barely see five feet in front of them. They swam around to the bow of the ship, going up to the top edge. They examined the length of the ship and back down to the sea bed. So far, no men walking around under the water, one of the divers mouthed to the other. He turned to let the third man in on the joke. He was gone. He pointed to the other diver and mouthed, "Where's Sam?" Their partner was nowhere to be seen. The younger diver followed the older man to the dark opening. He pointed to the hole. Maybe he went in, he mouthed. They turned the beams of their flashlights into the darkness. The sight before them threw the seasoned men into a panic.

There, just inside the hull on the floor, was Sam. His face was pointed up toward the light. Inside the torn mask they could see his face. It was contorted in a silent scream. The water around him was dark. They shone their beams farther into the chamber and saw three of the creatures surrounding him, their teeth sunk deep in his flesh. The young diver cried out in fear and dropped his light, its beam making dizzying ripples across the interior of the hull. Briefly, they could see the image of dozens of misshapen heads and bodies huddled in the darkness.

Before the horrified men can escape, the hordes are upon them. The older man is covered and taken down by a half dozen of the monsters. The younger man gets away, almost to the safe zone, before he looked back to see his buddy's fate. He hesitated. For a second, he considered going back to help him. His indecision sealed his fate. Two of the creatures caught up to him. He drew his knife from its sheath and slashed at them. One got a hold on the diver's leg and sunk his teeth into it. He stabbed at the zombie with all his might. The blade gashed a whole in its neck. It did not let go. He sliced the other one, severing its arm. Momentarily thrown off balance by the blow, it falters. The diver slams the butt of the handle onto the skull of the ghoul attached to his leg. It falls back and sinks to the sea bed. The Navy diver was unsure whether he had killed it or only stunned it. He started to pull through the water when he felt a hand grab onto his arm. He jammed the blade of the knife into the putrid flesh of the creatures arm, severing rotted tendons and muscles, cracking desiccated bones. The rotted hand and 1/4 of the arm comes away, staying attached to the swimmer.

In his panic he forgot the boat was probably still overhead, instead of swimming straight up he makes for the shore. When he was shallow enough he got to his knees, then onto flippered feet. The frogman burst through the surface only feet away from the little shoal. Angus and his man were scanning the horizon for any movement, when the diver's head, suddenly, appeared. The diver spits the mouth piece from his mouth and yelled for help.

The two men on the beach slung their rifles onto their shoulders and ran into the knee deep water. The man made a few more weakened strokes, reaching out his hand to them. The younger man on the beach hauled him onto the shore and pulled off his mask.

The Scotsman swore loudly, "Christ! What the hell happened down there?" The diver's eyes were round as the moon. He moved his mouth but nothing came from his lips. Then, he seemed to gain control of himself and said, "They got Allan and Sam. They swarmed us out of the cargo bay. They were eating him! One had my leg but I knocked him out, maybe he's dead. The other grabbed onto me. I cut him loose..." he stopped. His eyes rolled and he passed out.

Angus looked down at the man's leg. He saw the
torn wet suit and the gaping wound. He grabbed
his partner and pulled him back, looking him over
for bloodstains. He was clean. "I don't know how
contagious this sickness is, or how it is transmitted.
We better take care." Neither had touched the
dying man anywhere but the front of his suit,
which looked clear of blood or materials. He bent
to take a closer look at the wound and jumped
back. Hanging from the man's elbow was the
putrefied, severed hand of the zombie.

One of the many things that he had brought to this
fight was a supply of plastic tarps, body bags and
gloves. He had fought in too many third world
countries, where disease and illness was a daily
reality, not to come prepared. They unfolded one
of the tarps, spread it over the man. They used it
to cover his wounded body while they transferred
it into the body bag. They left his face exposed so
that he could breathe, zipping it up to his chin.
The younger man brought the truck closer down to
the sandy beach and lifted the bag into the back of
the truck. They removed their gloves and tied
them into a plastic garbage sack and pushed it
down into the side of the zippered bag with their
comrade.

As they were loading up the man onto the truck
they heard noises behind them. Walking up out of

the waters of the bay was a line of men, if you could call them that. The first three were completely out of the water and onto the sand bar when Angus turned to see what the noise was. Whirling around, he threw the MP5 to his shoulder and began hosing the line of me with lead. He could see pieces of their bodies flying off, but no blood spray. But, more importantly, they were not falling.

Stanley joined him in the firefight. Now, the second line of rotting, decomposing bodies were slowly coming up out of the water. Staggering and ungainly, they continued to come. The high powered shots were having no effect on them. The next row began to surface. They were getting too close for the men to continue firing with no consequence. They couldn't afford to be splattered by the contaminated fluids. Angus gave the signal to retreat. The men ran to the truck, turning and firing as they fled. The bullets might not stop them, but they'd noticed it slowed them down. The appalling damage that the zombies suffered was cumulative. One creature lost part of a leg and was dropping behind. Another, being hit several times in the abdomen, was listing to on side from the damage to his skeletal structure. They continued to fire. Stanley cranked the truck as Angus jumped into the back with Josephs. As they dug out in a spray of sand, one creature grabbed onto the tailgate and was being dragged along. Just out of sheer anger and lack of other body parts to aim at, Angus pulled out his Glock and put a round into its forehead. The head ruptured and the zombie dropped off like a bag of rocks. Relieved, Angus sat back. "Well, shooting them in their muzzy heads surely works ." He said to Josephs who was unconscious and no longer listening.

Angus had just learned the first rule of zombie extermination. Aim for the head.

24

Jack Jackson was getting worried. It was nearly midnight. His wife, Selena had not made it to the diner earlier in the day. She had not been seen since she left the house after their conversation about the Russian ship. She often went off to herself, but, rarely for this long. Murphy had offered to go with him to look for her but, to his chagrin, now, he had tarried.

"Wait a little longer. She was a little miffed with me when she left. I could tell. She goes off to see her sister when she gets like that." He'd told Angus. "Did you call the sister?" Murphy asked. "No, they don't have a phone out there. I tried to call Selena, but she left her cell phone here. She is probably out there with Amorosa, telling her what a nincompoop I am. She knew we were not telling her everything. That always gets her steamed up. Let her get it all out. She'll come home when she feels better."

He had thought, then, that maybe he was wrong about it, but, he hated scenes. If she was out there, blowing off steam, it would just turn into an argument when he tried to get her to come home with him. He didn't want to give his brother in law the satisfaction of seeing them wrangling. "I'll give her 'til midnight. Then I am going out there." He said.

Murphy looked skeptical, but, didn't want to get between a man and his business. "Well, call me if you don't locate her soon. You have my number." Murphy said. He had his hands full with the business on the key, but, it still worried him about the woman. He hoped his friend was right. Unfortunately, for them all, the Captain was wrong.

At 12:15 Captain Jack headed out to his sister in law's house. Amorosa lived at the far eastern end of the island. It was just past the East End Ferry docks. Most of that area was undeveloped and rather wild and woolly. His sister in law's husband was a local from way back and didn't like company or intrusions of any kind. They lived on a large stretch of low land filled with scrub and spiny weeds. It had a sandy track for a driveway and a tall wooden fence surrounded the entire property. The enclosure could be called a privacy fence but calling it that gave it much more distinction than it deserved. It was made with any type of wood that Roger Gassaway could scavenge. From old plywood to used street signs to broken crates and pallets that he nailed together. The man cared nothing for the looks of the place, only that there was a barrier between his world and the prying eyes of the rest of the island inhabitants.

Roger Gassaway was six feet tall and weighed in around 280 pounds, none of it muscle. He was born on Deluna Island and had lived on the property at the east end of the beach all of his life. He inherited it when his father died in 1989. Roger was a football star in his school days and often referred to those years as the best years of his life. He had a full scholarship to Florida State until he suffered severe injuries to his back in a car accident the week after graduation. A drunk driver, who happened to be the son of the richest family on Deluna Island, veered into the other lane of the Bayway and hit him. The family paid for all his medical expenses and gave the family a large cash settlement to withhold making charges against the son. The Gassaway's grabbed the money and agreed. Roger's needs fell to the back burner. They often hit the family up for additional payments for 'therapy' that Roger never received. His back healed badly and caused him considerable pain and suffering, which he poured out onto his wife. Roger held on to his bitterness and anger, letting it rule his life. He became a reclusive and abusive man who thought that everyone owed him a living, because of the accident that stopped his football career.

With every new disappointment in his life, and in his dreams, he became even more enraged. His property was like an armed camp with motion detectors and spotlights on every corner, and electronic surveillance cameras on the gates. The only way into the property was with Roger's permission, or by having the security code for the gate. Anyone arriving would have to buzz in to ask for admittance.

That was why Captain Jack Jackson found himself talking into the speaker at the front gate of Roger Gassaway's home at a little after midnight.

Gassaway did not like Jack Jackson. Big surprise. Gassaway liked very few people. Jackson's heart was not broken up about it. He could hardly stomach his brother in law. He knew how he treated Amorosa and the kids but he could not get her to do anything about the situation. It had been an ongoing anxiety for him and Selena. They had begged and pleaded with her to come and stay with them until she could divorce him but she was so beaten down that she could not do it. He knew the day would come when they would hear news of a tragic ending to the marriage. It frustrated him that there was nothing he could do.

He hated for Selena to go there, even for visits, especially when she was upset with him for something. He did not trust Roger Gassaway. He tried to explain this to his wife but she would only say that Amorosa was her only sister. Where else would she go? Tonight, he thought, I hope, for once, that you are with her, Selena.

He pushed the buzzer once again and Gassaway growled into the night air, "Who the hell is it?" "Roger, it is Jack. I am looking for Selena." He said, gritting his teeth to be civil, hoping, "tell her to come to the intercom."

"What the hell are you talking about, Jackson?" he snorted, "I ain't seen her. She ain't in here. Now, get out of here and let me sleep." The click of the button echoed in the silent night. Jack pushed the button again. "Gassaway! Let me in! I need to talk to Amorosa. Selena is missing." He yelled into the plastic box that was nailed onto a rotted 2x4. "You hear me? You better open up or I'll drive this truck right through this pile of crap you call a gate!" He heard the electronic buzz as the rusty piece of crap gate squealed open.

Amorosa met him on the steps of the buckled plywood deck in front of the double wide trailer that had seen better days. A scowling Roger Gassaway, in his stained T-shirt and baggy boxer shorts, stood in the doorway. "What is it, Jack? What'd ya mean you can't find Selena?"

His sister in law's dark eyes were round with concern. "She went out to the diner just after lunch time and she didn't come home at closing. I called in Deke to cover, thinking she would show up late. She didn't. I figured she came out here and would be on home after a while...you haven't seen her?" He said finally. Amorosa shook her head. "No, I haven't seen her since day before yesterday. Do you think she might have gone over to the Elks Club?" the woman asked. The captain and Selena belonged to the local chapter of the club out on the beach, as did Roger and Amorosa. It was the one place that Roger went to socialize and he, generously, allowed Amorosa to go with him. The club served food and drinks until 2am most nights. Sometimes, Selena would go to see one of her friends who was a bartender there.

"I don't know. I didn't think of that. I guess I will go back by there and see. If she comes by here, give her this." He quickly handed her Selena's cell phone so that Roger wouldn't see. He didn't want his wife communicating without his oversight.

"Take this. It is set for silent. The keys won't make a noise when you push them and it will vibrate instead of ringing in. Tell her to call me, or if she won't, you call me." He whispered. Amorosa nodded and put the telephone in the pocket of her big housecoat. "I will." She told him, "You call me if you find her. I'll keep it with me." She whispered to him, glancing at her husband on the porch. Jack nodded to the man on the porch in grudging thanks and put the truck in reverse. He backed around the broken toys and strewn junk in the yard and passed back through the opening out onto the pot hole filled road. The screeching gate closed behind him.

Jack didn't find his wife at the Elks Club or any place else on the island. Where could she be, he thought, slamming his hand onto the steering wheel? Where she was, he would never imagine, nor would he ever see her alive, again.

25

Selena woke up with a start. It was pitch black in the truck and her head was pounding. The foliage covered the windows, enclosing her in a jungle world. She couldn't remember where she was and just how she got there. Looking around at the inside of the truck she thought she was in a cave, hiding from the white rabbit. Am I Alice? She wondered, feverishly. Her body was on fire. She was burning up from the inside.

She sat up in the seat and was overtaken with a violent attack of shuddering. She was suddenly freezing. Her teeth were chattering so hard she thought they might break. She had never dreamed it was so cold in a rabbit hole. She was sweating profusely. She realized her shirt was soaking wet. "I must have been swimming and fallen into this hole. Now, the tide has gone out." She muttered to herself. I must get out of here before it comes back, she thought.

She began feeling all along the dash and the wheel for a way out of the hole. She ran her fingers over the door and finally locked them around the door handle and pulled. Oh, it is a secret door, she smiled to herself. The warm night air billowed into the van like a down comforter. She rolled out onto the sand trying to wrap it around her. It felt so warm, so soft. Her bones were aching now like the joints were pulling apart. She writhed in pain on the sand, still unaware of her real surroundings. It hurt her. It was like when she had the baby. Hurting and hurting.

In her dementia she thought she was in the hospital, again, giving birth. She writhed and rolled on the ground. Don't push, don't push. She kept hearing the doctor say it. Don't push. Don't push. She wouldn't push, she told him. She would wait. She didn't want to hurt the baby. Maybe that was why the baby died. Maybe that is what caused the crib death, she thought. The doctors said they didn't know what caused it but, she knew. She knew this time. This time she wouldn't push and cause crib death. The words echoed in her head like yelling down a well. The pain was growing stronger. She began to moan.

Maybe she should walk. That will help the baby come. She pushed herself up onto her hands and knees. Then onto just her knees. Her head was spinning furiously now. She was no longer in labor in the hospital. She was on the Tilt a Whirl ride at the fairgrounds. She was spinning it,

around and around, faster and faster. Seventy two
times, around and around. She had counted them
when she was 14 years old. She and Amorosa set a
record that night. They were doing it again.
Around and around. She knew she was going to
be sick but she couldn't stop. It wouldn't stop.
Amorosa, she cried out in her fevered mind,
Amorosa, make it stop. Make it stop.

She was sick into the sand. She was looking down
the dark rabbit hole again and the blackness
surrounded her and blocked out the lights of the
midway and the sounds of the screaming riders.
The memories faded, the delusion disappeared.
The spinning world went as dark as night. No
more sounds echoed around her. She was in a
deep coma from the virus. She would awake
again later but she would never be Selena again.
When she woke again, she would not be Selena
Jackson; she would be a flesh eating zombie.

26

As the sun rose on the house on the bluff Dirk was up making preparations. Sometime, during the night, he had made up his mind to take matters into his own hands. He didn't need to wait for more bodies to pile up to prove to him what he already knew. There were zombies on his island.

He sketched out his strategy in his head in the wee hours. This morning it was just a question of how to get it into action. Unknown to the zombie expert, other plans were being made on the west side of the island. Soon their efforts would overlap and the secret would be out, at least to a small number of the inhabitants, but at this time, Dirk thought he and Randall were the only ones who suspected a problem. The men at the RV Park only understood part of the situation. They grasped the contaminant aspect, the virus, the dementia, but they had little comprehension that these 'men' were no longer sick. They were dead bodies that were being controlled by a mutated brain function. They didn't know how to effectively kill them, destroy the bodies or contain the contamination. Dirk had spent many years learning...the hard way. Even though they didn't know it yet, Angus, Captain Jack, and their team would need Dobbs' help, and it would happen soon.

Dirk spent the early morning listing and laying out what he needed. He checked his watch. Just enough time to pack his gear bag and get out to Bayside Beach. He made a quick call that set a few things in motion and mentally, ticked off his list of things to take. He had, on hand, most everything he needed to do the job he might be called upon to do. Always a minimalist, he believed in doing the job with the least encumbrances and least wasted movement as possible. It was more efficient that way.

He opened the hidden panel in his bedroom closet. Inside were several safes, some large, some small. Spinning the dials, he opened them all and took stock. Since it would be nighttime, and he hoped to be at a distance of at least twenty-five yards, he would take his Bushmaster XM15-A3M4. He would need four or five 30 round magazines filled with MI 93 5.56 mm ammunition. He fitted the rifle with his Aim Point ML2, a red dot scope that would help his shots be more accurate in the darkness. He also attached a Surefire weapon light to the hand guard on the side of the gun. The light would be used to illuminate the target. The light, as he taught his co-hunters in training, also served to keep the shooter in the shadow and less visible to attack.

He hesitated at the handguns. He usually did not favor a handgun for zombie disposal. In a zombie attack, you never wanted to get that close. Splatter, in this case, could be lethal. In the end, he decided on taking one handgun. Just for the screw up factor. If the worst happens, as he also told the students, if you run out of ammo, lose your weapon, get separated from your weapon, a handgun is better than a machete or a knife, and a machete or a knife is better than throwing rocks. But, not much better.

He grabbed his Glock 17 and chambered in a round of Federal 9BPLE hollow point ammo. It fired 115 grain jacketed hollow points, and at 1300 feet per second velocity, he knew it would open up a zombie's mutant brain in a heartbeat. If he was going to rely on a handgun, this one would be this one.

He laid out his hard shell helmet, the night vision goggles attached. He knew the helmet wasn't necessary since he didn't expect to receive return fire, of course, but it would make a good place for the goggles to rest until he needed them. In the heat of things, it was good to have everything handy.

From past experience he knew that the roar of gunfire could zap fine hearing skills in a second. Without hearing protection you could handicap yourself. It was essential to, not only protect your hearing but, hear the approach of your enemy. Conventional earplugs wouldn't suffice for this activity. He tossed in a pair of Pro Ears that he had used successfully in other attack situations. Without them, after two or three shots from the M4 or the Glock, about all he would be hearing would be the ringing in his ears. That was a good way to become lunch for a zombie, he often said.

From underneath a shelf he pulled out a long box. From it he selected trip wire and several flares. The trip wires would be lined up to set off the flares. Although that could be a disadvantage with the night vision equipment, it was a necessary risk, and it could be worked around. He planned to set up a perimeter around his camp as an alert system. The trip wires would set off the flares if an attacker moved into the radius of his area and let him know which direction to aim his defense.

One of the most primary calculations made in this type of scenario would be to let the 'enemy' come to you. In conventional warfare, conventional wisdom dictates that you should plan to outnumber your attackers and overwhelm them. In zombie combat, numbers do not matter as much as preparation. With a human foe you must calculate the risks, predict the strategy of the enemy before your attack can be successful. In this case, there is no enemy strategy. Zombies have no capacity to plan strategy and they do not comprehend risk. They know no danger. As the seasoned zombie killer knew, with the proper preparations in place, all you must do, to win a zombie battle, is identify the target, wait for them to come to you, and shoot them in the head.

In most cases, with this opponent, you do not have to find them. They will find you. They are searching for food, and you are it. Dirk knew that, if there were zombies on the island, they would be out in search of their next meal. All he had to do to find them was to go to an area where they had fed and wait. They would come, and, when they came he would be ready. One thing about zombies, they would follow the food, no matter what. It was a matter of 'point and shoot'. Shoot one and then the next, and the next. Their fallen comrades will not deter the next one from walking right into the next bullet, over and over again. With enough ammunition and directional alerts, you can pick off as many of the undead predators that come your way. The largest danger with the undead is being caught unaware. Zombies are not fast. Their muscles are in a constant state of deterioration. Their balance, flexibility and reaction time is poor. Their eyesight is little more than shadow. Depending on their state of decay, they may or may not have a sense of smell or touch. Their greatest strength is in numbers. A normal, reasonably healthy human can easily outrun or defeat a mutant zombie, but can be overcome by a number of them. Rule number one is "always be aware". Their greatest attribute is their relentless pursuit. They will not stop until totally incapacitated, by losing the ability to move, or by destroying the mutated brain. Rule number two is "always aim for the head". Nothing else will kill them.

Knowing all these things, Dobbs re-checked his list, made sure he had all he needed and headed out. He picked up his supplies and weapons and took them out the back way, being careful not to wake his sister. Since Jimmi didn't know about his zombie work, she would not understand why her peaceful, quiet brother was arming himself to the teeth for a day trip. He hoped she would never need to know about this, or any other, campaign.

Dirk made several trips, quietly carting the supplies out to his 'work truck', a red Ford F250 with camper shell. He had outfitted the truck for just such a situation as this, never thinking he would ever use it on his own island. When he was finished there, he went into the garage. He picked out a large gas can and put it into the bed. He gathered matches, tarps, ropes and other tools and stored those in the tool box.

Once located, any zombies he killed would have to be destroyed. Otherwise the remains could infect other healthy people. Within 24 hours the virus would take over their bodies, mutating in their brains. Then, there would be even more zombies with which they would have to contend. Burning the bodies of the zombies, and any other humans killed by a zombie, was, as he knew, essential.

Satisfied that he had all he needed, he slammed the camper shut and turned the lock. Dobbs knew that it was always more practical to hunt zombies in the daytime but he also knew that anything could happen. He would stay on the beach all day and through the night. Several nights, if necessary. It was possible that this was a small outbreak and could be taken care of quickly. It was, also, possible that it wasn't. If it turned out that it was more than he could handle, he would have to call in help from *ZARC*.

ZARC, Zombie Attack Response Corps, was a worldwide organization for zombie neutralization. Dirk had co-founded the core group with his Egyptian friend, Gassim Al-Fayed after the Middle Eastern outbreaks in the 1970's. *ZARC* had many different affiliate groups such as EZARC, in

Europe, AZARC, in Africa, and, the newest, NAZARC in North America. The league was still in its infancy in the western world, but, if help was needed, it would arrive. Until then, Dirk would be on point, with Randall as backup, if necessary.

By the time Dirk was finished he could hear his sister banging around in the kitchen. She met him at the kitchen door. "Where are you off to so early in the morning?" she asked, cracking eggs into a bowl on the counter. Dirk told her he was meeting Randall to go fishing for a couple of days. He had filled Durham in on his plan while he packed up the truck. "Well, you aren't going off without some breakfast!" she shook her spoon at him and winked. "Jimmi, I'll grab a bite at the Biskit Shack..." he started, but she cut him off. "You most certainly will not! That place has the lowest health score on the island! If you can't sit down for a real meal, I'll pack it up for you." He knew better than to argue. "OK," he told her, "I will finish packing up while you fix it." She grinned at him, knowing he would have rather run out the door. He didn't have a wife to take care of him and until he did, she thought, I will just have to do.

Jimmi fussed around, packing breakfast and lunch, before Dirk got back into the house. "You catch some big ones, Dirk." She said as he pecked her on the cheek. This was one time he hoped he would come home empty handed. He took the bag of sandwiches and biscuits she gave him and bid her goodbye. He could hear her singing, slightly off key, as always, as he got into the truck. It made him all the more determined to keep the island clear of the taint of evil that had washed onto its shores.

27

Randall took off his gloves and shook his head. "Damn. This doesn't look good... In so many ways." The young girl's body on the table was in bad shape. There were multiple injuries, punctures and slashes with what looked like a blade, but that was not all. There were tears and bites, as well. When he'd been called out to Red Point Park to examine a DOA, frankly, he had expected to find another obvious zombie victim. He had been surprised to find (only) a possible homicide. He cringed at the interjected 'only' that his mind had placed in that thought. It was hard to be a coroner and not do that. He didn't mean to minimize murder; it was just a defense mechanism to steel you to the work.

Detective Law seemed oblivious to the implications of the wounds, which wasn't surprising, Randall thought, since he is oblivious to most everything. There was little love lost between the investigator and the doctor. Law had been more help to the criminals on Deluna Island than he was to law enforcement. Durham could never decide if it was complete stupidity or total arrogance in the man, or both. His money was on both. The officers on scene had complained that he had tossed evidence into the bay and trampled the scene like a bull in a china shop. Neither surprised Randall. He told the CSI techs about the bottle and hoped they could retrieve it. Whether it would be of any use or not, they said, was questionable.

The victim had definitely been stabbed multiple times, slashed across her face and chest, and, possibly sexually assaulted. The other wounds were definitely bites, flesh ripped away by teeth. There were bits of debris in those wounds that looked suspiciously like decomposed tissue. He couldn't be sure until he tested the samples. There was a dramatic loss of blood. Which would be the cause of death, he wasn't sure. One thing he was sure of though, he thought, Dirk will be interested in this latest development.

He picked up the phone and dialed Dobbs' cell. He had spoken to him earlier that morning before the writer had gone out to set up camp at Bayside Beach. They had planned to meet up later in the day. He told Dirk he would be out to help him out after lunch. When he was called out to the murder site, he had to postpone the meeting. He hadn't had time to update his friend since then.

"Dirk? Hey, it's Randall. I've got a ... situation here; can you get away from camp and come over?" He asked.
Dirk took a look around the camp. He had finished setting up only minutes before. "I am still a little tied up over here. Can you come out here or do I need to come over there?" he asked, wondering at the doctor's memory. He knew that he was on stake out for a reason. "What's up?" he asked, suddenly, realizing that Durham wouldn't interrupt him for nothing.

Randall looked at the body of the blonde teenager on the table. "You better come out here. I have several things to show you."

"OK, I'll be right there as soon as I nail things down safely." Dirk said as he began locking up the RV. He had gone by Captain Jack's and rented a motor home for the stake out at the beach. He needed an operations center, in case he had to stay out here a while, and a place to secure the weapons. He was glad he'd decided to do it, now that he would have to leave the beach. Captain Jack had been a little gruff with him when he'd shown up at 6:30 in the morning, banging on his door. The funny thing was that he had been fully dressed, like he'd been up all night. Usually jovial and talkative, the man had been almost rude. He seemed to be in a hurry to get back into the house.

That, in itself, had been strange, Dirk mused as he gathered gear and locked the doors. Jack had come out onto the screen porch, pulling the door shut behind him, to rent the vehicle to him. Usually, no matter what the hour, he did all his business on the kitchen table. It was almost like there was something going on in there that he didn't want anyone to see. Weird. Thoughts of Jack and the mystery faded from his mind as he got into the truck and considered Randall's terse call. What now? He wondered. Five minutes later he was rolling down the Bayway toward the East End and the morgue.

The morgue was cold and clammy, as usual, when Dirk walked into the lab. "So, what's up, Durham?" Dirk asked as he noted the frown of concern on his friend's face. Randall motioned to him to follow him to the cold room.

Randall pulled back the sheet from the body on the table. Dirk sucked in his breath. The condition of the body hadn't shocked him as much as the victim. He hadn't expected to see such a young girl under the covering. "Who is it?" Dirk asked. "I don't know her name, yet. I just got her this morning. She was out at Red Point." He stopped, looking at his friend, suggestively. Dirk caught the look and knew what he was getting at. Red Point was just around the curve of sand from Bayside Beach where the couple was found.

Dirk took a closer look at the body. He had seen
the slices and puncture wounds the first time. This
time he saw the bites. "Uh-ho..." he whistled,
"but..." Randall finished his thought for both of
them, "which came first, the chicken or the egg,
right?" Dirk grunted his assent. The body was so
mutilated it was hard to tell if she was attacked by
the creatures then stabbed or vice versa. Either
would have done the job, but he had never heard
of a zombie attacking a dead body, or of a killer
stopping a zombie attack so that he could murder
someone. He voiced these errant thoughts to the
other man.

"I know. I have been trying to decide that
question, myself." He said as he pulled out a sheaf
of papers, "The preliminary tests have given me
one answer, for sure. There are strains of the
Solanum virus on her tissues...and, in her blood
stream." Dirk looked up. He went on. "And, the
debris in the wound had decomposed tissue in it.
So...this is what I have so far. She was attacked,
stabbed, obviously, AND she was attacked by a
zombie." Dirk started to protest that zombies do
not attack dead bodies, but Randall held up his
hand. "I know, I know...but, from what I can tell,
she was not dead when the zombie got to her. The
virus was IN her bloodstream. If she had been
dead, the virus might have been in the BITES and
on her skin but not in her blood. Her heart had to

be pumping when she was attacked to circulate it into the system." He went on to tell the open mouthed man that, even if her heart was faltering, near death, it would still move the virus into the bloodstream enough for it to show up on the tests.

"This is what I think happened. This poor girl was attacked by person, or persons, unknown. She was brutally stabbed, her throat cut, and, yes, sexually assaulted. Then, the perp left her for dead, but she was still clinging to life, bleeding out onto the sand." Randall said, leaning against the cabinet, shaking his head. Dirk looked thoughtful for a moment, and then took up the narrative. "Yes, that's why... She, somehow, attracted the attention of the creature, which probably was in the woods wandering, or came up from the bay. Hungry, it wouldn't turn down the chance to feed. She probably never knew it happened..." he trailed off. Randall agreed. "Yeah, I am sure she was past knowing or caring, at that point. That leaves us right where we were afraid we were..."

Dobbs nodded. "In the middle of a full blown zombie outbreak. I knew it. I prayed it wasn't, but I knew it had to be after seeing the other bodies." The Medical Examiner covered the girl and rolled her into the freezer. "The question is, now what? I mean, I have three viral explosions ready to blow in here" he said, pointing to the refrigerated room used as a holding room, "And, unless I miss my guess there will be more. I already have the Cheries' next of kin calling for the bodies to be released to the funeral home...This girl's family will be next. What do I tell them?" Dirk could see his dilemma. There was no way these bodies could be released to the embalmers. They would contaminate the mortuary, the attendants and the director, and would re-animate! He told Durham that he would have to stall them, and by all means, keep the corpses on ice! "Thanks, Dirk, I would have never thought of that." He said dryly.

Dirk, despite the circumstances, or maybe because of the stress, had to laugh. "Yeah, Durham, what would you do without me to help you along?" he asked, as they left the icy room. They compared notes on the situation, the beach and the bodies, and Dirk left with Randall promising to stay away from the beach. Dirk didn't want him to put himself in danger. He assured his friend that he could handle it alone. Durham agreed only to shut him up. "All right, but call me if you need anything, OK?" Dirk agreed. He was back at the beach in ten minutes, his mind returning to zombie control. His resolve even stronger than before. He searched the surrounding areas while it was still daylight. He would try his best to locate the tainted beasts before darkness fell. Those he didn't find in the sunlight he would lure into the camp in the dark. It was going to be a long weekend.

28

Gerald "Gerry" Johnson woke up. He stared up
into the tops of the trees, wondering, what the dark
leaves and palm fronds were. To him they looked
like the wings of black crows covering the sky. His
head spun with every move and pain beat at it like
a blacksmith on his anvil. Despite the pain, he
knew he had to get up. He had to get help. The
birds would get him if he stayed there. He had to
get away.

Seriously injured, but alive, the man pulled himself
to his feet, out of the gully and started toward the
road. He was infected with the virus. He didn't
know about the virus that was coursing through
his veins. He didn't know that he had only a few
hours to live. He, also, didn't know that he would,
soon, become one of the fiends who attacked him.
He wandered around deliriously in the woods. At
dawn, he came out onto the jogging trail. He was
no longer looking for help. He was past help. His
wounds were festering at an accelerated rate.
Decomposition of the tissues had set in. Within a

very short time he would succumb to death, but it wouldn't be the everlasting death that comes with a normal illness. He would return to life, but, he would not be alive. He would be the walking dead.

Just behind him, around the bend a couple was out walking their two dogs. They often took their pets out to the park at dawn to enjoy the peace and quiet. Their dogs, although of the larger variety, were docile creatures. They had never attacked anyone, or even bit. The leashes were on the dogs to keep them on the path, so that the owners didn't have to chase them through the trees, if the animals caught the scent of a rabbit or squirrel. They held the leashes, limply, in their hands, enjoying the foggy morning. Suddenly, both dogs tensed and came to attention, sniffing the air. Before the walkers could react, the dogs began to jump and try to pull away, but the man and woman held on. The smell from Johnson's inflamed wounds filled their noses. The wounds he had received the night before had begun to decay. The putrefied flesh emitted an oozing liquid that dripped along behind him, leaving a snail trail of smelly slime on the pathway. When the couple's dogs came across the seepage they went ballistic. The wild, rotting, decomposing emanation was more than their primal instincts could contain. They pulled free of their leashes

and took off, growling, snarling and barking down
the trail.

When they saw the infected man ahead of them
they flew into the air, leaping the last few feet
between them. The dogs hit Gerry Johnson and
took him to the ground. Snarling, biting and
pulling they attacked him viciously.

The couple ran toward the scene in horror. As the
dogs attacked in frenzy, they dragged the man up
the trail to a place in sight of the main road. Just
at that moment, two men in a construction van
drove by. They saw the attack and pulled to side
of the road, jumping out to help the downed man.
They grabbed two large limbs that lay on the
roadway, leftovers from the high winds, and began
beating at the dogs. Unwilling to give up the
animals hung on, briefly. The men continued their
beating until, finally, they gave up. The dogs
yelped and ran away a few feet, then, enticed again
by the smell, ran back to the body. The workers
jabbed and beat at them, again and again, until
they ran off with a trophy piece toward the nearby
kennel entrance. The entryway had a small
enclosure to the side of it. The dogs hunkered
down inside, away from the men, and continued
their gnawing on the parts they had won.

When the ambulance arrived, the man was in a
deep coma. The viciousness of the attack was

blamed for the condition of the body. He was pronounced dead at the hospital the next morning and taken to the morgue. The dogs were taken to Animal Control and their 'trophies' were bagged and sent along to the emergency room.

Gerry Johnson had no identification on him. He was tagged a John Doe and transported to the morgue. He was placed in the freezer with Anna Knox, and the Cheries. They would have more company before the weekend was done.

Randall Durham looked over the unidentified man and knew that the dogs had not killed him. The man was killed by the Solanum virus. He cleaned up, changed to his street clothes and headed out to the beach to lend his friend a hand in getting rid of these things. He left strict orders that anybody that came in should be frozen immediately, no exceptions. No bodies were to be released to anyone without his permission. He couldn't know that his orders wouldn't be followed.

29

"Oh my God, Dirk! Did you see this paper? They found that poor man all chewed up and missing one of his hands" Jimmi Dobbs exclaimed as her brother entered the den of their Deluna Bay home. He'd found one of his ammunition cases empty and had come back to get another. "Are you the town crier these days, Jimmi, or what?" he asked, jokingly, referring to her tendency to announce everything she reads to the house at large.

Dirk had seen the paper. He was not convinced. He spoke with medical examiner's office on his way to the house. Randall was not convinced, either, but, did admit that until all the tests come in he couldn't be sure. The bites on the victims didn't really look like dog bites but, at this point, it was hard to tell. There was so much tearing, and the wounds looked suspicious. Dogs do tear when they bite so it is possible he thought. He would just have to wait. He'd know more when Randall got the tests back.

Jimmi turned on the television in the spacious den and flipped to WDEL, Deluna Island. Dirk stopped to hear the latest. He was not surprised to see Reporter Angel Kraig outside the Deluna Island Sheriff's office. She began her report.

"Earlier today our cameras caught up with the alleged dog handlers from the Easy Life Boarding and Kennels as they voluntarily came in for questioning."

The cameras panned the complex and stopped as the door opened and the two men emerged. Jeff Kelley and Bubba Lambert made their way across the gravel drive. A sheriff's deputy stopped Lambert for a moment. Kelley continued on toward the waiting car.

Angel Kraig caught up with him and turned the full force of her dimpled smile on him. "Mr. Kelley, could we ask you a few questions for the six o'clock news?" she asked sweetly. Jeff Kelley stood rooted to the spot as if glued down. He was a big, bony, lanky man who looked more like an oversized boy. He had slicked back short brown hair and dark soulful eyes surrounded by a fringe of dark lashes. He looked into the camera, a little confused, 'Huh?" he said, his voice breaking into two octaves. Repeating her question, he answered her in the same broken tones, "OK."

He was tall, lanky and a little clumsy, as if he had
not quite grown into his size fourteen feet, yet.
"Ahh, just a minute, I have to get Bubba...I mean,
Mr. Lambert." He loped off across the lot. After
much explaining and gesturing, he came smiling
back, practically wagging his tail, if he'd had one.
"He'll be here in just a minute...ma'am." He said
self-consciously.

The two partners could not be more opposite.
And have two more mismatched names. Where
Jeff was large, and gawky; Bubba was compact,
low to the ground with a cat like grace. Jeff had
short, sleek hair, was clean shaven and had dark
doe eyes. Bubba had a wild mane of soft, silver
beige fluff, a bushy mustache and icy clear blue
eyes. If either one should have had such a
common name as Bubba, it wasn't Lambert.

Jeff bumbled across the lot, tripping and righting
himself, as he headed back toward the bench. He
sat down to wait, gazing happily into the camera.
Bubba, on the other hand, moved across the rocky
expanse like he was floating above the earth. He
constantly kept watch where he was stepping and
what was around him for any potential risk. Jeff
sat with his long legs apart, hands pressed palm
down onto the bench between his legs, shoulders
hunched slightly inward. His head was in constant
motion looking around in awe at all the equipment
and crew. Bubba sat down gingerly, perched

lightly on the edge of the seat, as if he might spring away at any second if the need arose.

Jeff's hair was mussed and there were stains on his shirt front from lunch and probably breakfast, as well. Bubba brushed unseen lint from his immaculate pullover, picked at his perfect manicure and, licking his fingertips, he smoothed down and groomed his feathery whiskers. The camera man came over and told them that the reporter would set up the scene then ask them a few questions. Simple, he said, just look into the camera and talk.

"Angel Kraig, WDEL TV.
Tonight we have with us the owners of the kennel and boarding facility where the unidentified man was mauled by dogs this afternoon near National Seashore Park, Mr. Jeff Kelley and Mr. Bubba Lambert."

"Mr. Kelley, do you know how the dogs that attacked the victim got out of their enclosures?" she asked flashing him her famous grin. Jeff Kelley looked into the camera, swallowed, and said, with his irregular tones, "No...Uh, ma'am."

Lambert let out a snort and was impatiently gesturing to the commentator, "Ms. Greg" he said, purposely mispronouncing her name, "Those dogs were NOT from our kennel!" He shot a look at his partner. The camera panned the other man, who was watching the cameraman adjust his settings, unaffected by his friend's displeasure. Lambert sat up straight, pinning the camera with a vicious look, "We do NOT board or breed THAT TYPE of animal." He stretched out the negatives.

"But, you DO board dogs at your facility, don't you?" Kraig asked innocently.

"Yes, but we have VERY stringent requirements for the pets we accommodate." Bubba said imperiously, with a slight lift of his head.

"So, Mr. Lambert, it is your contention that you have NEVER SEEN these two dogs before on your property?" she asked.

"Most Definitely NOT." He replied, repulsed by the very thought.

"But, you DO board dogs there?" she reiterated.

"Yes." Lambert replied shortly. The reported looked toward the camera for a full beat.

"And, do you BREED dogs there, as well?" she asked, as if it were a crime, for effect.

Before he could answer, Jeff piped up, looking into the camera with his puppy dog eyes, and said, with all his guilelessness, "Oh, no ma'am. We don't do THAT. The dogs do that themselves."

It was all Kraig could do to keep from breaking up into peals of laughter. Before she could resume her poise, Bubba looked at his partner in disgust and rolled his eyes. He put one soft hand over the camera lens and said, "That's enough." He sprung from his perch on the seat and disappeared around the camera crew and was gone.

"More at 11. Angel Kraig, WDEL TV". The reporter signed off.

Dirk smiled at the television, but soon lost his sense of humor as he sped across the island with his replacement ammo. The weight of the situation was weighing on him. He hoped he could put a dent in the numbers of the creatures tonight. He was too much of a realist to think that he could get them all at once. At least, he was in the right place. He just hoped it was the right time.

The sky turned black as he pulled in to the camp. The night sky matched his thoughts.

30

Captain Jack had exhausted all the ideas he had on where his wife, Selena, could be. Since she had stepped out of the kitchen the day before, she had not been seen. He had checked with her sister, but so far she hadn't been there. Amorosa had called and told him a friend of hers had thought she'd seen Selena at the beach where she'd gone before. He secretly wondered if she had left him. They had been having some troubles lately. She said he was too remote and cold to her, he had confided in Angus. Jack had told her she was just imagining things. He told her she needed a hobby, he cringed as he thought of how that might have sounded to her. Maybe she had had enough of him and had decided to take off. She had done it before when they were fighting. She was gone for a whole week once. He thought he would go crazy before he found her. She had gone down to Destin and rented a condo. I was giving you time to think, she'd said. "That's probably what she is doing now. Making me think." He said to himself, as he stared out at the swaying palms. He hoped so.

"Wouldn't she have called you, Amorosa, if she was just angry with me and out there?" He asked the sister. "No, Jack, she doesn't have her phone and she knows she can't call here. She knows he is home this weekend and that he has been on a binge." She whispered, not wanting her husband to hear, "She will probably come out here tomorrow because he will be gone. I told her." That thought seemed to settle Jackson a little. That did sound like what she could be doing. Amorosa told him not to worry, "You know how she gets, Jack. She just needed some time to think." Jack agreed to call her, if he heard anything and hung up. He decided she was probably right and put his mind on the business on the key. If Jack Jackson had been thinking straight he might have been more proactive in looking for Selena, but, as it was with the epidemic on the ship in the bay, he was on overload.

He busied himself around the kitchen, tidying up the charts and plans on the table and pulling a couple of faxes from the basket. He saw where the café had sent in their order for the week's groceries. Selena usually handled that but he guessed he better get it done himself. It was another hour before he looked at the clock. "I wonder what is happening at the ship?" he thought. The plan was to get the charges set and then come back in to regroup before blowing it.

They had decided to do it after hours. The ferry quit running then, and the chances of anyone being out on the bay were minimal. The clock was ticking on this thing. He wished Angus would get back. He had tried his cell phone earlier and it went to voice mail. He guessed that they were busy and he didn't hear it. He would try again later.

Suddenly he heard the sound of a car pulling into the gravel drive. Before he could get up, the door burst open and Angus and one of the team came in carrying something. "What? What happened? What's that?" he stammered. "It is not a what, my friend, it is a who. It is Josephs. Clean off that cot over there and let me get him down." He ordered.

Jack swung into action, his problems forgotten. They got the injured man onto the cot. The park owners started to unzip the bag. "Wait, Jack! Don't." Angus commanded. Jack stopped. "The man has been injured, possibly infected. I don't know how contagious he is but let's not take any chances." He said. "We have to get him to the hospital, then." Jack said, picking up the phone. Angus stopped him. "Jack, we have 200 pounds of illegal explosives out in the bay, 24 illegal sub machine guns and any number of other weapons violations they could charge us with... We can't just call 911." Murphy said quietly. Jack put down the phone.

"You're right. But, the others have medical training in battle injuries and so do I. We will have to do it ourselves." Jack said. Angus told him that the bleeding had stopped and that he was all right for the moment. "We will just keep an eye him. We can't afford to take chances with the infection unless we have to. He is stable right now. We will have to get more information before we do anything else...safely." The Scotsman wondered to himself exactly where they would get information on an infection that they knew little about and couldn't confide in anyone about.

Murphy gathered together the rest of the ammunition and called in the other men for the team. These men were the second wave. They didn't have the underwater expertise of Allan, Waters and Josephs but they were seasoned in what is known as CQB, close quarters battle. If what happened at the beach was any indication, they would be in very close quarters with more of these sickened men who could, apparently, hold up under heavy combat inflicted wounds...and, walk underwater. He didn't understand this. The men were, obviously, terribly emaciated, sick, wounded, but, they keep coming. The bullets didn't faze them, only made it harder for them to get along, he explained to Jackson when the truck was loaded. They stood outside under a heavy magnolia tree, talking quietly. The Captain

listened, knowing the Scotsman would not
embellish, but having a hard time giving credence
to the things he was describing.   "And, you say,
this man in here," he motioned toward the house,
"was wounded by one of...them?" Angus nodded.
Jack understood, now, why he was stopped from
touching the injured man. He shuddered to think
how close he was to possible infection. He vowed
to stay clear of him and keep anyone else away, as
well.

Murphy rounded up the men and started toward
the loaded truck. Jackson tried to talk them out of
going back down to the beach.   "Jack, this is an
honest tale of what happened on the beach, and I
gather, under the bay out there. We have to go
back." He said seriously. "We doona want those
corrupt things coming up on to the island to roam
free," he said fiercely, "And there is this, as well,
we canna know what went on down there by that
ship. Josephs is hurt and may be having strange
imaginings on the status of the situation. We may
have two men left behind, alive, and possibly
injured, down there." In the Special Forces ranks
the unwritten law is 'No man left behind', living or
dead. He was right. They must go back.

The men showed up as Angus was putting the last
of the ammunition into the truck bed. "I am
taking Johnson and Stanley back out to the key.
Send the others on when they arrive...ASAP!"

Murphy said. With that he jumped into the truck
and the three men drove away as the sun faded. It
would be in the darkness that the men would go to
face the remains of the undead army that got
away.

31

The night had come down quickly and deeply. The clouds obscured the stars and the bay was black glass. The only light was coming from the campfire Dirk had built near the RV. So far, nothing. Not a sound or a sighting of anything more than the cicadas chirping. Dirk was alone at the beach encampment with his Glock 17. He had picked this particular weapon because the stock configuration holds seventeen rounds, with a plus two base and one round in the chamber, he could easily fire 20 rounds ; not the weapon to use if he were trying to conceal it in a crowd but just the thing for zombie target practice while he was facing the undead alone at the campsite. At least he thought he was alone. Unexpectedly, he heard a car coming down the sandy drive. He stood, putting the Glock 17 back into his holster, and walked out away from the fire. The last thing he needed was some nosy tourist snooping around his set up.

He relaxed when he saw the nose of the white
SUV enter the light. Across the front it read,
Emerald County Medical Examiner. It was
Randall Durham, one of the few people who was
privy to what he was doing out on this isolated
stretch of sand. "Randall, he said as the M.E.
rolled to a stop, "what brings you out here?" The
zombie hunter asked, his hand shielding his eyes
from the headlights.

"I missed you." Durham quipped, laughing.
Dobbs grinned; secretly glad his old friend had
shown up. "No, I had a new case come in after
you left. I thought I would bring you up to date."
The men went over to the fireside where Dobbs
pulled out another folding chair and set it up. The
doctor settled into the woven plastic seat and
kicked his legs out near the fire. The wind had
picked up and it was a little nippy in the open,
despite the season.

"I got another victim in this morning. Somehow,
it didn't get logged in until after lunch. I didn't
know anything about it until that idiot attendant
came back. He couldn't find his..." Durham
shook his head. He had often complained about
the boy to Dobbs so, further words were
redundant. "Anyway, the victim was in the final
stages, just about dead, when some joggers' dogs
smelled him..." they both wrinkled their noses at
the thought, understanding the dogs' response,

"Well, you know. They went crazy and took him down. By the time a couple of guys saw it and knocked the dogs away, they had torn him up worse than he was."

Dirk nodded, waiting for the rest of the story. Durham went on. "They tore off a hand and a few fingers and ran off with them. The EMT's got them from Animal Control and sent them in. The general consensus is that the vic was mauled to death by the dogs."

"Yeah, I saw the news report. Looks like the Sheriff is going that way. What are you telling them?" he asked the doctor. "Not much at the moment. I just let them think what they wanted for now." Randall, being an animal lover, hated that the dogs were being accused of a mauling that wasn't their fault, but, there were human lives at stake and that had to be the top priority. If this got out, before they had the outbreak under control, people would panic. They would run, possibly spreading the virus farther. They had to contain the story for now, he told Dirk. Dirk agreed. He felt badly for the innocent animals, too, but it was what had to be done.

Suddenly there was a loud "Crack!" Dirk and Randall both turned toward the southwest side of the island. "That sounded like a gunshot." Randall said. Dirk nodded. "It sure did. Like a 9 mm.

speaking of, you got yours with you?" They both waited to see if they heard another. Even though no further noise was heard, Dobbs was alert. He wondered who would be shooting a gun on the island. It could be someone taking aim at a snake, but something told him that it was something more. They turned back to their conversation. Dirk still remained alert, listening as his friend spoke.

"Not a Glock, but my old magnum wheel gun." He pulled back his light jacket on the right side to show a holstered hand gun. "I usually keep mine on me anytime I am near you." He quipped. Although, with what he had been seeing at the morgue lately, this time he carried it for protection. Dirk grinned. "How'd you get out of the dungeon?" he asked.

"I was bringing these latest reports out to you, about the new vic, but, honestly, I had to get out of the office for a while. The place is a zoo. I called in Hanrahan from Pensacola to take over. He is not what you would call a 'mover and a shaker', so, he won't get too ambitious, but, just in case, I have all the, uh, questionable cases filed under assumed names for right now. So I am taking a well-deserved night off." Durham handed Dirk a written report on the cases so far.

"And why aren't you home with your wife?" Dobbs asked him, hoping he would be able to stay on at the camp. "For your information, Mindy and the girls are gone to her mother's in Brewton. I thought I better get them out of here till this is over." He told him, then added, "You want some company or not, Dobbs?" "Sure, as long as you got your wheel gun with you and all." he said, partly joking, partly serious. The last thing he wanted to do was get his old bud in a position to get hurt. Yet, he was glad to have him. Randall had been in the trenches with him before. He could handle himself. And, most importantly, he knew the two main rules of this particular combat. 1. Head shots. 2. Don't let them catch you off guard. He could deal with anything that came up, with or without Dirk. He had done it before. Dirk just like to give him grief.

Randall asked about the camp. He explained the set up to him and showed him where he had placed the perimeters. He adjusted the alarm system and showed his friend how to work it. Just in case something should happen to him, he would want his friend and his island to be as safe as possible. The only way to be safe with this threat looming over them was to have a knowledgeable individual or individuals on the job. There was always the chance that Dirk could get attacked and then someone else would have to take over. His friend knew the other rule as well. If Dirk became infected he was to shoot him in the forehead, immediately. There is no room for sentimentality in this war. He knew that Dirk would do the same to him. Neither wanted to become one of the ghouls they chased. A fate worse than death. By a long shot.

Despite all his misgivings for his friend's safety and the jokes, aside, Dirk was glad to have company. The night would be long, and along with everything else, Alexandra was on his mind. He'd gotten a letter from the doctors. She had relapsed. The drugs had become ineffective. They had her back in the ward she was on when she left. The nightmares were back, but she wasn't responding to treatment. She hadn't spoken to anyone but her mother since she arrived. She thought she was back in college and her mom was visiting her in her dorm. The doctors said that it was easier for her to exist in that world than the one that held such frightening memories. She had retreated to a time before such things dwelled in her world. It was because of the state she was in that Dirk had led such a solitary life. He tried to insulate the people he loved from his work. Now, he was faced with his worst nightmare. His work had found its way to his home. He was more determined than ever to clear this threat off of the island.

Randall settled into one of the chairs and took a long drink of the beer he'd pulled from the cooler. Dirk told him about Alex. Randall let him talk. He knew that his friend was feeling the guilt and the pain, all over again. He would never get over what had happened to her on his watch. As the night wore on, Dirk and Randall kept watch. They were glad to have something to do to help the people on the island who knew nothing about the dangers.

What Dirk and Randall did not know, as they sat on the beach waiting for their prey, was that just around the point, Angus and the others were having their second encounters with the walking dead.

As Angus' men were under the water fighting for their lives that day, Dirk was stringing trip wire and setting flares. As Stanley and Angus were wrapping Josephs' body in the plastic and putting it into the body bag, Dirk was checking out his gear and going over his plans with the ME. While they were trying to mow down zombies as they came out the mingled waters of the bays and the Gulf, Dirk was listing the reports on the dead and missing. As Angus was blowing the head off a zombie from the back of the truck, Dirk was checking on his surveillance system and audio alarms to warn him in case he should doze off. Now, as Randall and Dirk were sitting by the fire at the camp, waiting for zombies, Angus and his new team were set up on a beach across the island watching for the same thing. The shot Dirk and Randall heard had been one of Murphy's men taking a shot at a coyote. The jumpy man, hearing something running through the underbrush, capped off a shot before making sure of his target. Red faced and head low, he took the gruff reprimand from his superior. Angus laid into him with a little more vigor than necessary, but, his nerves were as raw as the volunteers were, and, the folly could have had a much more serious outcome had that been a local teen looking for a make out spot. The time would come for shooting, he told the man, but make sure who, or what, it is before you pull the trigger again.

32

Dirk and Randall were just about to take turns on watch when Dirk's cell phone rang. It would change the face of the whole operation. It was Jimmi.

"Dirk, you better get back over here. There is a big, foreign man here demanding to see you and he is scaring me to death." Jimmi wailed. His sister didn't like to deal with anything out of her comfort zone. She had a way of making things a bit bigger than they really were, but, Dirk didn't think so this time. She sounded frantic.

Dirk, clicked off the phone and explained to Randall what was going on. "Do you think you can hold down the fort till I check this out?" he asked his friend. "Yes, Dirk. I was a Marine not a hairdresser!" he quipped, "I know what to do if we get a tumble. I will call you to bring the Mounties and blow the head off everything dead that is up walking around." Dirk frowned at him, "All right,

just hit 'Z' on speed dial." He said as he handed
Randall another cell phone. "I set this up for you.
I knew you would show up." He grinned.

Randall laughed at his friend's choice of hot keys.
"Yeah, 'Z'. How cute. Go on." Randall assured
him, "I got this." Dirk grabbed his key ring off the
table and told him, "OK, I'll be back ASAP." Dirk
waved as he drove out and headed for the bluffs.
"What the hell is this all about?" he growled under
his breath. The sun was still hanging part-way
over the horizon as he bounced down Northside
Drive, heading back to his house. He didn't know
that he would be quite a while rejoining the doctor.

The night had gone by without incident on both
sides of the island. The sun was peeking up over
the palms as he turned out of the park. He sped to
the bluff house as fast as he could go in the heavy
truck. He couldn't imagine what this was all about
but he didn't like the thought of a strange man
beating at his door at all hours, foreign or not.

Jimmi met Dirk at the door, wringing her hands.
"My Lord, Dirk. I thought I was gonna get my
throat cut! This big foreign man was banging on
the door, hollering something in some Ay-rab
sounding language. All I could understand was
Dirk this and Dirk that. I never been so glad to see
you walk in the door in my life!" she finished her
tirade as they made the glass doors to the patio. "I

put him out here with some tea, which he made a face about! The kind of weird stuff those people eat and he makes a face at MY sweet tea!"

Dirk looked through the glass door to see a man, indeed dark, of medium height and a husky build, sitting with his back to them. Yes, he thought, "Ay-rab" was pretty close. He smiled as he recognized his old friend, Gassim Al-Fayed.

Jimmi, it's OK. This is one of my oldest friends from my Navy days." He told the frantic woman. "Come on out and let me introduce you." She backed up. "Oh, No! I've seen enough of him today. Besides, it sounds like he has something important to talk to you about." She said, "Now that I know he isn't going to kill us and feed us to the vultures or something, I think I'll go back to bed! I'm flat worn out." The woman went toward her room shaking her head, still muttering, "Ay-rab" to herself. Politically Correct was not in Jimmi's vocabulary.

Dirk stepped out onto the flagstone patio and greeted his friend. "Gassim, how are you? What are you doing here?" His smile froze on his face when he saw the look in Al-Fayed's eye. "Where?" It was all he had to say.

Gassim said, "Where? Here!" he said, emphatically, "Do you not know? I have come all the way from Khartoum to tell you there are zombies in your backyard!" Dirk put his hand on his arm to calm him, "Yes, I know, now. We have just confirmed three deaths as zombie kills and we have a host of other problems. How in the world did you find out?" Dobbs asked.

Gassim Al-Fayed went on to tell him about the conversation he overheard in the café and how he had recognized the name of his island. "I know that if zombies are on Deluna Island then my friend, Dirk, needs my help."

"Glad to see you, man. I do need all the help I can get." He said. Yes, they would all need help, and fast. Gassim caught Dirk up on the chain of events that led him to the island and through their own set of contacts; they tracked down the arms dealer who, after assurances from them and his own contacts, told them about Angus Murphy's order.

"Then, we have to get over to the RV Park. The Captain and Angus have no idea what they are dealing with or how to handle it. "Dirk said as they both strapped on their guns and jumped into the truck. On the way Dirk told his friend about the camp he set up and his plans to find the zombies. "Once we get Angus and Jack up to speed we will go from there and finish up at the beach." Gassim, on his own gut instincts had brought two of his men with him to help out. He didn't know if Dirk had called *ZARC*, yet, but, if not, he knew they would need more manpower. The two Egyptians were in the van that Gassim had rented at the airport. Gassim laughed that it was a good thing he had not brought the men to the door. "Your poor sister would have barred the door and called in an air strike!" Dirk nodded his head, laughing, as well, "Yes, Jimmi would not have taken it well." "An understatement", Gassim replied.

Dirk gave the men in the van directions to the camp and called Randall to tell him the cavalry was coming. Randall protested that he did not need help, but, was glad for the backup. This was serious business and no time for false bravado. Dirk explained about Captain Jack and Angus Murphy. Randall told him to get there, by all means. Both Jack Jackson and Angus were well known to the doctor. He didn't want them to face this foe alone, or uneducated. Dirk told him he would call as soon as he knew anything and rung off.

Dobbs and the Egyptian pulled up into the circular gravel drive in front of the RV office, which was in the front room of Jackson's house. The Captain came out the door as they were hurrying up the drive.

"Dirk! What are you doing back out this way? I figured you'd be off in the RV, writing another book." He seemed nervous, Dirk thought. "Jack, this is my old friend, Gassim Al-Fayed, of Egyptian Military Intelligence." The man looked startled. He didn't know that Dirk had friends in military or intelligence circles. The two shook hands.

"I won't beat around the bush, Jack. Gassim heard through the grapevine that you and Angus got some Semtex and quite a bit of it. Along with some heavy duty firepower." Jack Jackson was stunned. How did Dirk, a low key mystery story novelist have contacts high up enough to know about the arms deal? And, know an Egyptian Intelligence agent from halfway around the world well enough to bring him here? This was just too fantastic.

"Well, Dirk, I, I ...don't know what you mean. Weapons? I..." Dirk cut him off. "Jack, are you involved in this problem with the ship and the sickness on board?" he asked the man, looking him in the eye. "You don't have to worry. I know about it."

Jackson looked like he might pass out. The strain of his missing wife, the ship, the injured man and all the strange stories were just about to get to him. "Look, Jack, let's go inside. This is not something we want to talk about out here." They headed to the door.

Jack stopped. "Now, Dirk, there's a lot you don't understand about what's going on here. This is very serious. It is deadly to the people here on the island." He said. "No, Jack, there's a lot YOU don't understand here. This is not just a sickness. These men who are infected are now zombies. The living dead. They eat flesh. If they bite or otherwise contaminate you, you will die and reanimate into one of them. You better take us in and tell us what you know." Dirk told him.

The captain stopped again and turned, "Zombies!" he looked at the man like he was crazy. "Are you working on one of your books, or what? Zombies!" He snorted. Even knowing all that he knew so far about the sickness and its results, he couldn't believe in zombies! Dirk took his arm and made him look at both of them. "Jack, this is serious. Deadly serious." Gassim looked the old captain in the eye, "Captain, you have seen much in your life but you have not seen what I have seen...what we have seen together." Looking toward Dobbs, Jackson began to see they were serious. "The sickness you know about makes men into flesh eating, blood drinking monsters. They are no longer living men. They are dead. They walk and attack, but they are dead. If you are exposed, YOU will become like them."

"You mean everybody that gets infected turns into those...things?" He asked, turning white around his white mustache, thinking of his close call with the sick man. The three men walked into the house. As they entered the room, Dirk and Gassim heard a moan from the man on the cot in the corner.

"Who is that?" Dirk asked. Jack explained about the attempt to find the ship and place the explosives, about the loss of the two men and how the man in the corner was bitten over 12 hours ago. "I was about to tell you..." Dirk cut him off. "Bitten? Did you or Angus touch him?" Dirk said sharply. "No. Angus and Stanley wore gloves and wrapped him in plastic and zipped him up in a body bag. We unzipped it but we haven't moved him." The captain said guiltily. He should have taken him to the hospital where they could help him but we couldn't with the illegal operation we were involved in..." Dirk shook his head.
"It won't do any good." The man moaned once again. Dirk and Gassim look at each other decisively.

Dirk grabbed a comforter off the couch and threw it over the man's head. They both drew their guns and fired; two rounds each, into the man's head. The blanket absorbed any splatter or flying purulence. Captain Jack Jackson jumped at the roar of the guns. "What are you doing? Are you crazy?" he yelled.

"It is the only way." Gassim said as both men holstered their guns. "You must shoot the head." "Yes, Jack. First and most important rule to killing a zombie: AIM FOR THE HEAD." Dirk said as the ex-military man sunk into a chair. He could not comprehend that his mild mannered neighbor, who looked like an accountant, was a full- fledged zombie killer.

"Where is Angus, now?" Dirk asked as they rolled up the man's body and took it out to the incinerator. "Oh, hell! He, Stanley and the new guy, Phillip something, have gone back down to the key to make sure none of the zombies are on the island." Jack exclaimed. He had forgotten all about them.

"We have to get down there. Jack, stay here and wait. I have more help coming. I'll call and give them your number. When they get here, tell them where we are." Dirk ordered as he and Gassim rushed out.

While he and Gassim had driven to the RV Park, the EMI officer had put in a call to *ZARC*. The organization had taken the coordinates and promised to have men on the ground in 24 hours. Dirk, Gassim, Randall and team on the key would have to hold the fort until then. He signed off as they turned into the sandy tracks that Murphy's truck had made.

Bumping across the sandy ruts, Dirk held on with one hand and dialed Randall with the other. He gave him a quick rundown on the situation and told him help was on the way. "Until then," he said, "Watch yourself, man. There are probably some stragglers on the ground that didn't go back into the water. So watch your monitors and watch for the flares. If one goes off, be prepared for them to come from that way. If more than one directional flare goes off...Get the hell out of there." He said sternly. "Live to fight another day, right man?"
"You got it. I'm on point, dude." Randall replied, jokingly. That is how the men handled the seriousness of their respective jobs. They joked, they threw insults and barbs, but they both knew the gravity of the circumstances.

Dirk hung up and dialed *ZARC*, again. "Tell them to get those men on the ground ASAP." This was no regular outbreak, this was his home, his island, and he couldn't be impartial in this one.

Gassim floored the truck, sliding around stands of palms and outcroppings of monkey grass. "Do we have an ETA on the guys from *ZARC*?" Gassim asked using the shortened term for *IZARC*, *International Zombie Assault Response Corps*.

"They have a *ZOOM* Team that just landed in Atlanta. Getting the equipment would take a little time. They will be here in three or four hours, the rest will take longer. 24 at the latest." Dirk explained.   Gassim nodded. "So it is up to us for now?" Meaning the two of them, Angus' team, Randall and the two men at the beach camp. "Yes, that is about the extent of it." Dirk said, dourly, "but, it is better than what I had a few hours ago."

They rounded the bend and slid to a stop beside Angus' truck. The men were nowhere to be seen. Dirk and Gassim got out, grabbed the MP5's they had gotten from the Captain's stash, and several magazines of ammunition. They slung the rifles over their shoulders and started down the path to the key.

Just as they started down they hear a burst of suppressed fire. They made their way down to the end of the trees in a low crouch in time to see Angus and two of his men firing on five or six zombies coming up out of the water. The men, in their panic, are still shooting randomly at the bodies of the ghouls. Occasionally, they are getting in a head shot but don't seem to realize the head is the objective.

They are still far enough away that the two experienced zombie exterminators know that there is time to spare. Dirk and Gassim hit their stance, train their sights on their heads and begin picking them off, one by one. Angus and his men, thankful for the assistance, fall in beside them, panting. Before they can see how to get the job done, the battle is over. Five zombies lay motionless with their mutant brains spattered on the white sand. A sixth one is still trying to crawl up from the breakers where one of the Scotsman's men blew off his legs. The little cove is an unholy mess.

Dirk explained how he learned of the threat on the island and the proper way to quell it, while Gassim instructed the men in the proper way to dispatch the living dead and dispose of the contaminated bodies. Angus, when he had time to take a breath, was just as flabbergasted as Jack Jackson was to find out that the writer was more than he seemed. He could have never imagined that he would owe his life to the man.

"All I can say, Mr. Dirk, is that I was never so glad to behold a site than I was to see you and your big friend taking aim at those beasties." Dirk and the Scotsman laughed. It was good to be alive when you have been surrounded by death and survived.

33

While Randall Durham was out at the beach on zombie watch, the dental records came in on the John Doe who was mauled by dogs. The young man's name was Gerald Thomas Johnson, known as Gerry or "G". The attendant on duty put the file on Durham's desk and shelved the body in the drawer. Durham had left strict orders that any bodies that came in were to be put in the freezer. The aid had been called in to fill in for the regular attendant who had taken ill. The order from the ME had been verbal, so the part timer hadn't heard it, nor been informed. Usual practice was to place bodies into drawers until the examiner saw them, but this was not a usual day. These were not usual corpses.

As soon as the guy came in the phone started ringing. Funeral directors, families, policemen; everyone was in a tizzy over the release of the bodies in the morgue. The problem was that he could not find the names in the book. The book listed them as completed and released. He didn't want to tell the loved ones, or the police, that the bodies were, apparently, missing. He would have to make sure, he thought, as he entered the freezer.

He pulled two bodies out of the freezer to check the toe tags for identification cross referencing and found a problem. For some reason the Doc had listed the couple in the freezer under the wrong name! No wonder he couldn't find them. Their families were calling, raising the roof, to have the bodies released to the mortuary for burial and he had almost told them the bodies were lost! He was relieved but dreaded the task of straightening it all out. It took the better part of two hours to find out the correct information, talk to the family and the funeral home. He'd had to forego the other duties he'd been assigned. He hoped the doctor would be impressed with his quick thinking. It was nearly quitting time when he finished the required updates to the records and was headed back to the freezer with the last of them when all hell broke loose.

He heard glass breaking, metal tables being overturned onto the cement floors in the big empty examination room where he'd left the bodies. "What the Hell?" he said, running for the autopsy room. Slamming the swinging doors back against the wall as he hit them, he came face to face with what used to be Mr. and Mrs. Cherie. They reached out their disfigured limbs before he had time to turn and run, grabbing his arms in their still frigid hands. The decomposition had stopped when they were frozen but now that they had thawed it had started again. A thin red liquid ran out of their mouths and dripped from their bodies onto the floor, leaving a trail from the gurneys to the doorway. Their sodden feet made slipping noises as they shuffled across the floor. In seconds they had the orderly on the floor and were ripping muscle and flesh from his neck like it was Thanksgiving and he was the turkey.

Since the couple was the first in and the first out, their counterparts had not quite defrosted. Anna Knox was silently staring at the ceiling, her eyes as unfocused as her brain. The hunger was beginning to gnaw at her insides, making her still frozen limbs ache. She had no reaction. Her brain function was limited to only one thing...flesh. She was overwhelmed with the need of it. Clumsily, she pushed herself up on the table and heaved her unresponsive body over the side. Anna hit the floor with a spongy thud, the metal table followed. The noise was deafening in the tiled room. The creatures did not react. The attendant was no longer concerned with the things of this world. He was beyond it, but, he would be back.

As the corpses defrosted and re-animated at the morgue, Randall was having problems of the zombie kind of his own. Moments before a flash lit up the night sky in the northwest quadrant of the perimeters. It was the warning flare. The doctor and the two operatives jumped to their feet, at the ready. The flare could have been set off by an animal, a stray dog or coyote, but they were on alert, just in case.

Randall, his senses tingling, pulled out the night vision goggles and peered into the trees. Night vision goggles do not depend on heat to capture an image, as some might think. They can be very helpful in spotting the creatures in the dark. NVG's take the ambient light, such as starlight and tiny particles of reflective light, capture them and increase them. This gives a brighter picture of the surroundings. In this type of lens, heat is not the deciding factor. In NVG's it is the magnification of the existing light sources and a question of contrast. The more contrast the subject has to its surroundings, the better view you will get. If you are looking for a white dog in the dark woods, you have it made, but, if you are looking for something that is dark against the darkness, it will be less visible with NVG's. There is also a problem with NV equipment when you have a bright area to search. Unless you are, now, looking for a black dog, the increased light will lessen the ability to pick out shapes. Yet, for what he was working with, NVG's would work. That is, once the light from the flare dissipated. He could see very little at that moment.

He had the infrared goggles or the IRG equipment, as well, but he was doubtful about its ability to display the walking dead creatures. To say that zombies had no heat signature is not precisely correct. The process of decomposition in a normal human body produces a small amount of warmth, as with the decomposition in a compost pile. However, with the acceleration and concentration of the process involved with the Solanum virus, the amount of heat generated can be significantly more than characteristic decay. The doctor changed to the IRG's.

The two men from Gassim's unit were patrolling the perimeter of the camp, weapons ready. Randall searched the wooded area for anything. There! About 150 yards away there was a weak image moving through the trees. He alerted the men and continued scanning. There were two more images but were so faint that he couldn't be sure. He changed back to the NVG's. The intense brightness from the flare had dissipated, leaving a slight glow that aided in illuminating the area.

There! Again, on the left, two more, stumbling toward the camp. Zombies are slow. The disintegration of the muscle structure can only function in a partially effective way. There was no real hurry to the situation. The men had to just let them walk in. Still, the hair was standing up on the back of the medical examiner's neck. He signaled to the men. One shot rang out, taking the one out. He continued staring into the darkness. So far, he could see no more of them. Intent on the trees, Randall failed to be on alert for sounds from the water. The two men had ventured farther into the wooded area in search of more of the creatures.

Suddenly, a crash sounded behind him. He turned quickly, just in time, to see the figure of a man coming up the beach from out of the water. It had run over the campfire, knocking the rack and coffee pot over in its persistent pursuit for the food it knew was on the beach. Namely, one Randall Durham. Randall pulled up his weapon and fired two shots, rapidly, into its head. The creature fell in its tracks, onto the fire. The sodden clothing refused to burn but the smell of burning flesh permeated the area.

Randall Durham sat down on the, luckily nearby, camp stool. He continued to survey the area, turning his head in all directions. He was not going to be surprised, again. After a few minutes the men returned to camp explaining, in their broken English, that they had cleared the area. No more of the creatures were found. They looked, in surprise, at the zombie kabob steaming on the near extinguished campfire. The smell was difficult to stomach. The decomposition and the burning of what flesh that was left was not a scent they would forget soon. After a moment, they went into the storage area of the recreational vehicle and came out with tarps and a body bag. They had on Plexiglas masks, rubber gloves and moon suits, ready to clean up the mess. Randall didn't offer to help them. They knew more about the disposal process than he did. They did this for a living, he thought, incongruously. Like the movie said, "Dyin' ain't much of a livin', son". Well, neither is 'undying'.

He wondered how Dirk was faring on the east end. He hadn't heard from him for a while. He took out his cell phone and hit speed dial '0'. He and Dirk had a running joke. Dirk had Randall as zero on his speed dial, as Randall had his number listed. The phone rang several times. He was about to hang up when Dirk answered. "Yeah", he said. Randall told him about the stragglers with whom they had dealt. "Yes, I spotted them and the guys took them out, but not before one nearly got me." Dirk was instantly alert. "What do you mean?" he inquired quickly. Durham told him about the zombie from the water. "If he hadn't knocked the coffee pot over..." he left it hanging. Dirk told him to watch his back and explained what had been going on over on his side of the island. Randall gave him the same advice, "Watch your back, too, Durham." And, clicked off.

Once the cleanup was finished Randall and the two man team settled down to keep watch again. While the time ticked by, Dirk and the guys at the key were under another attack. It wasn't pretty.

34

Later, near the wee morning hours, a storm kicked up in the Gulf of Mexico. It was a tropical storm of little consequence but it blew into Deluna Island with a fury. It lasted for less than an hour, but in that hour, it was fierce. Not a serious squall, just big enough to keep the zombie hunters at bay and enough to drive the zombies into hiding. Zombies may not be rocket scientists but they do know to come in out of the rain. The physical sensation of being pushed back by the winds was enough to stop their forward motion and send them into a more sheltered area. Unfortunately this did nothing to help the men searching for them, trying to destroy them.

Many of the infected Russian crew members, who had wandered inland in search of food, ended up in empty buildings, shacks or beach enclosures. Others simply walked back into the bay. One, it was found out later, walked out into the Gulf, and marched out to sea. Three found their way onto the west end dock and onto the ferry that was docked there for the night.

The citizens of Deluna Island didn't realize that just outside some of their doors were beings, hidden in the shadows that would kill and eat them. Too fantastic to imagine. They would not only do that, but would infect them with a curse that would make zombies of them as well. It was science fiction. Midnight movies. No one would be able to grasp the danger until it was too late.

When the rainstorm was done, Randall came out of the RV. He and 'the boys', as he had come to call them in his mind, had taken shelter there. They were safe enough inside and they knew that the creatures would, most likely, find some dark corner and stay there for a while. The beach was strewn with seaweed and palm frond, but the air felt fresh and clean. The sun was just about to come up. The black was turning gray. Soon, it would be golden pink, turning the island to an ice cream colored paradise. As the doctor stood, gazing out across the bay, his phone rang. It was Dirk.

"Hey, you get wet?" he asked, as Randall settled into one of the chairs. "Nope, some sucker rented a big motor home and left it for me." He chuckled, knowing his friend probably hadn't fared as well.

Dirk barked. "Yeah, but did they have it fumigated before you slept in it?" Before Durham could answer he went on, "Oh, wait! I got that backwards! Fumigate AFTER you slept in it, not before!" They both released their tension with a good laugh.

"So, how did you fare in the storm?" the doctor asked him. Dirk related his experiences with the creatures and Angus' men. "They guys were doing pretty good. They had the right idea, just didn't have enough information." He explained how they had planned to carry the fight to the zombies until the rain drove them into hiding. Dirk and the guys from the key sheltered in an abandoned shack in the trees next to the key.

"So, what is the plan for today?" Durham asked. "I need you and the..." Dirk started. "The boys." Randall put in, with a chuckle. "Ohhh, kay. 'The boys' to stay put. We are going to start your way and flush anything we find to you as soon as it gets light enough." Randall agreed and rung off. He relayed the message to 'the boys' and they all took up points and stayed there. They didn't want to miss anything.

35

Being attacked by flesh devouring zombies was certainly not something that entered the somewhat pickled mind of Cammie Sherrer. It was just another night on the beach for her. She was sitting on a barstool at her favorite bar. All was well with the world. The Star Fish Pub was a quaint little beach bar where many locals hung out. The building was nothing special. It was a little cinder block structure with a large outdoor patio surrounded by palm trees and sand dunes. The front section was the dining area with mismatched tables and chairs. The back area was the bar and opened up onto the deck. There was a big open grill at one end. Every few weeks they would have a big cookout. Many of their customers were fishermen and would sell them the freshest catch of the day.

It was a mixed crowd at the Star Fish. You had bikers and businessmen, maids and the military, drug dealers and debutantes, well, at least, FORMER debutantes...all walks of life.

Residents and tourists covered a broad socio-economic range in the tiny melting pot. Life on a small island made it that way. That 'melting pot' mentality is how Cammie Sherrer came to be rubbing elbows with some of the richest people in the area.

Cammie was a skinny, bleached blonde who spent her days cleaning rental units for Deluna Properties, one of the local real estate companies that specialized in vacation homes and condominiums. She occupied most of her free time downing shots of tequila with the patrons of the Star Fish. She had been on the island less than a year but was well known on the club circuit. Within days of moving to Deluna Island she had met up with John Tolbridge, owner of Deluna Properties, at the Star Fish. When she beat him at darts, matching him, shot for shot of tequila, during the game, he asked her to join him at his table with several other businessmen. They closed the place down. By 2am she was hired as a maid, even though he had no idea of whether there was a need or not. He put in the call to his secretary at home, getting her out of a warm bed to tell her that his 'good friend' would be in to fill out the paperwork the next morning. Ahh, the bonds that alcohol can knit...

Cammie was on the job by the end of the week. John Tolbridge had real estate all over the area.

When one of his deals fell through and he was
stuck with a small house on the east end, he
offered to rent it to Cammie for the amount of his
mortgage payment. The amount was ridiculously
low for a three bedroom house on a cul de sac in
an upscale area. Too low for any house on an
island paradise for that matter. Sherrer jumped all
over it. She and her family had been living in a
small travel trailer at the RV Park. She left owing
a week's rent and never looked back.

Cammie had three children, none of whom lived
with her on a regular basis. They were all in foster
care in another state. She had lost custody of the
last child a year before when she had left him at
daycare for hours after closing. The police were
called when the proprietor had been unable to
reach her by phone. The officers sent a car to her
house. They found her passed out in her car in the
driveway. She was drunk. Family Protection
Services took the child. It had been the third time
Cammie was found unable to care for her children.
After the latest episode, the woman decided she
needed a fresh start. She told the court that she
had a job and lodgings in Pensacola with relatives.
It was a lie. She went there for a vacation, using
the money from an emergency aid fund she
received at a local charity. When she got to
Florida, she decided she would stay. She met the
real estate man in the pub that night.

Back in her home state she was well known to the local police and on the local bar scene. Her bar fly career had started back in the late 70's as the hippie scene was taking a last gasp. She was one of the free spirits that could be seen walking the dark streets in ankle length skirts, halter tops and sandals, pupils the size of saucers. She was particularly enamored of consuming several large bottles of Nyquil and eating hallucinogenic mushrooms. She purported herself to be a witch, a fortune teller, and a former handmaiden to the Queen of the Nile in a former life. She had a swirling dragon holding a crystal ball tattooed on her left shoulder. The words "Psychedelic Witch" were engraved under it in flowing script.

By the time she made her way to Deluna Island most people had changed the first word of her moniker from "Psychedelic" to "Psycho". Shortly thereafter, "Witch" became the "B" word. It was becoming well known that Cammie Sherrer would grind you into dirt if you got in her path. Her co-workers at Deluna Properties had learned this truth fairly quickly. They found that she would take credit for work that she didn't do, steal things from the units being serviced by the other workers, and, despite her reprehensible behavior, she would report the most minor infractions to the owner. She, consistently, caused great difficulties for the other workers. She was not a popular person in the workplace or in the community at large. She tended to handle her personal life in the same way she handled her work life. Neighbors complained. Parents of her children's friends had refused to allow their kids to visit at her house. Eventually, they would not allow her children to come to their homes, either. There was just too much drama where Cammie was involved... unless you were her drinking buddy. She would extend any support to those folks. until they were of no more use to her. Then, she would walk right over them. To her, they were just in her way and a stepping stone to where she planned to go.

Cammie had taken in a young homeless boy named Mickey and allowed him to live in the garage of the home the businessman, Tolbridge, had rented to her. The young man was sullen, angry and rebellious. Neighbors had complained of multiple problems involving him, including thefts, bullying and threats. When the nearby residents confronted her, Cammie would have none of it. In her opinion, which she shared often and loudly from the front porch of the rental house, the neighbors were all stuck up preppies without the brains of a tree slug.

The people never knew that the boy, whom she stood up for so publicly, was terrified of her. She often railed at him and threatened him with beatings or jail. The boy, whom she also used as her own personal slave, took all his frustration and rage out on the people and property around him.

Mickey was often seen carrying her into the house late in the night after she had, somehow, made her way home from the bars. Neighbors were often alarmed to see her car parked crookedly across the lawn or nosed into a tree on the side of the road where she had driven it after a binge. Cammie was a one woman party that had been going on for over 30 years. Who knew that late this night, during the sudden storm on the island, Cammie's party was over for good.

Cammie Sherrer had been shooting pool at a bar on the Bayway Highway called, appropriately, Shooters. "Last Call" was looming and she was not ready to give it up. In her opinion, she was only half buzzed, when the call came. The lights came up and the doors were locked. It was time to go home. Cammie weaved out to her late model Chevrolet convertible. She had recently bought the car at one of the "Buy Here, Pay Here" at "Car City", the strip of car lots along Pensacola Boulevard. She knew that she would end up paying twice as much as the car was worth, but, with her credit problems, it was the only way she could get a car loan. She was determined to have the car, so she weighed her choices with a thumb on the scale.

The rain had stopped and the fog had rolled in.
She stood dreamily imagining the thick mist was a
fluffy blanket. She staggered into the side of the
car, shaking her head. She had almost passed out.
A few more long blinks, she thought to herself, and
she wouldn't make it to the Star Fish before
closing. The Star Fish was a couple of blocks up
the beach beside the Elks Club, backing up to the
Marina. She often wound up her nights on a
bench outside the "Fish", looking at the bobbing
boats. Cranking her car, she pushed the button
that lowered the canvas top. She needed the rush
of air to wake her up a little.

The Sheriff's deputies rarely patrolled the strip area
between the bars and the beaches. They had an
unspoken rule during tourist season, "Let the
tourists enjoy themselves and don't interfere unless
absolutely necessary". The rule spilled over onto
the residents, as well. Due to relaxed patrol, the
drunken woman swayed and reticulated her way
across the island without restriction. This night
was just like many others.

She pulled into the parking lot at the Star Fish
barely missing the cement posts at the entryway.
She followed the drive around to the back and
parked crosswise of the opening. Cammie began
to feel a little sick. She decided that a few minutes
more of the nice soft breeze wouldn't hurt. She
laid her head back on the white leather headrest.

She heard the sound of steps slowly coming up on her left. She presumed that it was one of the men leaving the Elks Club next door, since it closed down a little earlier than the Star Fish. She opened her bleary eyes just in time to look into the rotting face and fetid breath of one of the living dead, out for a late snack. Before her boiled brain cells could assess her situation, the Psycho Bitch became Zombie Brunch. She didn't even have time to scream.

Next door, Roger Gassaway was having supper at the Elks club with his friends. The booze was flowing and they were feeling no pain. He had left Amorosa alone, at home, worrying about her missing sister. "You make me sick. He told her. "Your uppity sister takes a little vacation down to Destin, just like she did last year, and you go all to pieces." Gassaway hated Selena. He knew she had tried to get his wife to leave him many times. He begrudged her the strength she had to stand up to him and the freedom she had from her husband. He didn't want any of that rubbing off on Amorosa. Jack had always been easy going and let Selena live her life the way she wanted, as long as she loved him and stayed true. Roger Gassaway saw this as a sign of weakness.

"All I know is, Amorosa," he growled into her face as he gripped the front of her blouse, pulling her close, "is that YOU better never get any fancy ideas about taking a little trip off this property without my permission. If you do, it will be the last trip you ever take." He shoved her away from him and slammed out the door.

He had treated his buddies to several versions of the story throughout the night. Each version got more violent and less coherent with the telling and with each drink. His companions, who were loud talking, obnoxious drunks in their own right, had stopped agreeing with him several versions ago. None of them liked the look in his eye. They knew Amorosa and had been witness to his rough treatment of her in the past. They were trying to talk him down a little now.

"Aw, man, you got a good wife out there at your place. She would never do you no wrong." One said. "Yeah," chimed in another, "Your ole' lady knows which side her bread is buttered on. You don't need to worry about that." Gassaway pushed his chair back, almost tipping it over, and stood up. "Yeah, well we're gonna see what she thinks she is gettin' away with. I am goin' out there and come up real quiet from the beach. I'll look in that window and just see what she is up to!" He staggered to the door, righted himself with an effort, and threw up his hand in farewell. His friends shook their heads and counted themselves heroes for even trying to help Amorosa. After all, they all agreed, she was his wife. They couldn't interfere. They ordered another round and forgot all about the woman out in the Gassaway compound.

Roger Gassaway was paranoid, among other things. Many other things. He was sure everyone was out to get him and his belongings. That is why he always parked his camper truck all the way at the end of the parking lot by the marina, under the big spotlight. He thought it less likely that someone would try to steal his truck if it was bathed in the yellow glow of the bug light. He, apparently, never took into account that it was the farthest away from the building and the safety of numbers.

There was a lot of foot traffic up by the road and the entrance, but, back by the bay, it was lonely and desolate. The big yellow spotlight hung over the dumpster and the storage shed where fishing tackle and other odds and ends of the marina patrons were stored. The clouds had made it a pitch black night. The rain had begun to let up, but, the wind was still kicking up quite a noise. Gassaway did his best impression of a highly inebriated penguin running in a blizzard as he fought the tempest. Weaving, and out of breath, the blob of a man dug for his keys in his pocket. He found them, fumbled them to the door lock and dropped them. As he bent between the truck and the storage shed he let out one gargled scream as two zombies drug him down to the pavement and had him for dinner.   Amorosa didn't know it yet but this was her lucky day.

It might have been Selena's sister's lucky day, but, it wasn't lucky for Selena. Selena had lost the life that she had known. She had lost her memories, her thoughts, and her feelings. The infection had raged in her body, eventually, killing her, but, she did not stay dead. She had risen up and was, now, wandering the east end of the island in search of a meal. Her friend, Angus Murphy, would see her once more and, when he did, he would have to kill her.

36

Dirk and the men had spent the time during the storm planning their next step. "We have to go and look for them, now." Dirk told the group, "They are sheltering somewhere. In dark corners, stands of trees, abandoned..." "Cabins?" Murphy interjected in reference to the structure they were currently in. Dirk smiled, "Yeah, just like this" he gestured around to all the darkened corners. "Luckily, we got this one first." He went on with his talk. He laid out his proposal. They would split up into groups of two, each group going separate directions. They would walk 'the grid', search party style. They would cover the east end and the north side of the island, the areas nearest the downed ship.

The men gathered their weapons, radios and flashlights and headed out. As they congregated on the sand for last minute orders, three deformed and decaying men came out of the stand of trees to their left. Dirk and Gassim drew their weapons and fired. Two of the zombies dropped into the sand. Angus took aim with his Glock 19 and dropped the remaining one. They went into alert mode. They patrolled the perimeter of the little key, searching in shadows and light, alike. They found another nest to the west of the key. The anxious ex-military men let loose with all they had. The suppresser units on their rifles could only dull the sound, not silence it. The men returned to camp where they stood, back to back, keeping their eyes on every inch of ground. After a few minutes, they relaxed somewhat. They knew that the zombies would have come had there been any more.

"Now, we will be getting some company out here very shortly." Angus said, "There is no way that this cracking gunfire will not reach the ears of the police, one way or the other." Dirk agreed. "We will just have to hope we can convince them to keep it all quiet," he said, "If it gets around there will be a panic on this island. With no bridges, only the ferries to get people out of here..." he trailed off. Angus nodded, grimly. Both men had seen what panic can do to normally rational people. Dirk's phone rang. It was his contact from *ZARC*. He turned away and spoke quietly into the receiver.

Lt. Rindy Baker was eating breakfast at the Captain's diner when she heard what she thought were rapid gunshots. She had just returned from

an eighteen month tour in Iraq and had no doubt
what the staccato bursts meant. Someone was
firing an automatic weapon over near the key! She
called the Sheriff's office.

Within minutes Dirk, Angus, Gassim and the
others heard a siren coming their way. "Well, here
we go," Angus said to the men. Dirk cut his call
short and joined them at the crossing tracks of the
little road to the key. The flashing blue lights
bounced off the white sand and the palm trees.
Dirk caught sight of the top of an SUV in the trees.
He hadn't seen it there before. He knew that it
meant tragedy to someone. He didn't have time
to discuss it but pointed it out to Murphy. "Oh my
God" Angus said sadly, "that is Selena's van. She's
been gone since we found the laptop..." Dirk hated
to meet his eyes but nodded to him. "You think
she..?" Angus whispered, hoping he was
misunderstanding. "Yes, Angus, it is probably the
case. The van, running into the trees likes that...
She was probably infected somehow and tried to
get home but was too sick..." Dirk stopped. The
police cars had stopped a few feet ahead of them.
Angus put the dismal thoughts from his mind to
focus on the dangerous situation in which they had
found themselves. He knew, as he hoped the
others understood that these policemen could
easily misunderstand what they were seeing. Men
with guns, dead bodies...It could go badly.

The deputy got out of his car and started toward them. Seeing the mess on the beach, he drew his gun. The men immediately dropped their guns on the ground. One twitch and they would be joining the zombies on the sand. They put their hands up, waiting. The man spoke into the radio on his shoulder, calling in backup.

"Throw down your weapons and put your hands on your heads!" he yelled, obviously so shaken that he didn't realize they had done both things already. He motioned for them to back up by the trees so he could go nearer and see what had happened on the sandbar. "Get back! Get over there by the trees!" He told them. Just then the men heard another sound in the nearby bushes. There was a low, moaning, keening sound as a woman appears out of the brush.

Selena's long black hair was a tangled mass of twigs and seaweed. The clothes she was wearing were covered in dried blood and sand. As she moved nearer they could see that her right arm was swollen, with the decaying flesh hanging in long strips. Her once pretty face was bloated and gray with patches of skin and muscle missing from her cheek, bones gleaming through in the flashing light. Her once blue eyes were white and rheumy. In her left hand she had the torn carcass of a cat. He must have been the owner of the blood on her clothes. In her feeding need she had found the unfortunate creature. Her craving had not been satisfied by the animal. She was tracking the smell of the men on the key.

As she neared the group of unarmed men, Dirk shouted to the officer, "Don't let her touch you! She is contagious and dangerous!" He prayed the man would understand.

The deputy whirled around at the sound and gasped. He was a long time resident of the island and, despite her appearance, recognized Selena Jackson. "Oh my God, Selena! What hap..." he started. Angus yelled to him, "She won't understand you! She is too far gone!" The officer started toward her anyway and one of the men ran over to stop him. The policeman unholstered his weapon with shaking hands and ordered the man to stop. "You don't understand, Officer! She will kill!" the man pleaded with him. He didn't listen and kept walking. The team member ran forward again and grabbed the officer's arm but it was too late. Selena saw the men and reached out and grabbed onto the closest man, sinking her teeth in his neck up to the gums. The unarmed man screamed a gurgling scream. The deputy instinctively began to shoot. Dirk cried out to him, "You have to shoot the head!" but the frightened man just kept shooting at her body, bewildered by the lack of response. The gun began to click. He was out of ammo.

Selena turned toward the sound and found another victim in the young deputy who stood frozen on the spot. His empty gun dropped from his hand into the sand.

"Ahhgg, poor lamb. Ahh, Selena." Angus cried as he looked at her and started to her. "No! Angus!" Dirk's voice brought him back from his grief in time. Dirk quickly retrieved his weapon, raised it to his shoulder, but Angus was faster. He looked to Dobbs and said, "I will do it. I will release her from her misery." He pulled the trigger and blew the left side of her head off. Jack's wife fell to the ground. Her ordeal ended in almost the same spot where her nightmare started. Angus turned away, tears on his rugged cheeks. He would have to tell Capt. Jack that his wife was gone. He hoped he would understand that he had done it out of his love for her.

The first man that Selena attacked lay dead at the foot of a tall skinny pine tree. The deputy was not dead but was very close. Gassim went to each one and put two rounds into their heads. Angus and the last of his party sat heavily on the ground. Dirk calls out to them, 'Come on, men. Get back up. There are more around here. Don't let your guard down." His words galvanized them into action. The two ex-Navy men got up, grabbing their weapons once again, searching the trees and water line for any signs of more living dead killers.

A swishing sound in the water got their attention just as the sounds of the wailing sirens announced the arrival of the backup units. Two sheriff's department cars rolled up and an officer got out of each one. Once again the men were forced to drop their guns on the beach and clasp their hands behind their heads. This time it was different. The officers had arrived in time to see what was happening on the beach. The new officer was much more discerning and told them to put their hands down. One of the constables knew Angus and asked "What the hell is going on out here, Murphy?" he said, gesturing around the beach. Angus told them quickly about a virus that caused extreme delirium and violent outbursts, such as what they had seen from the road. He left out the whole 'zombie' part, for clarity. It would only prolong the explanation. Murphy told the officer that there was an epidemic, brought in on a Russian ship, and that the crew members had, somehow, made it to the island. "The sick men are roaming loose on the key, delirious and violent, "he said, praying that the man would believe it and help them. "We have been trying to round them up..." he stopped. Dirk finished it for him, "There are still a few around us here, and we are in danger as we stand here unarmed." He said, patiently as possible, "We need to pick up our weapons for your safety and ours. You saw what happened to your friend, over there?" he asked, pointing. The man looked at the torn man he had known for years. The deputies agreed to let the men arm themselves "Until we find them all I will have to let you have the weapons. After that...I'd just as soon they would disappear." Angus nodded. They would have to get the weapons out of sight when this was done, unless they wanted to try explaining them to a judge. They started toward the wooded area and the ferry dock. Angus kept up a running dialogue with the men to keep them calm and informed of the situation. He didn't want any one getting nervous and mistaking their actions or movements. Someone could get killed that way.

"This virus mutates the brain, you see, and the victim becomes homicidally violent. Unfortunately, even a scratch from one of the infected ones can make you ill, so you canna let them get near you." He prattled on. "What kind of virus is this? Is there a vaccine?" the younger deputy asked. "It is a deadly sickness. There is no cure. It is 100% lethal. The only thing you can do for these poor souls is to destroy them before they infect you or those around you." Dirk told them. "And don't make the mistake we made and the other officer made." Angus said. "We couldna' din why we could shoot them and they wouldna' fall. Hits to their bodies don't work." "When you shoot. Shoot to kill and shoot them in the head. Destroy the brain. It is all that works."

At that moment they had come down onto the sandy key where one of the wounded zombies lay, still trying to claw his way up the beach. The officers were able to get a good look, and smell, of the creatures. They saw the damage done to the thing's body, and how it continued to live, still trying to attack. They saw the decomposition and the rotted body.

Dirk told them about how the thing would go on and on, trying to get to another victim until its brain was destroyed or until it completely rotted... The deputy, appalled, raised his service revolver and tried to shoot it in the head. He missed. The other officer took the Remington 870 he had pulled out of the patrol car and pulled the trigger. The zombie's skull disintegrated. Like it or not, the local authorities were now involved.

37

Jenna and Adam had been hiding out in the empty locker room at the school for, what felt to Jenna as, an eternity. "You ok?" Adam asked her, timidly. They hadn't talked much. Jenna was propped up against the cement wall in the corner with her legs pulled up to her chest. Adam had found a blanket in one of the lockers and she was wrapped in it as tight as a burrito. She didn't open her eyes, she just nodded. He tried again. "You want to go out in the gym and stretch out on the bleachers?"

This time she raised her head and opened her eyes, "Yeah. I guess so." She stood up, stretching, and rewound the blanket around her. It gave her a sense of security that she needed badly at the moment.

Adam peered out into the cavernous space. In the semi-darkness he could see that it was empty. No different than the last time he checked. He opened the door wide and the girl in the blanket passed through. They walked slowly, but alert. Adam felt sure they were safe here. No one would think of looking for them there. And, there were none of the awful creatures there. He had checked it all out and locked the doors that led out into the empty school building.

"You probably need a little exercise. You've been balled up in there for a while." He said with a jerk of his head toward the locker room. Jenna didn't look up, but replied quietly, "Yeah, I am sort of stiff. That floor is pretty hard." Adam felt hopeful for the first time in days. "I know what...let's just make a few laps around the floor. Not running, I mean." He added when he saw her startled look. "No, I mean, let's just...take a walk. Around a couple of times. It will get our blood circulating." He saw her wince as he said the word "blood". He looked down at his clothes that were smeared with it and thought about the horrible attack she'd witnessed and kicked himself. "Come on. We will start at the south end and go around two times...or three if you feel like it." Jenna nodded and they started their circuit. No talking. Just walking. That is what he kept chanting to himself to keep from pushing too hard. After the second round Jenna said, "I think that is enough, don't you? I think I want to, you know, like you said, stretch out...on the bleachers." She still felt so uncomfortable talking to him, which seemed so strange. They had always talked so easily to each other. The thought made her sad so she took off, on her own, to find a place in the stands. Adam followed.

She went all the way up to the top. That was her favorite place to sit. You could see all over and that was a good thing right now. Being able to watch for trouble. She could always slip down on the floor between the seats and be out of sight before anyone could see her. She picked a place near the steps in the corner. Adam sat just below her, one step down. "You rest. I'll keep watch." He told her, feeling a little stupid, like a kid playing war games. She smiled at him, and laid full length on her stomach, struggling to cover herself with the blanket. He took it from her and spread it over her, tucking the edges in around her. She had such mixed feelings, some were even good. It surprised her. She whispered, "Thanks." And turned her head to the wall. Adam didn't feel snubbed by her actions. He knew this was as hard for her as it was for him. He just wanted her to be safe and, hopefully, clear all this up. Get back to normal. If that were possible after all they'd been through, all they'd seen out there at the beach. He hadn't told her what he was thinking. She was coming around, understanding that the rumors Anna Knox had spread around school were not true. He didn't want to rock the boat, but, he was frightened. He couldn't remember all that had happened to him out there. He rubbed his hands on his jeans and felt them drag against the damp fabric. He looked at his hands and his pants. There was blood all over him. It froze his heart and left a hard knot in the pit of his stomach. What had happened out there? he thought, and hoped that Jenna wasn't thinking the same thoughts that he was thinking. He didn't think that she was, though. As far as he could tell she thought that it had come from his fight when he was trying to save the man at the park. It hadn't. It had come from the camp. From Anna. He hadn't gotten any of the blood on him when he was fighting. The pole had kept him away from the worst of it. He was more worried about what had gone down with...her...on the beach.

He was still unsure about what had happened out there. He had been so angry. So angry that he just remembered yelling at her and pushing her down. She fell. She had screamed. He remembered her scream. When he tried he could only remember looking down at her, clenching his fists. They were sticky. She had blood on her. He remembered looking at his hands and clothes. He had blood on him. That is all he could remember. What did he do? Had he hurt her? He wanted to hurt her. He wanted to kill her. She ruined his life. She made him lose Jenna! She made people think he had...done those things. People will never forget what they saw in those pictures and the rumors they heard, he thought, the weight in his stomach twisting. No matter what, even if he showed them proof...they would still wonder. The images will still be in their minds...and on the Internet, forever! That witch! The anger was still there, bubbling under the surface. It took effort for him to get a hold on his feelings. They were so strong that it frightened him. He knew how angry he had been. How angry he still was.

He wished that he had someone to talk to about it all. He wished that he had never gone on that picnic. Glancing back, Jenna was still quiet but he didn't think she was sleeping. He wished he could just tell her! He wanted to tell Jenna everything and make her understand but how could he? He wasn't even sure what he had done. What if? He couldn't tell Jenna. What would she think? She might think he did it! She would leave him, again. He couldn't stand the thought of that. He couldn't take the chance.

He rubbed his hands together. The blood was dry but he wanted it off of him. "Hey," he whispered to the girl, softly, "I...uhh...need to go...to the bathroom. Will you be o.k. out here on your own? Or..." he could feel himself blushing. He didn't want to tell her he was going to wash the blood off. He'd rather not bring that up. Jenna turned over and sat up, pushing her hair back behind her ears. "Yeah, I'm good. I can't sleep, anyway."

He hurried across the big floor. He didn't want to leave her too long, but when he turned the faucet there was no water. He remembered that the coach said something about the plumber coming to fix something. He got a few drips out of it but it didn't do much good. It just made it sticky again. He looked around. In the window sill there was a spray bottle of window cleaner. It would probably eat the skin off his hands, he thought, but it is better than nothing. He sprayed his hands and scrubbed them with a handful of brown paper towels. It didn't get it all but it got most of it. His clothes were hopeless. He searched around for more clothes but had no luck. He would just have to wear them until they could get home. It would be just brown stains by then, he told himself, and nobody would think it was..blood. .

Meanwhile, Jenna was in her own mental dilemma and, at the moment, it wasn't about Adam. It was about the guy she'd brought to the beach. Where was Gerry? He was supposed to have met up with her at the car. He hadn't shown up by the time she ran into Adam. What if he had been attacked by those creatures? What if he was lying, sick and hurt, somewhere? She should have tried to find him. But, she had seen something out there that she couldn't understand. She was afraid. The things she'd seen at the Point were horrifying. The 'things' that had attacked that poor

man and Anna. Blood and death...she couldn't go
back. She put her face in her hands. She felt so
guilty for running away and leaving Gerry out
there! Yet, she didn't know what to think about
what had happened...to Anna. The
creatures...she had no way of knowing whether he
even ran into them. He may have been far away
from the parking area where they were. Or, he
could have seen them and gotten away from there.
Who knew? He was probably on his way home by
now. But, the creatures were not the only worry
she had on her mind concerning him. Back in the
farthest parts of her mind there was another
thought about Gerry.

Gerry had been angry with Anna Knox. Furious
with her. She had ruined his life with those same
posters and rumors about him. She had seen what
had happened to Anna, and Gerry had been
headed to the beach. What if he got his revenge
on her? The very thought scared her beyond
words. She liked Gerry. He was a nice guy, but,
thinking back, he was acting very strangely and
was talking awful funny at the end. How far
might he have gone to make sure she didn't hurt
anyone else? Or, to make her pay for how she had
hurt him, and Adam. The thoughts swirled
around in her mind.

Until one thought stopped them. She had done
the same thing to Adam. It had never occurred to

her that Adam was as angry as Gerry. Adam was as hurt as Gerry. Until that moment she had never thought about Adam's anger. All thoughts of Anna's other victim had slipped from her mind.

She looked toward the big doors at the end of the gym where the bathrooms were. Adam had gone to clean up…clean up…Adam was covered in blood… The new thought terrified her. She would not believe that her Adam, the polite, loving, sweet Adam, could do what she saw done to that girl! No matter how angry he was! She hadn't realized that she had come to think of him as 'her Adam', again. She pushed all thoughts of it out of her mind as she saw the boy coming back from the washroom. Seeing him there, walking across the shiny wood floor that she'd walked across with him so many times, made her heart skip a beat. He was her Adam. She knew that, suddenly, in that moment. Although, she still felt the hurt, the doubts, she couldn't make it go away that easy, even though she knew what Anna had done. It was like having a broken bone in an accident. You would know that the injury was not done on purpose, but that wouldn't make the pain go away..she thought to herself. She was feeling a bit better. Then, the cloud of doubt came back. Not about what Anna had made people think Adam had done, but, what she wouldn't put into words. About what happened on the beach. She was still unsure. Was it Gerry or was it 'her

Adam'. She squeezed her eyes shut, refusing the very thought. When she heard him coming up the stairs she had pushed the bad thoughts out of her mind and could only think of how much he had suffered.

Adam sat down on the hard painted wood of the bleacher. He felt so awkward, with his dirty clothes and splotched hands. That is why he was surprised when he felt the warmth of her touch on his shoulder. Afraid to turn, he felt her run her hand down the back of his head. As the sun went down and darkness crept across the gym floor, the two found their way back to each other.

The sky was a smudgy indigo black outside the big windows that hung high up near the ceiling of the locker room. Adam and Jenna had moved back to the relative safety of the locker room. Adam was concerned that they would not detect an intruder in the vast inky depths of the gym. They were still locked in a comforting embrace when they heard noises outside.

Adam sat up, instantly alert. "Adam?" Jenna whispered, frightened that the creatures might be outside. "Shhh..." he said, quietly. He walked to the door they had locked and barricaded with the gymnastic equipment. The noise was not coming from the gym. He made a slow circuit of the room and bathrooms, Jenna on his heels. In the boy's

bathroom they could hear mumbled voices. A
loud bang made them both jump. The continued
metallic rattling told Adam that it was one of the
burn barrels that the wood shop used. It was
rolling down the sloped drive behind the atheletic
building. They listened so hard they both thought
their ears would implode. Then, they heard
laughing, giggling. "It definitely is not
those...'things'." Adam whispered, assuringly,
"It's some kids. Probably someone we know." He
finished, with a wry grin. Jenna relaxed her death
grip on his arm. "Do you think they know we are
in here?" she asked. Adam shook his head. He
pointed to his nose and gestured for her to sniff the
smell that was filtering in on the light breeze. She
took a deep breath through her nose. Marijuana.
No, they were not there to find them. They were
just enjoying a joke on the 'school', smoking a few
on the back steps. Thumbing their noses at the
authorities.

Adam motioned for her to sit down. They would
listen for a bit, just to be sure. After a few more
giggles and the crashing of a few more pieces of
school property trash receptacles, they could hear
the group shuffling off, their catcalls and laughter
receding into the night.

"I hate to say this, but I am getting hungry." Jenna
said, grimacing in the semi-darkness. Her words,
spoken quietly, still echoed in the cinder block

room. "It's O.K., "he replied, "I was just thinking the same thing." He got up and paced along the line of metal lockers. "I will go out and get us something..." she jumped up and ran the short distance to him. "NO! You can't go out there. They may be looking for you...and..." she hesitated. He spoke up. "It will be alright. I have been thinking about it. There is that little gas station across from the field. I can get in there, easy. I'll stick beside the building and be back in no time." Jenna didn't want him to go, but she knew that they would have to have something to eat soon and, at least, it was dark now. Still, she was frightened, "Adam, what about those...men? Do you think there are more of them?" she asked. Adam gulped, but tried to put on a brave face for her. "I..I..don't know. I think it must have been some sort of illness or something. I don't think there are any more of them out there." He lied. "You'll be fine here. You can lock the door and there are no windows in here, or other entrances. Just don't open the door for anything, or anyone, except me." "But, what about you?" she asked, worried. " I'll be fine. I will keep my eyes open and I have this." He held up the long lead pipe he'd found in the trash pile at the road. "Just stay here and don't open this door." Jenna promised she wouldn't.

He kissed her lightly on the lips and promised that he would be back in an hour. She had a sinking feeling as she replaced the heavy 'horse' back in front of the door. Adam had pulled it as close as he could to the door and still be able to get out. Before he left he found a mop and bucket in the closet. She did as he said and mopped around the legs. Then, just like he said, when she pushed it, it just glided across the cement and lodged tightly against the door. Within a half hour the floor had dried. She tried giving it a push and, once again, he was right. It wouldn't budge. Once she was out of work to do she huddled up in the corner and wrapped herself in the blanket, again. Her mind went back to all that had happened in the last day and a half. Seeing those awful pictures, seeing Adam leave with that awful girl...seeing them, together, at the beach. She thought she could not see anything any worse than that, but she was wrong. Finding Anna, bloody, on that blanket... She shivered. Then, seeing Adam fighting with those horrible creatures. What were they? Why were they attacking that man? She just couldn't think about that anymore! She looked around the, now, nearly pitch black room. Oh Adam, please come back soon!

To keep her mind off of the horrors that might be lurking in the dark corners she thought of Gerry and Adam. Anna. It was her fault. She could almost be glad she was dead. Poor Adam. Like Gerry, none of this was his fault. He did nothing. It was all that girl. She did it, all. As horrible as it all was, Jenna couldn't feel sorry that she was dead. She got what she deserved. Her attitude about Anna even surprised herself. She was not an angry or vengeful person, but, this girl had hurt so many people. She couldn't believe that Adam could have done that to her, but, Jenna wasn't going to abandon Adam, now. He couldn't remember anything about what happened. He was in shock. She didn't believe it, but, she was standing by him. He had, finally, broken down, out on the bleachers, and told the her what he feared. He was so afraid and confused. He couldn't go home until he was sure that he hadn't been the one to kill Anna. Jenna would not go until he was ready. Besides that, there were those creatures. She admitted to herself, she was afraid to leave the building. She just prayed that Adam wouldn't run into any of them while he was out there.

Had they been older, wiser, they might have realized they should go home or to the police about the man on the beach, but Adam was afraid of being arrested, and, they were teenagers. Teenagers seem to think that running away and hiding from adults will solve any problem. So, they chose to remain hidden. Jenna worried when the boy hadn't come back in an hour. What if he didn't come back? What would she do? What should she do? She started to panic. Stop it, Jenna! She told herself. She put those thoughts out

of her mind.   He is fine and he will be back.
Nothing is wrong. She believed he would be back.

After Adam left the gym he skirted the dark trees.
Across the street was a dry cleaner. The owner
was a sponsor for the football team and lived
upstairs over the business. Adam knew him. He
knew Adam. If they were looking for him, and the
man saw him he would tell the authorities. He
turned the opposite way. Beyond the trees was a
junk yard and the field. It backed up to an old
service station. It should have been torn down
years ago, but, the old man who owned it and the
yard, wouldn't give it up. He only opened a few
hours a day. Adam knew that he had some food,
snacks and such, inside. And, he knew the locks
on the doors were no good. He headed there.

Adam went through the yard. He stayed in the
shadows of the stacked cars and far away from the
office. There was usually someone there. He
crouched down behind an old van to look around.
The coast was clear, as far as he could tell. He ran
the last few yards to the old building. The lock
was basically worthless, but, there was little inside
that anyone would want. Adam jimmied the lock
in seconds and was inside.
He grabbed a plastic bag from behind the counter
and went to the cooler. He grabbed a two liter
soda and bottled water.   He knew where to find
everything since the kids from school came to the

station for snacks during the day. He cleaned out
the candy and chip aisle, which wasn't really very
hard since the old man didn't stock very much. He
grabbed two toothbrushes and a tube of
toothpaste, deodorant and a roll of paper towels.
He couldn't think of anything else. He left twenty
dollars on the cash register for the old man. He
didn't want to cause him any problems. He hoped
that it was enough.

He went back out the door he came in, locking it
behind him, shaking the lock to make sure it held.
It did. He went back through the yard, through
the trees and slid into the gym. He rapped on the
door. "Jenna, it's me." He heard the sounds of her
mopping the floor and scooting the horse. She
opened the door a crack, then wider. When he put
the bags down, Jenna threw her arms around his
neck. "I was so afraid you wouldn't come back!"
He wrapped his arms around her, grateful to have
her back. "It's OK. It took me a little longer than I
thought, but, I am here, now. Don't worry." He
patted her back and whispered his feelings into her
ear. They stayed in an embrace for a few moments.
He felt guilty about Jenna being involved in this.
She didn't have to be here, hiding out, he thought.
She needed to go home. This was his problem.
She hadn't done anything. He knew he should tell
her to go but, he couldn't. He wanted her with
him. He needed her strength, but, mostly, he was
afraid to let her go, afraid she would leave him. It

was stupid to hang on so tight. She knew the truth, now. She was on his side. He held her tighter. Jenna relaxed into his embrace. She had been afraid while he was away. She had a million thoughts running through her head. Mostly about Anna Knox and how she did the same thing to Adam that she did to Gerry. She wondered about Gerry, what he might have done, where he was now... He was so angry. Could he have done that to Anna? He was mad enough to have done it. If so, would that make her an accessory? She wouldn't think about it. She couldn't. She lifted her face to the young boy. It was a few minutes more before they got to the food.

While Jenna finished her meal of corn chips, brownies and a lukewarm drink, Adam showed her the other items. "I thought you might want to...freshen up. You'll have to use the bottled water." He said, slightly embarrassed at the personal nature of the moment.

"Thanks, Adam. I would LOVE to brush my teeth, wash my face and brush my hair." She hadn't even considered what she must look like. She disappeared into the bathroom. Adam cleared up the trash from their meal and thought about their situation. They couldn't stay here forever. He had to figure something out, but, before he could think of what that would be, the locker room door slammed open, hitting the wall with a crash. They hadn't put the horse back in place.

"Get Down on the floor! Put your hands on your head and lace your fingers! Police!" Adam immediately went to the floor on his stomach, putting his hands behind his head. The officer stepped over him, squatted on one knee and told him to give him an arm, slowly. The cuffs went on, one arm at a time. They pulled him to his feet.

"Adam Moore, you are under arrest for the murder of Anna Knox. You have the right to remain silent..." The boy didn't hear any more. The whole world was spinning out of control. He vaguely heard Jenna calling his name as they took him away. He didn't struggle or try to explain. He just went along, moving his feet, bending his legs, with no more idea of what he was doing than a rabbit. He just kept telling them that he did not do it and, please, not to hurt Jenna.

Later the deputies would say he was acting guilty. They were telling the truth. He was acting guilty, but, for different reasons than they thought. He felt guilty. He could not be sure that he hadn't hurt Anna.

After they got him to the station he was booked and fingerprinted. The boy went through the process without a word. They put him into a stark, ugly room with a battered table and three chairs. There he waited. It was an hour or more before they got back to him.

Detective John Law sauntered into the interrogation room. Adam's first words since the door slammed open at the gym were, "Where is Jenna? Is she OK?"

Taking a toothpick from his mouth, the detective said, "She's dead as fried chicken!" he replied, smirking. Adam went white. "Dead? How...she was fine when we left the gym...What happened to her?" he was becoming frantic. John Law just laughed at his emotional outburst. I'm not talking about that little girlfriend, I'm talking about a cute little naked blonde girl. Dead, wrapped in a blanket out on Red Point." Adam sat back, breathing heavily, relief rushing through him. Nothing else mattered to him at that moment. Reality slapped him in the face moments later when the detective demanded to know why he killed Anna Knox. "I didn't do anything to her!" the boy sputtered, even though he wasn't sure it was true. "You were out there with her, weren't you? We got witnesses that will put you in the car just before sunset. We got your fingerprints on the beer bottles all over the campsite. You gonna say you weren't out there?" the detective growled into his face. "No, I wasn't gonna say that. I was out there, sure. I stayed out there till, I don't know around midnight, then I left." He said, trailing off, miserably.

"How'd you leave, you have a car out there?" Law asked.

"No. No. I walked." Adam stuttered.

"Who else was out there?" he shot back.

"Nobody. Nobody I saw. I mean, I guess somebody must've been out there later, to ..kill...her. I mean, that is kind of obvious, but nobody when I left." He was saying too much but he didn't know how to stop. He couldn't tell them what he saw. They would never believe him. And the only other person who saw it...He couldn't tell them about Jenna. It would get her in trouble. He couldn't do that. It would put her at the scene. "Did you see anybody on the road when you were walking, or on the beach?" the other officer asked.

"N..No. It was dark. I couldn't see much of anything." He stammered.

Detective Law knew the kid was lying but he decided not to call him on it. Law was sure he had his man so he would get the whole story sooner or later. A few hours in the tank and he'd be more likely to want to talk. "I'll give you a little time to think over that story, boy. Maybe next time I see you you'll have a better lie cooked up. Lock him up." The detective said and strode from the room.

Adam jumped up from the table. "I didn't kill anybody. You gotta believe me." He yelled as the officer began taking him away.

They put the dazed boy in a smelly cell and left him to his own thoughts, which were jumbles of dark, frightening snapshots. He remembered the beach, the picnic, the girl. He gasped as he remembered that she was the one who had started all this. It made him feel sick.

He lay down on the cot and covered his eyes with his hand. He didn't want to remember it. Any of it. What lay behind the blackness in his head, but even as he fought it, it came. It opened up like a black flower, layer by layer. At first, he relieved the picnic like a grainy, black and white newsreel, then the pictures in her purse, the shock he had felt when he realized that she had done it all. He could see her, begging him to listen to more of her lies, standing there, naked in the light of the fire. It made him feel sick, disgusted with her, furious with her. He remembered pushing her away, onto the blankets. Then, it was foggy, dark and blank. He curled over into a ball, forcing his brain to think, to remember. The mist began to clear and he saw himself wiping blood off his hand onto his jeans. What had he done? No! He nearly cried

out in the cell. He would stop asking that
question! He knew he couldn't have killed her.
He was furiously angry, yes, but he didn't have it
in him to kill another human being. Not unless he
was in danger of his life, he threw in rapidly,
remembering the fight to save the man at the park.
That was different, wasn't it? He questioned
himself. Yes, that was different. The man was
being attacked, overwhelmed by those...men,
creatures, whatever they were. He had to kill them
or let them continue to attack. The man was dead
by that time but he didn't know that at the time.

He pushed those memories away. He was getting
away from the point. There were too many
frightening, unsettling areas in that portion of his
memories. He must remember what he did before
he left the beach, and Anna. He said a silent
prayer, beseeching the God he hadn't called on in
quite a while. Please, God, make me remember.
Let me be sure...let me be innocent of this horror.
The tears came, silently, but ferociously. He
shook with the spasms, as tears wet the dirty
mattress. Somehow, he fell into a deep, exhausted
sleep. As he slept the wall crumbled down.

He woke, an hour later, with a start. He rubbed
his eyes and wondered where he could be. Slowly,
the cell came into focus and his heart sunk. Jail.
The beach. Anna. As if it were a silent movie
coming into focus he began to remember. The

black flower he had shoved his painful memories into began to unfold again. It opened, one petal at a time, and he could see the scene on the beach. The pictures went backwards, to the minutes before she had come back from the trees. He could see himself sitting on the blanket, the horrible pictures spread out before him. He was still reeling from the realization of what Anna had done to him when he heard her scream. He jumped, startled. He hid the folder and turned to see her come out of the trees.

"Sorry! Something slithered over my foot! Thank God it had fur. I hate snakes." Anna said as she ran out of the woods.

He turned and went back to the fire. He was unsure of what he wanted to do or say. It was all just like a jumble in his head. He couldn't decide whether to throw the things in her face and demand an explanation or play it out and make sure she was the one, the only one, involved. He sat down on the blanket and opened another beer. Anna, unaware of his discovery chattered on about the moon and the pretty stars. She wrapped herself in the blanket, inviting him to come back.

He stared out at the water, thinking about how much he'd like to strangle her, but, instead he walked down a step or two to the water. He didn't notice her squirming under the cover until she said, "Hey, what're you thinking about so hard? Hmmm.?" Blissful in her own little fantasy world, she didn't notice his tight jaw and rigid shoulder muscles. She went on about how wonderful he was, and said, "Give me one of those beers, huh?" He handed her a beer, still not looking at her. She used the edge of the blanket to open the bottle and leaned back against the pillows. He had just about figured out how to trick her into telling him about the pictures when she said, "Adam, I thought we had things to finish when I got back." He didn't answer her. At some point, he couldn't remember when or how, the girl stood up and let the blanket drop. She was standing there naked in the firelight. It infuriated him that she thought she could play him like this, and think he was a fool. Before he realized it he was standing by the crumpled blanket , knocking the beer from her hand. It fell onto the ground, hitting something hard, it shattered and lay in shards on the tufted material. He gave it no thought. He had come to the breaking point. He couldn't hold it in any longer.

"Tell me, Anna, is this what you want me to do? Is this some disgusting fantasy or something?" he cried out shoving the pictures she had altered into her face. The perverted images fluttered to the sand. "Is this what gets you going? Is this what you want to do?" He grabbed her and threw her down onto the heap of blankets and held her wrists over her head. She cried out in pain because he had unknowingly pushed her down onto the broken bottle. With every movement it was cutting into her back, her side, her arms. She screamed again in pain, bringing him back to reality. He pushed her aside and let her up. He grabbed up the pictures and the faxes and shook them at her. "Why Anna? Why would you do this? To ruin me? To break me and Jenna up?" he yelled. He ripped the pictures into shreds and threw them into the fire. "Who was in this with you? Did you do this by yourself or is there someone else who has it in for me?" He fired questions at her, giving her no time to answer. He jumped up and stood with his back to her, shaking. She pleaded with him to forgiver her. "I'm sorry, Adam. I love you." She blubbered. "LOVE? You don't have the first idea what love is! Is this how you show someone love? You make them into a laughingstock? You make people think they are perverts? You RUIN their lives? Is that your idea of love?" He was yelling in her face, his hands burning to grab her and shake her until she rattled. "My God, Anna! You are sick. Do you think I could ever love someone who would do something like this? I can't even stand to see your face. You're nasty. I can't stand the thought that I've even touched you." He grabbed up his jacket and another beer. "I am getting out of here."

"NO, ADAM!" she screamed, "Don't go! ADAM, ADAM!" He took one look behind him. She was standing, naked, holding her arms out. It didn't register that there was blood streaming down them, down her side. He felt something sticky on his hands. That was when he noticed there was something on them. He wiped them, unthinkingly, on his jeans. The fact that it was blood from her cuts didn't even sink in. He didn't listen to her, he just kept walking. He could still hear her calling out as the firelit trail turned dark. When he left her, she was ALIVE. She was still calling to him as we went up the trail. He didn't kill her!

He sat up on the dirty cot, suddenly. He didn't kill her! He REMEMBERED! He did not kill her. She was alive when he left! The thought made him feel light, like all the weight in the world had been lifted off him. That is, until he remembered that he was still under arrest. He had, finally, convinced himself, but there was someone else he would have to convince. He would have to convince the police. With a heavy heart, but, with a clean conscience, he lay down, again, and thought about how he would make them understand. In minutes he was fast asleep. Exhaustion and relief had finally combined to let him rest.

When the cops had busted into the locker and cuffing Adam, the officers found Jenna in the bathroom. They pulled her out. Jenna saw them putting cuffs on Adam. "Don't hurt him! He didn't do anything!" she cried out, kicking at the policeman's shins. "Stop! You are hurting him!" she said as she saw them pick him up by his cuffed arms. This intensified her attack on the policeman trying to take her out of the room. The officer was forced to pick her up and take her to the car. "Where are you taking him?" she asked, beating on the grated metal between the back seat and front seat of the patrol car. "Miss McLain, you need to calm down before I have to charge you with obstruction." he told her, tersely. His shins still smarting from her blows. "We are taking Mr. Moore to the station where he will be questioned about the murder of a girl on Red Pointe beach. Do you know anything about that?" He turned to give her the tough stare he reserved for the rough customers. Frightened, Jenna sunk back into the seat, crying. "I know that he didn't do anything to her. He didn't kill her." The officer decided not to press her until she could be interrogated at the station. "Well, the best thing you can do, Missy, is sit back and calm down. No one is going to hurt your boyfriend, but we will have to get a statement from him about what happened out there...and from you, too."

When they got to the station, the McLain's were there. The policeman took her into one of the empty interrogation rooms and left her with her grateful parents Jenna told them the whole story, except for the part about the sick men. She couldn't tell them about that. Adam had killed the two...men, after all. Her father called Adam's parents and told them that their son had been found. He also had the unhappy news that he had been arrested for murder.

"What?" Mrs. Moore cried into the phone. "He has been arrested, Mrs. Moore. The girl he went with out to the beach...Anna Knox. She was murdered last night. They think Adam did it." Mrs. Moore dropped the phone and collapsed into tears. Her husband took up the receiver and finished the conversation. Mr. McLain assured him that they didn't believe that Adam had done such a horrible thing. He gave him a number to a good lawyer in Pensacola. Mr. Moore thanked him and said he would be down at the station as soon as he could get there.

After she had finished her tale and was assured that his parents were on their way, Jenna wanted to see Adam. The desk officer told her that it would be quite a while before he would be allowed visitors. Later, that night, after she had answered all their questions, they allowed her to go home. Alone in her soft bed, Jenna tossed and turned, worrying about what was happening to Adam. Eventually, just like Adam, Jenna fell asleep. The terrors of the past hours forgotten for now. But, in her dreams, she could see the bloody young girl, the rotting flesh of the men as they chewed into the poor man's flesh. She could see the pieces of bloody, rotten skull as it flew into the air when Adam hit them with the pole. She woke up, screaming. Screaming for her life as they decomposing men chased her down the beach. Her mother soothed her, asking her what she meant when she was crying out "they are after me!". Jenna claimed she couldn't remember, but she could remember. All too well. They were out there and she was afraid there were more than they knew. More of them coming for them as they slept.

38

After the scene at the key, the police had to be informed. Randall, Dirk, Angus and the men from the beach were questioned. Dirk took point and explained exactly what happened and what else would happen if they didn't let them get back to work. The only reason they were released was the fact that the deputies backed up their story. But, mayor, Jim Maddox, was not buying a word of it.

"He's a psychopath! A PSY-CHO-PATH!" Maddox said, punctuating each word with the stem of the pipe, "Dirk Dobbs is a lunatic!"

"Zombies! Walking dead! What kind of idiot thinks he could get by with a story like that?" He yells as he pounds the desk.

"I don't know, Jim, Dirk Dobbs has been a standup guy around here for a long time. I can't see him...making things...up." the sheriff stops, remembering that Dobbs IS a writer, and shakes his head, knowing what's coming.

"Are you kiddin' me? He makes up stories for a living and has a house full of guns and explosives. Standup guy?" Maddox sputtered, "We don't know half of what he has up there on the bluff."

"Now, Jim, Deputies Long and Waters say..."

Maddox interrupted again, "Deputies Long and Waters were scared spit less and they know as well as I do that they could have ended up in that pile of bloody bodies on that beach! Easy as pie! They'd say anything to save their butts from a crazed bunch of killers, armed to the teeth!"

"No, I don't believe that. If that was true they wouldn't be holding to their stories now, after the danger is over." The lawman told him.

"Out of danger? Who said they are out of danger? They're not safe; none of us are safe here on this island with a raving maniac living down the road. We're a captive audience for him and his buddies' antics." Maddox stomped around the room blowing smoke, in more ways than one. The mayor wasn't used to having his ideas questioned. To think he let that lunatic move up there, on those bluffs!

"Jim, I think you are overstating this situation.
There is some validity to the situation on the key.
There was something very strange about the whole
thing...and not on Dirk's part. The bodies were
taken out by the tide before we could get down
there to do a proper crime scene investigation.
Without going into a lot of detail, I can say this;
we found decomposed body parts all over that
beach. Storm victims or from a flooded cemetery,
we concluded, but it was really weird. Bodies gone
and decomposed parts washed in...It was
gruesome! The boys were going to bring
the...parts in, but Dirk and Murphy warned us not
to touch them. They had some kind of team there
by then. They were dressed in those suits that
keep contamination out. It was like some movie
or something. They scooped them all up into body
bags but it was an awful sight. And, Dirk and the
men stayed and supervised the collecting..." he
stopped, realizing what Maddox was going to say.
Contaminated crime scene... but it was too late, he
tried to explain, and "He didn't touch a thing." As
a matter of fact, he wouldn't let anyone touch
anything. He had that team there in those Haz
Mat moon suits that we got when the storm
washed up those barrels, remember?"

Maddox just glared at him. He went on. "We took
it all to the coroner's office and they froze it so that
we can get to it later." He ran out of steam.
"Anyway, I don't think those guys are our

336

murderers...On that little girl, out at Red Point? We got the guy who cut her up on ice at the station. Hands covered in blood, admits he was there and fought with the girl. Then, he just clams up."

By this time Maddox had settled down a bit. The picture of the young girl, cut to ribbons, had settled into his mind, overshadowing the previous one of bloody massacre. He couldn't understand what went on at the key, but he sure as hell could see what happened to the girl at Red Point. It made him thoughtful. He would be sure that boy got what he deserved for doing that to that poor girl. Still, he couldn't let go of the writer and his military buddies shooting up the beach.

"That is pretty strange that they knew how to take care of a scene, but it doesn't change the fact that Dobbs is a gun nut who is out there roaming the island armed like a Bosnian rebel. And, I want your assurance that he will be reined in and disarmed. No one on this island will be safe until you do it!" He pounded on the desk, weakly. "And keep all this 'walking dead' crap quiet. I'll have my staff get a statement out about a flu virus that makes people disoriented and violent. They'll tell them it is contained and under control."

With that, and the wind taken out of his sails, he turned to stalk out of the office, but made a miscalculation. He turned short and walked briskly into the hanging plant by the door. He righted himself and nodded to the sheriff sheepishly, gathering another head of steam to cover his embarrassment, "and, as for that boy, what was his name?" he snapped. "Adam, Adam Moore." Sheriff Richards told the fuming mayor. "Well, you wind Adam Moore up tight and don't let him loose! At least, we have one maniac off the streets!" He growled, and left.

The sheriff, glad that he had gotten off the Dobbs' subject, turned his attention to Adam Moore. He knew that boy that juvenile delinquent was holding back something and, by God, he was gonna get it out of him. He turned and left by the door the mayor had exited and headed toward the jail with a new determination to break the boy down.

39

The men at the key had been joined by some of the local off duty deputies. The Sheriff and the Mayor were brought into the loop, but the mayor was still skeptical. The few others who were let in on the outbreak of 'flu' were sworn to secrecy. They were told the men were extremely contagious, deliriously violent, and were told to kill them on sight. The news filtered down through the ranks. From one mouth to another ear, slightly revised, until the story was twisted out of proportion. This was added and that taken away until the most important detail was left out of many accounts. The part about aiming for the head. The part about destroying the brain to destroy the threat. Many men and women were going out to a fight without their most significant implement of warfare. Many would not survive to fight another day.

Dirk, Angus and the men scoured the beach and surrounding areas. They found no more zombies. There was a chance, a small one, that those left were washed out to sea in the storm or, simply walked back into the water. They decided to regroup and lay new plans.

Later, back at the beach camp with Randall, over hot cups of coffee, the three men went over the layout of the traps laid earlier by Dirk. With a few additions and alterations they settled down to wait for Angus and, what remained of, his team. They had gone with the deputy to round up what supplies they could round up for the additional team members. While Dirk, Gassim and Randall planned and waited, Angus and his men were loading up all the supplies that they could from the local constabulary and various military types around the island. Angus called in every favor he was owed, and thanked God that there were quite a few. With the truck bed loaded, they took off for the campsite in a shower of sand.

Captain Jack, still grieving over his lost Selena, rode shotgun, barking directions to the driver, who was unfamiliar with the back roads. Angus sat in the back, rifle at the ready for any obstacles that might be encountered. Sliding sideways around the sharp turn onto Dewey Street the truck passed the entrance to the ferry dock. As the truck hit the pot holes in the sand and shell road, the men in the back of the truck had to scramble to find a hand hold to keep from being tossed out the back. None of them had time to watch the scenery or take in the grisly sight just beyond the entrance sign. None of the men saw the crouched figure by the dock house that was just finishing his supper. A meal that featured ferry boat captain on the half shell. Not as if it would matter to the poor man. He was way past saving.

As Angus and his team bounced away, three of the infected former ferry workers wandered around the bowels of the automobile transporter. They were coming into the later phases of the virus. No longer capable of rational thought. They were confused, dazed but still a few hours from the inescapable hunger that will drive them to feed on other uninfected human flesh. The boat had become an incubator for the walking dead. The workers wandered the ferry, unaware of where they were or who they had been. Yet, they stayed near the place that was familiar to them.

Since the attack that infected the crew came as they were preparing for the next trip, all was ready to push off. The mooring lines were unattached; the motors were fired up and running. The course was set for the mouth of the Gulf of Mexico, where, then, the captain would have turned toward the Pensacola Harbor landing.

As the last course of the ferry boat captain was served on the dock, the Deluna Dolphin Ferry pushed out into the bay, as if the captain was at the wheel.   While the truck sped toward the base camp to finish off the zombies on Deluna Island, a deadly surprise was headed out of Deluna Bay into the open waters of the Gulf. Next port: unknown.

40

Randall had to get back to the morgue. He had all those bodies chilling in the freezer, and he needed to make sure they stayed there. Dirk shooed him away like a mosquito. "Go! Get out of here! You've done your bit. You got stiffs waiting," he taunted him. Durham laughed, "Yeah, they are more entertaining than you, anyway", he said as he got into his vehicle. The men waved as he pulled away.

When the medical examiner entered the building, he knew something was terribly wrong. The silence was as thick as mud. He could hear the ticking of the clock over the door. "Oh, ----!" He swore as he pulled out his gun. He had worn his own weapon when he left the beach. It was a Model 29 Smith and Wesson, a .44 Magnum revolver. It was a powerful handgun, one of the most powerful in the world. It would take a head, preferably a mutant one, 'clean off', he'd told Dobbs, quoting the movie cop. The problem was, the zombie hunter told him, that it only held six shots.

"I won't need more than six, if I hit what I aim at! And, I will," the doctor had exclaimed, confidently. "Yeah, you can aim at six of them and hit six, but you better hope you don't meet seven!" Dirk ribbed him. He had refused his friend's offer of one of the Glocks as he was leaving. A Glock could hold up eighteen rounds of 9mm with a full load magazine and a round in the chamber, Dirk had said, tauntingly. He might have cause to re-evaluate that decision, he thought, as he listened to shuffling sounds coming from one of the offices.

He stared down the dark hallway and hoped there weren't seven.

The doctor put his back against the hall wall and moved slowly down the hall. - He came to the first office. The door was ajar. He could hear muffled moaning. On high alert, he kicked the door back and looked inside. The room was a shambles. The computer monitor lay on its side on the floor, the desk lamp beside it. Just beyond it he could see a white work shoe. The shoe moved as he watched. He slid, back to the door, against the office wall, inside the room. On the floor lay one of his assistants. He couldn't make out which one, as there was a full- fledged zombie feeding on his neck.   Randall pointed the long barrel of his gun on the monster's head and pulled the trigger. With a deafening roar the Model 29 lived up to its reputation. It took the head clean off the creatures shoulders, the rest of the decaying body fell to the floor. Randall moved cautiously over to the injured man. It was too late to save him. Knowing what was to come of him in the immediate future, Randall put two more rounds into his head. The shoe stopped moving.

He cleared the rest of the office and moved back out into the hall. He opened his cell phone and called for back- up. He didn't know what he would encounter farther into the morgue. Dirk and Gassim flew into action. Leaving the men to keep watch, they headed to the county office.

Randall decided to hold down the fort in the hallway until the two men arrived. He had left the extra firepower at the camp, not expecting to encounter trouble at his place of business. He had a few shots left in his gun but, if he found a nest of the things, he would be in trouble. He would hang loose in the entrance way and take out any that showed their ugly faces.

As he finished that thought, he heard a shuffling sound coming out of his clinic. He trained his gun on the direction from which it was coming. Moments later, the disfigured face of Roger

Gassaway came into sight. The man was in deep decomposition. His face was a mass of hanging, decayed flesh, his, once strong, arms dangled at his sides. He looked in the doctor's direction with dead eyes, but, alerted to the new source of food. Selena's brother in law started toward Durham, dragging his big feet. Randall had little trouble taking him out.

Just then the glass door the reception area opened. "Randall, it's us," Dirk told him. The doctor nodded, keeping his eyes on the hallway. "I came in and knew it was bad news. It was silent as a tomb." He told them, grimacing at his choice of words. "I cleared the hallway and found one feeding on an intern in the first office. I think it was Cherie," he said sadly. "It was hard to tell. He was in pretty bad shape. We'll have to get a crew in here to clean this up before someone walks in." Dirk inclined his head. He had already put in a call to *ZARC* for help. The *ZOOM* team was hitting the beach in less than an hour, the others would follow.

ZARC would send in enough people to contain the outbreak, clean up and do reconnoitering of the entire island. Once they had exterminated the creatures, that crew would go around the island to make sure they had gotten them all.

The three men, with Durham on point, moved down the hall to the inner offices and the laboratory. It was a nightmare. Blood was on almost every surface. Several bodies were lying in mangled messes on the floors. Zombies are not known for their good manners. They took their feast, part by part, with them as they wandered the rooms, casting them aside when they were done. Even Dirk hadn't seen a scene of such gore. It got to him. Maybe it was the fact that this was his home, his safe place, a place where he had come to see his friend. It took all he had to keep focused. Randall was experiencing the same emotional response. Gassim saw that this was harder on the two men than it was on him, a visitor. "Let me go first, Doctor," he said in his gentle accent, "I can see that this is hard for you. Some were your friends." Randall and Dirk let him pass, but shook off the blanket of emotions that had engulfed them, momentarily. Dirk concentrated his mind on the job at hand, once again, a zombie hunter. Finding none of the creatures in the outer offices, they headed for the lab. One by one they cleared each area, moving on to the next until they were in the laboratory office. The small office held a desk, phone and filing cabinets. The door to the lab was directly ahead. There they found the unfortunate technician who pulled the bodies out of cold storage to re-tag them. The log book was out on the desk, toe tags in a small pile beside it. It was obvious to the medical examiner what had happened. "He must have noticed the discrepancies in the book and tried to clear it up," he told the men, quietly. "He pulled them out into the lab to re-label them, but it took too long. They thawed out..." he trailed off. He felt responsible for the young man's death, for all the deaths. Dirk spoke softly to his friend, "It wasn't your fault. If you hadn't taken control of the bodies the last few days, it would have happened sooner...and worse." Randall knew his words were true, but, it still pained him.

Inside the laboratory the men encountered another of the beasts, but, no more. They found one more victim there, a lab tech that had come in to catch up on some research, his computer opened, files on the desk. In all, they had four of the walking cadavers who had been taken out of the deep freeze, and three victims. The victims were in deep coma. It fell to Gassim to put them out of their misery. This was the hardest part for any zombie hunter. You are still taking a human life when you kill the victims, but, if you did not do it, you would be letting another monster loose to kill.

The men left the building to the team from *ZARC*, who had arrived just in time. Dirk and Gassim headed back to the beach, Randall stayed there. "I'll have work to do when they are done. I will call you when I am through." He told the men. They left him standing under the green striped awning, staring out at the white sand dunes of the beach. Usually, it was a good place to daydream. Not this day. This day all his daydreams were nightmares.

41

ZARC had come through for the islanders, sending in several teams to help with the infestation. The *ZOOM* team, Zombie Outbreak Observation and Mitigation Team, was usually called in first, to see if the problem was, actually, a zombie outbreak. If so, they would handle it. If it was bigger than what they could take care of, headquarters would send in another *ZOOM* team. After *ZOOM* was done with their job, a cleanup team would be dispatched. The *RAID* team, Reanimation Incineration and Disposal team, would then come in, clear the area and dispose of the remains safely.

Randall watched as the last *RAID* member carried the plastic bag to the specially equipped van. The operative, who spoke very little, ducked his head in farewell and the van pulled away.

The examiner entered the building with trepidation. He was amazed. No one could imagine that there had, only a few hours ago, been a scene of unspeakable carnage inside the doors.

The entire area, as he walked from office to office, was perfectly arranged, floors and walls clean and gleaming. The faint odor of paint was much preferable to the odor that had emanated from the dead, as it had been the last time he was inside.

There were a few items missing, a monitor here, and a lamp there; but, all in all, it was back to normal. He refused to think of the human life that was lost there. People could not be replaced as easily as a lamp or piece of carpeting. He entered his office. There had been no bloodshed in this room. He had locked the door before leaving the day before. He only wished he had locked the freezer, as well. All could have been avoided. He shook his head to clear the thoughts. He had lots of work to do.

He pulled a sheaf of papers from the fax machine. It was the test results from the young girl who had been killed on the beach. He hated to see what it would say. Adam Moore's parents were close friends with he and his wife. They were invited to the same parties and had the same circle of friends. He had known Adam since he was born. If this proved that Adam Moore was the owner of the blood and DNA found on Anna's body, he would have to be the one to deliver the message to the sheriff. It was not a job he was looking forward to. In fact, he was dreading the idea of it.

He stared at the complicated letters and numbers on the page. He could hardly believe his eyes. Durham quickly found the file on the mauled man, Gerald Johnson. He slapped the papers down on the desk and dialed the sheriff. He dialed the number gladly. The murderer was not Adam Moore. The murderer was the mauled man, Gerald Johnson.

42

Detective John Law rattled his nightstick along the bars of the holding cell that held Adam Moore. "Get up, Boy!" he growled, "It's time for you to answer a few questions!"

Adam jumped up, startled out of a dead sleep. He rubbed his eyes clean and stared, open mouthed at the lawman. The remembrance of the past two days slowly poured into his mind, rooting him to the spot.

He was in jail, accused of murder. He couldn't help praying that this was a dream and he was still sleeping at home in his bed. It wasn't. He grimaced as the keys scraped in the lock and the cell door flew open.

"Come on, get yourself up, boy! What'd ya think, this is summer camp?" he growled through clenched teeth. These preppy boys just pissed him off. Thought they could do anything and get away with it, because mommy and daddy belong to the country club! Well, he thought, this little nitwit was going to find out that he wasn't any better than anyone else!

The boy got up from the cot and started toward the cell door. As he got to the seething man, the detective's hand shot out and backhanded him across the face. He stumbled backwards, stunned, but, didn't fall. "Hey! What was that for?" he shouted out before he thought it out. "That was for being a wimpy little ----!" the lawman erupted, furious that the boy would question him. He would get the boy to confess to what he did to that girl on the beach, one way or another! He drew back to strike him, again, when the Sheriff called out to him from the stairs.

"Law! Stop! Take your hands off that boy!" the head of the department called to the detective, who had grabbed Adam by the neck. Law released his vice grip on the boy and whirled around. He began making excuses. "The prisoner was trying to get my gun! I was only holding him until he let go!" the cop lied. The Sheriff knew better. He had caught Detective Law in these types of scenarios before. "Detective Law, you need to go upstairs and calm down," he shouted to the man, "Meet me in my office in ten!" He said, meaningfully. John Law whirled and stomped up the steps, knowing what was coming.

The Sheriff went over to the cell. The boy was wiping blood from his nose. He handed the boy his handkerchief. "I am sorry about all this, Adam." He told him, "Detective Law is a little too...zealous, sometimes." Adam looked at him, one eyebrow lifted. "Well, most of the time, but, between me and you, he is on his way out," he confided in the boy. The boy nodded. The Sheriff got to the reason he came down, "I am pleased to tell you, Adam, that you are being released."

Adam jerked his head up, "Really? Why?" he asked, suspiciously. After the little scene with the detective, he was a little less trusting of the police. "You have been cleared of all charges. They got the tests back and it wasn't your blood on the body, or on the knife." Adam's head was swimming. He couldn't decide if he was happy or angry. He didn't have to stay in jail. He was happy about that, but, he shouldn't have been there in the first place! He was angry about that!

"Wait. What knife?" he queried the officer. "We found a knife in the sand, by the water. It had the girl's blood on it, and it had fingerprints." He explained, "They weren't yours." The Sheriff went on to tell him about what they did find. "They found a broken beer bottle that did have your prints on it, but, it was matched up to the cuts on the girl's back. It looked like she fell on the bottle, at some point, pulled it out and tossed it aside. The fatal wounds were dealt by a hunting knife, the one we found in the sand." The boy's head was swimming. He was free. He didn't do anything, just like he'd remembered. Anna fell on the bottle, but he didn't do anything to her. The blood on his clothes and hands had been his own. He'd cut himself on one of the shards when he picked up his stuff to leave. Relief flooded through him. Suddenly, he thought if he didn't do it, who killed her? He asked the office in charge just that.

"A young man named Gerald Johnson. It seems that she had pulled the same stuff on him, out in Milton, last year. Caused him all kinds of trouble. Ruined his football career, humiliated him with all his friends." The Sheriff could see that this news wasn't new to the boy. "Adam, did you know him?" "No, but, Jenna told me about him. She met him a while back and he told her about it Friday night...Oh my God..." he trailed off, fearing he had just implicated his girlfriend in the murder. "Did Jenna have anything to do with this murder?" the Sheriff asked, perking up. Adam stammered, quickly answering, "No! No! She and Gerald came out to the beach to confront us, me and Anna. Jenna chickened out and went back to the car. That's where I found her. Gerald had gone down to the beach, alone." He told the sheriff all that happened that night, except for the horrible sight of the creatures and how he had stopped them. He couldn't tell him that. He would never believe it.

Adam was released to his parents, with the admonition not to leave town because they had more questions to ask him. He pulled the sheriff aside, "Will Jenna get in trouble for any of this?" "No, I don't think so. I put in a call to her parents. I am going out there to take her statement. It will place Johnson at the scene and help us close the case, since he is dead..."

"Dead?" Adam exclaimed. "How...when?" The officer told him about the dogs, the flu sickness. He left out a good bit of the details, since they had been sworn to silence on the subject.

"Flu, that makes people violent and crazy? I have a few more things I need to tell you, Sheriff." Adam told his parents to wait and followed Sheriff Richards to an interrogation room to tell the part about the two sick men he had stopped. Richards had to give up a little more information, since; the boy had seen the creatures.

He looked the boy over for any cuts or scrapes. He questioned him about the cut on his hand, "Did you touch them or did they touch you?" Adam assured him that he had stayed as far away from them as possible. He hadn't gotten any of their bodily fluids on him or anything like that, he said.

Sheriff Richards told him to keep that part of the story to himself, citing panic as his reason and sent a text to Dirk about the zombie killing site. He knew they would have to go over it, again.

With a clear conscience Adam left with his parents, thankful that the ordeal was over. He had no idea that, although over for him, the ordeal was still in full force at the beach.

The Sheriff went out to the McLain house, personally, to take Jenna's statement. The girl was crushed when she heard that Gerald was the murderer, and that he was dead. "Poor Gerry," she cried on her mother's shoulder, "None of this was his fault! It was all that girl's fault!" Even though the teenager was talking about a murdered girl, Richardson had to agree. From all that he had heard, from she and Adam, the faxes Mr. McLain showed him, it was a wonder that someone hadn't killed her sooner. "Well, it was understandable that the young man had plenty to be angry about, but, taking the law into your own hands is never a good idea. Had he not been taken ill and passed on, he would have spent the rest of his life in jail," he said, somberly, "It isn't worth the price he would have paid." Sheriff Richards told the McLains goodnight and headed back to the office, glad that one mystery was cleared up. Now, he thought, if only we can contain this other mess. As he got into his county vehicle, the men at the campsite were settling in to find the rest of the zombies.

43

Dr. Randall Durham was getting a little bored sitting at the beach waiting for his good friend to return. So far the most exciting thing that had happened was being dive bombed by a mosquito the size of a '69 Dodge Dart.

After finishing up the work at the morgue he met up with the men at the beach. The team was surrounding the little key, Angus and his men were working the wooded area south of the diner, and, Dirk and Gassim were following up on the north side. They felt that the highest possibilities of sightings had been in the wooded area between the key and the campsite. They had left Randall at the camp to watch the monitors and let them know when they got a hit. He had been watching the monitors, waiting for the flares to go off, and walking the perimeters of the campsite like a German shepherd in a POW camp.

Suddenly he heard what he thought was gunfire, and a shotgun blast. That got his attention. Something was happening on the west side of the island. His adrenaline began to pump and all thoughts of boredom flew away on the wings of his wild imaginings. He would soon find out that his thoughts were neither wild nor imaginary.

He tried calling Dirk on the cell phone, knowing that the chance of him answering in the middle of a firefight was zero. He'd be too busy. But the doctor called anyway. No answer. He waited until it had been quiet for several minutes and dialed again. This time Dirk responded with a curt "Hello!"

"Dirk! It's Randall. What in God's name is going on over there?" he asked illogically, since he knew very well what was probably going on over there. "Well, we are shooting off some fireworks, what about you?" He said, good naturedly. "Nothing here so far. Are you OK? What's happening?" he sputtered.

Dirk briefly filled him in on the scene on the beach. They had run into a couple of stragglers and taken them out. One had gotten away, into the woods. Dirk and Gassim were searching the sector. Randall blew out a lung full of air, "Whew! I am about sick of these nasty things! I'll be glad when they show up over here so I can take

them out!" Randall was still reeling from the losses
at the lab and the threat against the whole island.
"Well, you keep your guard up, man. They may
be headed your way and you will get your chance.
We ran that one into the woods and a few across
the point. They may have gone back into the
water, but if they didn't they are in a bee line to the
camp." He told his friend. "We are leaving here
on foot to track them that way, so I will be seeing
you pretty shortly... If I get into any of the trip
wires I will shoot off a flare from the flare gun so
you will know it's me. But, remember, Randall,
there may be a zombie or two in between us. Be
prepared; just make sure it's a zombie you're
shooting at and not me or Gassim." He ended
somberly.

"Hey, I only have one question. With your ugly
mugs, how can I tell?" He wisecracked. "Huh!
Funny, Randall. Real funny." Dirk said as he
clicked off the line, smiling. Nothing like a good
natured insult to break the tension after a bloody
zombie battle.

Dirk and Gassim indoctrinated the deputies Sheriff
Richards had sent out on the care and handling of
zombies and their victims, reiterating the rules
several times before leaving to trail the zombies.
One good thing about the walking dead, they
were slow as Christmas. There was nothing but
woods for about a quarter of a mile ahead of them

so the likelihood of them running into any more victims was small, but the probability of infection from the corpses was immediate. They had to take the time to explain it to those left behind to clean up the mess, in case the *RAID* team didn't get between sites in time.

He told the shaky men "Do NOT touch the bodies. Do NOT get their bodily fluids on you. Use the tarps and bags, if you have to, but, hopefully, the *RAID* guys will get there in time." He told them there was a large supply of body bags in Angus' truck and, that he had gone back to the house to get more tarps.

Gassim and Dirk were to follow the ghouls and try to push them toward the camp rather than the populated areas on the coast. When Angus finished with the supplies for the cleanup he was to go around the inland side of the cove by the diner. Hopefully, he and Gassim could catch the ones in the woods before the creatures got to the camp. If not, Randall had become pretty damn good at this zombie killing stuff. Dirk was sure he could handle it.

The two veteran zombie hunters were in their element. They spread out as far as they dared and kept in constant visual contact of the other. They went quietly. Any sounds they might make could cause the zombies to turn and come back toward them. They could wander out of the path they were trying to set them on and send them into the path of some innocent bystander.

They went quickly and quietly into the trees. After a few minutes of steadily covering ground they saw two of the zombies up ahead. There had been more in the trees than just the one they lost. The brushwood and tree trunks made it hard to get a good shot at the creatures. They had to keep following them along until a clearing. They had covered over a quarter of the way to the camp when they lost sight of one of the zombies. As they were trained, they panned the entire circumference of the area, back to back. You didn't want to let one get behind you. Dirk had taught that to the new recruits. Nothing.

There was nothing they could do but split up. There were several houses around the area and they couldn't take the chance of one getting to other human victims. Dirk motioned for Gassim to go ahead and made a circular gesture meaning that he would backtrack, circle the two houses and come back to this point and catch up to him. Earlier, he had shown the Egyptian the way through the woods to the beach where the camp was located and drawn a quick map of the trip wire perimeter. Gassim was a quick study. He would have no trouble finding the site. With a quick nod of their heads to each other in farewell and a bidding of good fortune, the men went their separate ways.

Dirk circled around the trees where they had lost sight of the zombie, finding nothing. He went back as far as he dared and ran a perimeter search from there to the water on the western end. Nothing.

In between, there were two dwellings. One was a vacation house and seemed to be empty. He made a quick circuit of the exterior of the house and out building. Everything was locked up tight, no openings for entry into the darkened recesses. He went on to the next house.

Coming up from the water, he wasn't sure where he was, or at least not sure who lived in the house, until he heard the yipping and yapping of several dogs. "From the sound of it, I must be back behind the Easy Life Kennels." He said to himself, breaking his own rule of silence. The kennel proper sat on the front side of the property, facing toward the main road. The residence of the owners, Lambert and Kelley, was behind, facing the bayside. He'd often wondered how these two ended up with such a large and extremely prime piece of real estate on which to put their little doggy motel. He finally found out that Lambert's family had owned the parcel since dirt was a baby, and they passed it down to their only son, the

persnickety badly-named Bubba Lambert. Jeff
Kelley had been Bubba's friend since grade school.
When his parent's died, Bubba let him move out to
the family farm to help with the animals. The two
found a common love of canines. When Bubba's
mother passed and left the farm to him, he had the
kennel built. After a few years he made Jeff a
partner. It seemed a very unlikely partnership but
the business was thriving with Bubba's business
acumen and Jeff's loving care of all the little
visitors. Dirk ran the story through his mind, but,
his focus was on his work.

Dirk's mind was jerked back to the present by a
screaming howl coming from up ahead. He
flicked on his flashlight and ran for the house. He
crested the small rise in time to see the zombie
munching down on a terrier. He fired, but his
foot slipped in the pine needles and he went down,
missing the creature. Before he could regain his
footing he saw a light come on in the back porch
of the house. The door opened and a big fluffy
beige head poked out, sniffing the air like one of
his lodgers. He saw the small dog in the creature's
jaw and screamed an agonized scream. Before
Dirk could call out a warning, he lunged out the
door heading straight for the zombie.

"No! Bubba! Stop! Don't get near the creature! He
will..." Dirk yelled until he was drowned out by
the resounding roar of a shotgun. Lambert had

pulled it from out of nowhere like the proverbial rabbit out of a hat. Bubba Lambert splattered the zombies head all over the tall pine trees that ringed his dog pen. The dead terrier dropped from the zombies grasp and hit the ground only seconds before the zombie followed with a squishy thud.

Dirk reached the furious man before he lowered the gun. He put his hand on Lambert's arm to keep him from rushing out to the dead dog. "Don't, Bubba. He's gone. There's nothing you can do. If you touch him or anything out there that's contaminated you will get infected and turn into one of the monsters yourself." Dirk said quietly.

"What is that?" the grief stricken man asked as Jeff came bounding out the door. Bubba grabbed his arm and told him what happened. He reiterated the warning Dirk had given him. Dirk explained the situation to them, about the ship, the virus, and the 'sick men'. He told them about the mysterious happenings on the island, missing persons and the attack on the key. He told them to keep their animals in; their guns loaded and, if any more zombies showed up, aim for the head. The last little bit of advice probably seemed a little redundant, considering Bubba's excellent performance, and he told him so. He congratulated him on his perfect reaction to the threat. Bubba was glowing over the praise, as if he was being stroked. He promised to keep his ears open. The men gathered their dogs and went in locking their doors and turning on the floodlights around the yard. They waved a good bye to him, with guns in hand, and he went on his way.

Dirk double timed it through the thicket to the waterfront and took a shortcut to the edge of the camp. He saw Gassim inland about 500 feet and whistled to him. Al-Fayed returned the call and came down to meet him on the shore. Dirk unfolded the events at the Easy Life Kennel. The Egyptian filled him in on the whereabouts of his target.

"He is there among those thick bushes. I couldn't get a good shot on him in the pines! He got in there and has not come back out. I think he is confused. It is like a maze in there from what I can see. I blocked the other entrance so that he will have to come back out this direction," he told Dirk.

"I will call Randall and see if all is quiet there." Dirk punched in the numbers and waited for the answer.

"Randall Here." The doctor answered shortly.
"Randy, Dirk. Any movement there?" Dirk asked.

"No. I thought I heard something in the trees off your way but no flares, no zombies." He said.

"That was probably the one Gassim has snared in the monkey grass over here. We can't get a shot at him but he'll be strolling out this way pretty soon. Once we get him, I will let you know and we will come in from the beachside." Dirk flipped the phone shut.

Gassim had a plan to flush the zombie out of the grass. He laid it out for Dirk. He agreed and set up his shot while his friend circled around the mass of thick fronds. In seconds a flicker showed, and then a bright orange flame licked up into the sky. Gassim returned with a rusty bucket he had found at an old campsite. He nodded to Dirk and went off toward the water. Just as expected the zombie moved out through the only opening that remained in the grass that was free of flames. Dirk took aim and put two rounds into its head. Gassim returned with a bucket of water from the beach and doused the fire.

Dirk flipped his phone out and let Randall know what was going on and that they were on their way up the beach. The last thing they needed was for Randall to blow them to hell thinking they were a couple of their putrescent visitors. When asked how the doctor would know if it was the two men or two zombies, Dirk replied, "Hey, you'll know it's me by the ugly mug." Snorting, Randall said, "Now, tell me again how that will help me tell the difference between you and these nasty looking creeps?" "Smart Ass." Dirk said with a dry chuckle, as he snapped the phone shut.

He followed Gassim through a small thicket of scrub. They set off across the sand at the water's edge. As they trekked toward the camp all was quiet. Dirk brought his friend up to speed on the action at the kennels and pointed out the periphery of his 'watch zone'. They avoided the trip wires and made their way around the point west of the beach, heading closer to the base camp and the waiting doctor. Only this last dark bend and they would be within sight of the glow of the camp's fire. They moved around the bend and walked straight into two of the creatures feeding on the remains of a woman. It was too late to help her.

Dirk took the left one and put three rounds into its putrefying cranium. The zombie flew backwards into the dark waters and sank out of sight. The other creature rose to his feet still holding a half consumed arm in his hands, his predatory instincts telling him that 'new meat' had entered his feeding zone. He stumbled forward, dropping the arm on the sand, in hopes of fresher fare. Gassim popped two rounds into his head, exploding it like a miasmic birthday balloon. Dirk and Gassim walked on with only a backward glance at the carnage left behind.

The moonlight bathed the beach in a soft glow. There was a gentle breeze blowing, rattling the palm fronds. Normally this was a sound that Dirk found relaxing. Under ordinary circumstances it would have been a perfect night for a beach party, but the kind of party they were attending was not the kind of get together he had in mind. This was the kind of affair where, if you ducked out for a bite, you might be the one to get bitten.

The two men spotted the campfire at the same time, with relief. They skirted the last clump of trees, warily, and made for the clearing beyond. Randall stood, seeing it was the cavalry, he grinned from ear to ear. "Hey, you zombies!" he hooted, "No meal here!" he joked, "Oh, it's you, Dirk. I took one look and thought..."

"Yeah, yeah, yeah. As I said earlier, Smart Ass!" the zombie hunter punched the good doctor in the shoulder, laughing. It was good to let off a little steam with their juvenile jokes. It was the way they let each other know that they were worried for the others safety and relieved to see that they were all there in one piece, literally. Men don't do that 'touchy feely' stuff.

Suddenly, a flare went off in the northern perimeter. The zombie hunters and the doctor flew into action. Several of the monsters came shambling into range. Each took aim and took them down. Another flare let go a few yards to the south. From out of nowhere Angus appeared, leveling his AR 15, he let go with a burst of gunfire. The two zombies who had set off the flare, disintegrated in a shower of decaying flesh and rotted bone.

"Good catch, Angus! Where the heck did you come from?" Dirk called out to the Scotsman. "I ran out of ghouls on my end and thought I'd scramble over here and pull your tails out o' the fire!" He quipped. There were no more warnings, so, the men sat down to wait.

Angus filled them in on what had happened on the other side of the island. He and his men had cleared their zone and met up with the RAID guys. The other ZOOM team had arrived and taken over the west side. "The boys say that there is two more coming in by boat to take over this side and search and recon the east end."

Angus pulled a sheaf of papers from his vest. "I thought you might want to read this." Dirk took the papers and began to read.

"Today, Islanders looked on in horror, as a disheveled man, apparently suffering from some form of degenerative skin disorder, attacked another man at the West End Ferry. The attacker, obviously delirious from his illness, grabbed an un-named Islander and began to bite and scratch him. The victim was somehow unable to resist the delirious man or get away, even though the man was obviously weak and emaciated from his illness.

An unknown team of men in military garb appeared from out of the trees and began shooting the feverish man without a word of warning or an appeal for him to stop. It was apparent that the men were more interested in proving their prowess with their firearms than they were in compassion for the sick.

"It was horrible. This poor man was out of his mind…Who wouldn't be if they were in that shape?" said bystander, Myra Morrison, "He obviously had some sort of that flesh eating bacteria thing and they just shot him". Ms. Morrison is the owner of Spaceburger Café, an internet restaurant on Deluna Beach Court.

Another witness to the outrage was Juliana Duffentone, editor for The Left Hand, the local newsletter for the Illuminated Latitude Organization. "When the men burst out of the bushes with all those high powered assault weapons, I was sure we would all be killed! It was ab-surd! The man couldn't have weighed more than 90 pounds and here these gun nuts come and just blow him away! Why, I ask you, could they not have gone over and pulled him off the man? Or, tasered him? They all LOVE their tasers so much! No, they were bent on KILL! " She said in disgust, "I even heard the leader call out for them to 'aim for the head'! Were they scoring points with this poor man's life?"

When asked about the so-called victim of the attack, Duffenton replied, "I do feel for him, but he was older and larger than the sick man, he could have gotten away if he had tried." She said, "I think he wanted to be in the limelight and was willing to let these gun lovers make headlines to get in it."

At the time of this report, the identity of the team of shooters is not known. Minutes after the shots rang out a caravan of vans arrived and cordoned off the area. All press and the witnesses, except for this writer, were shuttled away. I managed to slip away into the trees before detection. I found my way to my office and my keyboard to get the story ou...........................

"That was it, Dirk. We found his body, or what was left of it lying across his desk," Angus Murphy turned to face his new found friend, handing him the printed sheets, "there was not enough left to re-animate. I printed out the story and destroyed the hard drive. For once, the creeping creatures did us a service. "

Randall and Dirk faced each other. They both knew what he meant. If the reporter had finished his article and hit the 'send' button, all of Deluna Island would have known the truth. With that truth would have come the panic that the team sought to avoid. Panic causes people to do strange things. They would do desperate things like hiding their injuries, hiding their loved ones who had been infected. The teams would never be able to contain the outbreak. People would find ways to reach the mainland and the infection would spread. Loosed in a highly populated environment it would erupt like wildfire. From there the panic would spread. Infected people would pack up and head to the bigger cities, to the hospitals, to the disease control centers in even bigger populations. They would board planes, get on buses, trains and boats. Once the virus is carried in so many directions, there would be no stopping it. It would be the Zombie Apocalypse that they all feared.

Yes, they felt sadness for the innocent reporter, who was only doing his job, but they also felt relief that he was stopped. His one life lost was the savior of millions, even billions, of others. Angus

Murphy lit a match and held the flame out to Dirk. Dobbs placed the edges of the reporter's last words to the flame until the sheets ignited. He held them until the charred curls reached his fingertips. He let them fall into the campfire and made sure they were consumed.

As they watched the fire, a jeep arrived with four *ZARC* operatives. Dirk and Gassim consulted with them and were relieved of their duty.

By morning the island had been scoured and cleaned. One team stayed behind to make sure there were no laggards. Their final report would say there were no more zombies on Deluna Island. Their report was correct. There were none left on the island, but, the report did not include the surrounding waters.

44

"Now, we go out to the Easy Life Kennels for a story with Angel Kraig. Take it away, Angel!" The TV anchorman smiled broadly into the camera as Angel Kraig showed up on the screen.

"Thanks, Tom. This is Angel Kraig reporting at the entrance to the Easy Life Kennel, where a few days ago a man was mauled by two dogs. Since then, our sources have reported that the man who died that day had, only hours before, murdered a young girl at Red Point Park. The man's name was Gerald Johnson, from Milton. It seems he had been tormented for months by the victim, who seems to have been stalking him. He had come out to the beach looking for a confrontation on Friday night. It seems he got what he came for."

Angel paused for effect, and then continued, "When Johnson found Anna Knox had been stalking and tormenting another boy, Adam Moore from Deluna Island, he snapped. Johnson took out his rage on the girl, leaving her for dead. Strangely enough, Johnson had been suffering the effects of the Canine Flu that has ravaged our island. He wandered away, in a delirium, and in the early morning hours was attacked by the dogs of a local couple out for a morning walk.

The facts are still a little sketchy but it seems that the dogs were incited by the smell of the sores on Johnson's body that were caused by the infection. The couple stated that their dogs were loving, docile creatures that had never attacked or bitten anyone before. The local Animal Control is looking into the matter.

The facts of this case vindicate the animals and owners of the Easy Life Kennels, Mr. Bubba Lambert and Mr. Jeff Kelley, who I have with me, today."

The camera panned over to the smiling Bubba Lambert, his crystal blue eyes shining. Angel Kraig smiled at the man, then, back into the camera.

"Mr. Lambert, you and your kennel have been through a few rough days, haven't you?" she said, angling her microphone toward the man, for his answer.

"Why, yes, Ms. Kraig, it has been an or-deal." He smoothed his bushy, silvery hair and mustache, in a futile attempt to calm the mane. "The thought that our animals could do such a thing, well; it is out-rage-ous! We board only the BEST breeds here. We are just so thrilled to have our good name restored." Angel Kraig, smiling into the camera, told the man that the station was proud to be the ones to tell his story to their viewers. The camera returned to a close up of her face as she signed off. "This is Angel Kraig reporting. Back to you, Tom!"

The seasoned anchorman chortled and began his next story.

"Thanks, Angel. The flu that Angel Kraig mentioned in her report has devastated our small community. The sickness ran through the island this weekend has taken the lives of fourteen people, including two of our local deputies and the beloved owner of Capt. Jack's Diner, Selena Jackson. Captain Jack, who couldn't be with us today, sends his sincere thanks for the outpouring of love that the viewers have shown for his lost wife, Selena.

As for the flu epidemic, it has been contained and is under control. The danger has passed. I am sure many of you have seen the men walking around with the funny suits over the last few days.

The CDC in Atlanta sent in one of their epidemic teams to help us find the source of the infection and eradicate it. It seems the virus came in on a ship from Mexico City that sunk in the waters off the coast of our island. The authorities have gone down and destroyed the vessel after making sure there were no more infected survivors. The explosions you heard early today were the agents blowing up the ship."

The anchorman shifted papers on his desk and looked into the side camera.

"Many people have reported hearing what they thought was gunfire over the weekend on the island. Our sources have ferreted out that a local fireworks company, from Mobile, has used some of the more remote areas of our island to try out some of their newest mixtures for the coming holiday weekend. The spokesperson for the company said that they hope to amaze all with the show on the beach this year."

Tom shuffled again and looked into the front camera, again, and began the next story.

"In another story, local football up and comer, Adam Moore has been cleared of all charges in the murder of Anna Knox. It turns out that, although, he admittedly was on the scene the night of her death, he left the area before she was killed.

Allegedly, the girl had been stalking him, as mentioned in the earlier story from Angel Kraig. Rumors had been circulated throughout his school. They were started by Knox. She had altered photos of the young man, even posting them on the Internet. The stories and the pictures were all fabricated by Knox to gain the affections from Moore by alienating him from his friends, his football career and his long-time girlfriend, Jenna McLain. The ploy backfired when he found proof of her involvement in the scheme.

Anna Knox was murdered later, as we know, by Gerald Johnson, who had suffered at her hand the year before. We are glad to report that Moore has returned to school and has plans for college in the fall." The reporter went on to other mundane stories of the day. The biggest story of all would never be told.

45

Dirk pushed the button to mute the television in the cavernous den in the Bluff House. He leaned back in his chair and thought back over the events of the past week, when the doorbell sounded. He walked across the tile floor to the leaded glass door. He could see the form of Gassim and Randall through it. He let them in.

"Whatever you are selling, I am not buying!" he greeted them, happily. The two men smiled and entered the home of their friend. He called out to Jimmi to bring out some of her famous muffins and took them out onto the balcony.

Dirk, Gassim and Randall sat on the deck of the house on the bluff. The bay was a crystal clear, emerald green and the sun was high in the sky. The seagulls, diving for their morning meal, were twisting and splashing into the water only to come right back up, soaring into the air with their surprised catch. A gentle breeze alternated with tiny gusts, ruffling the table cloth and the palm fronds.

Jimmi stepped out onto the deck with a fresh pot of coffee and a basket of warm blueberry muffins. "Here you go guys, fresh out of the oven." She said, making a wide berth of Gassim. She was still a little unsure of him, remembering his wild eyed explosion into the house looking for her brother.

She hadn't known then, nor, in fact, did she know now, that the man had saved her brother's life. He had been rushing in, in fear for his friend's life, trying to save him from the infectious zombies.

Dirk and Randall, along with the local authorities, the Coast Guard and the help of ZARC had managed, miraculously, to keep the zombie outbreak at its most minimal risk. The residents of Deluna Island, had they known the extreme danger they had been in, had much for which they should thank the men. But, most would never know that they were only hours away from total devastation. Between Dirk, ZARC and the local authorities the real story was kept covered up. Most of the deaths were attributed to an outbreak of some strange Canine Flu. The more obvious incidents were purported to be from a band of drug smuggling pirates out of Jamaica, who had been caught and jailed. Those who, actually, saw the creatures were either dead, or in some cases, like the people from the Elks Club, dead drunk. Dirk was still amazed that it had been easier than expected to quell the truth.

Dirk's private mission was still unknown to the civilian locals, but not to the authorities. The majority of them were thankful that they had a man like Dirk Dobbs on their tiny island. A few were still unconvinced of his usefulness. The mayor contended that he was some sort of closet terrorist, just waiting for his chance to take over the island, but, to the others, he was some sort of mythical warrior, in a battle of good against evil. Some held him in a sort of reverential awe. His efficiency in preparing and taking out the zombies was mind boggling to them. The fact that amazed them the most was that he went in search of these things all over the world, by choice. It was more than they could get their minds around. Like most people who had lived through zombie encounters, they agreed on one point, they never wanted to see those creatures or what they could do to a person ever again.

In the aftermath, two local deputies had to be relieved of duty. They were admitted to a private hospital run by ZARC doctors in upstate New York. The experience had been more than they could handle. One was catatonic; the other suffered such horrendous flashbacks that he had to be sedated for most of the day and night. Neither would ever be the same. Their families had lost them just as much as if they had died at the hands of the creatures.

Had this been a battle, in the normal sense, Dirk would have been the first to receive honors, but with the hush-hush nature of the business, he would not see a medal or a ribbon. The limited knowledge of the situation was necessary, yet, his superiors at ZARC lauded as much commendation as possible on the island writer. Dirk smiled as he thought of the comments of his fellow warriors, especially the first timers, after the battle and cleanup was done. He had been a little embarrassed by their praise and awe. He realized that they were, still, a little in shock after the melee. They were relieved, too, considering the dangers to themselves and their families that had been averted. Dirk realized that, unlike them, and, indeed, most people, he had become accustomed to the sight of splattered mutated brains and the sound of zombies eating other human beings. Well, as accustomed as anyone could be to such things.

This, inevitably, brought his thoughts around to Alexandra. She had experienced this horror, just as these men had experienced it and, just like the deputies and countless others, she had walked away alive, but broken. Would she ever be whole again? He hoped so with all his heart. He knew she would never be able to be with him, again, but he hoped she would find love and a new life full of all the things she deserved.

In the bay, the horn of a ferry boat sounded and brought him out of his reverie. He shook the thoughts off, reached for one of his sister's prize winning muffins and took a big bite.

"So where to now, Gassim?" Randall inquired, slurping his coffee. Sometimes the doctor was still just like the kid Dirk remembered from grade school.

"I go back to Cairo on the 8:10 flight. I am to be at the agency on Wednesday to be reassigned." He said, glancing at Dirk, "I am in for a bit of a dressing down for taking off without checking in, but once I bring them up to date on the situation that arose here on Deluna Island, I am sure they will understand." Turning to Randall with a grin, he added, "Dirk is a bit of a golden boy around headquarters these days. They will be glad to know that he, and his home, is safe."

"I am sure they know a good bit of the story from their ZARC contacts in the field by now, so I wouldn't imagine that there will be much said about your hasty departure." Dirk intoned, "Besides you were on somewhat of a holiday when you overheard that conversation in the café, weren't you? Your hearing of which, let me say, I am extremely glad."

Gassim nodded, "I, too, feel very fortunate to have had my coffee in just that place at that precise time."

Randall finished off the last bite of his pastry, gulped down the rest of his coffee and ran a napkin across his lips. "Well, dear friends and gentle people, I must be off to the dungeon. I still have some loose ends to tie up and reports to file. The reports must be, umh, finessed to just the right amount of truth so as to pass inspection, without uncomfortable questions, as you know. So I must get on with it." He rose. "Yes, your skill is impeccable. You have done it before, but, God willing, never again on Deluna Island." Dobbs said. The three stood and shook hands all around and the doctor departed, hugging Jimmi on the way out.

Gassim and Dirk sat, quietly staring out to the nearby shores of Pensacola and Pensacola Beach. Neither man felt easy in his thoughts. Both men knew that there was always the chance that they'd missed one, or more, God forbid. The ZARC teams had scoured the Island, the boats and empty structures. They found none in hiding. They had burned the bodies and taken the remains far out beyond the horizon and dumped them in the Gulf.

There was one missing ferry but the Coast Guard had reported a large craft afire in the Gulf. The debris had sunk. Nothing could have survived the inferno on board. It, they both agreed, had to have been the East End Ferry vessel. Reports were that the ferry was readying to leave, their tanks full of gas. The craft could have made it out to sea and could have exploded from some type of overheating of the running engines. Divers would go down as soon as they could get in replacements that were cleared for security. Although the two men didn't speak the words, each knew the other was thinking the same thing. They could only hope that all aboard had perished.

The two zombie hunters sat in silence, drinking their coffee, eating their muffins, enjoying being alive. The wind stirred the palm fronds as the gulls continued their aerial ballet. All was safe, once again, on Deluna Island. They hoped.

46

While Dirk and Gassim sat on the deck, drinking coffee, the ferry boat drifted lazily into an isolated cove on the shores of a small island south of Mobile, Alabama.

The craft that burned in the Gulf had not been the drifting Deluna Island ferry. It had been a privately owned boat out of Miami, a floating Meth lab running their product up the coast. The cookers had become less than safety conscious after sampling their most recent batch and the boat caught fire and sank. There were no inquiries made to authorities, for obvious reasons. The cartel soon sent out their bloodhounds in search of the floating lab. They found nothing of their lab or their illegal drugs but when they saw the beached ferry they decided to check it out. That was when their bad karma caught up to them. They boarded the doomed ferry and quickly found out they had made a grave mistake. The zombies on the marooned ferry had an unexpected supper.

Night came. Dirk drove his friend to the airport
and Gassim boarded a plane for home. Dirk, lost
in thought, watched the take-off. The last week
had been one of the most terrifying sieges with
which he had dealt since his first encounter.
Having the creatures loose on his island was his
worst nightmare. And he was glad it was over. As
the lights disappeared into the dark sky he shook
off his dismal thoughts and made his way through
the busy terminal. His rumbling stomach
reminded him that Jimmi's muffins hadn't been
enough. He turned west, heading to Capt. Jack's
for dinner.

The place was busy, as always. He found a spot
near the kitchen and settled in. The tantalizing
smell caused his mouth to water. Everything
seemed to be the same on the surface but he
missed seeing Selena behind the counter, giving
him the thumbs up. Jack Jackson was there,
overseeing the job that his wife had done but it was
clear that he didn't have quite the enthusiasm he'd
had before the attacks. He spotted Dirk, smiled,
and came over.

"Dirk, glad to see you." He said, trying to sound
like his old self, but failing.

"How are you doing, Jack?" Dirk asked, quietly.

"I am not doing so well, Dirk," he confided, "I am just going through the motions until things make sense again." Dirk nodded. He knew, in sort of a way, how the captain must feel. The creatures had taken Dirk's fiancée, just as they taken Selena. She had lost her life just as permanently, even though her heart was still beating. Somewhere. Not here, he thought. It was an empty place that would never be filled.

Jack called out Dirk's order to the cook, but stayed by the table. The men talked for a few more minutes until the order came up. Jack took it from the server and delivered it to the table. "On the house," he said, with a weak smile. Dirk didn't argue. He knew it made the man feel better to do the small kindness for his friend. "Hang in there, Jack," he told him as he turned to go, "It will get better." Jack nodded and disappeared into the busy kitchen.

A storm was coming in. Dirk could feel it in the wind. He was glad. A storm would blow away the memories and cobwebs. He finished his dinner and headed back down the Bayway just as the first drops fell on his windshield. By the time it was a good downpour Dirk was home in his bed. He was overcome with exhaustion. He could no longer think about the possibility of missed zombies. He could no longer think about anything. He pulled the down comforter over his head to shut out the sounds of the storm. Then, he slept like the dead.

During the night the winds raged, the waves crashed onto shorelines up and down the coast. The tempest rocked the marooned ferry, releasing it, and the drug runners' boat, from the sandbar. The winds pushed them out into the gulf. The smaller boat was swamped, disappearing under the waves. The ferry full of undead sailed on, farther and farther, until it rammed into the legs of a deep water oil rig, splitting its bow. The creatures and their remaining victims inside knew nothing of the crash. Sated, the monsters lay dormant. Those still living were in the throes of death, expiring before the impact. They would re-animate in less than a day, left undisturbed. The ferry, with its unholy cargo, remained mostly intact as it sank to the bottom of the sea. It came to rest, lying on the sand underneath the oil rig. While Dirk slept the creatures stirred in the sunken hull. They knew no more difference being under thousands of feet of water than they knew on dry land, other than the slight impediment to speed caused by the pressure pressing on their bodies.

The storm raged above the wreck but there was barely a ripple in the sand down below. Winds howled, waves crashed over the rig's surfaces washing debris, as well as men, into the churning water. Many were lost along the southern coast over the long night. More would be lost when those wandering along the floor found their way to land.

The sun rose on the Emerald Coast. Crews were dispatched to repair damages and help the survivors. The day was as beautiful as the storms had been destructive. Those who walked the beaches, inlets and coves along the gulf coast, surveying the damage, searching for belongings and survivors had no idea what was creeping their way underneath the still churning waters.

Isadora Katz

A View of the People and Places

On Deluna Island

Dirk relaxes in the sun.

Dr. Randall Durham, ME

Capt. Jack's Diner, West Deluna Island

Dirk's house on the Bluff

View from Dirk's Balcony on Deluna Bay

Angus Murphy, Gassim Al Fayed, Randall Durham, and Dirk on the
key

Isadora Katz

Zombie Bay

About the Author

Isadora Katz is a mother and grandmother who lives near Atlanta, Georgia. She is married, after over thirty years, to her first love and high school sweetheart. The character, *Dirk Dobbs,* is based on a compilation of people, but, mostly on her husband, Rick. *Medical Examiner, Randall Durham,* Dirk's best friend and team mate is based on her husband's real life best friend, Randy. As in the book, they have been friends since elementary school. All of the weaponry and tactical issues were supplied by her husband, which helped the book have more authenticity.

Several of the characters in *"Zombie Bay"* are compilations of people, real and fictional. *"I think that makes the writing process even more enjoyable when you can put together these scenarios, have them do things that you know the real people would love to do."* Isadora says, *"It is fun to put them into the book and see how it plays out, using the different personalities to drive the plot."* She would only say, of one character, besides Dirk and Randall, to keep your eye on *"Angel Kraig",* the news reporter. She is one of the blends who is based on a real person. The *real* Angel Kraig is her daughter's good friend, Angel Craig, (with a 'C'). Angel is coming out in the sequel as a part of Dirk's Zombie Hunter team who is ready to change the Undead into the Dead with one head shot.

Isadora is an avid reader and loves to write. She began writing poetry when she was in her thirties and started several novels that remain unfinished. *"Zombie Bay"* was her first finished novel. And, her first in the Science Fiction genre. *"Zombie Bay"* was finished in 2007. Isadora has five finished, but unedited, works in progress. She plans to have a sequel to *"Zombie Bay"* finished in the coming year.

Visit Isadora Katz' Facebook page at:
http://www.facebook.com/#!/isadora.katz

or Email:
isadorakatz@hotmail.com

Now, available on Amazon.com
And Kindle!

Isadora Katz

Zombie Bay

Isadora Katz

Made in the USA
Charleston, SC
15 October 2014